Out of the Desert

TOM WALKER

For Aly, who taught me how to fly

CONTENTS

Egypt, September 1940

Chapter 1

The Bedford truck wound its way up the dirt road towards Helwan Camp, which lay to the south of Cairo. It travelled without urgency and its tired body seemed to groan and twitch at every bump and pothole it found.

For Peter Denhay, a thin, blond-haired Pilot Officer, the journey was drawing to its long-awaited conclusion. Many weeks had passed since he had left Liverpool, after an interminable wait for a convoy to gather. It had been necessary to travel in convoy because, although the Royal Navy controlled the waves, German U-boats lurked beneath them. The convoy travelled at the pace of the slowest ship and routed via the Cape, to avoid the intense combat taking place in the Mediterranean as fascist Italy asserted its claim to an empire in North Africa.

Even the longer route did not guarantee safety. One sultry night off Freetown, he recalled how an oil tanker travelling with the convoy had been torpedoed. Though Peter had not seen the explosion, he heard it from his bunk. By the time he reached the deck, all that was visible was the back of the vessel sliding into a spreading pool of fire. It lit the ocean for miles around and cast shadows beyond the other ships in the convoy. Here and there, the escorts rushed around to locate the enemy submarine and force it under the water. Men jumped screaming from the sinking ship into the oil-covered water and were instantly consumed by the flames. It was, he reflected, a perfect vision of hell.

Peter was just one young man amongst thousands of men and woman being transported to the Middle East to swell the ranks of the RAF. He was heading to Egypt to fight the war spreading towards that vital corridor, the Suez Canal, to defend Britain's maritime empire. Britain stood alone against the forces of darkness and oppression in the Summer of 1940. He knew, as well as any, that to lose the war here was to lose the war entirely. If that thought scared people, it did not trouble Peter; he wore the burden of his responsibility comfortably on his 19-year old shoulders.

He gazed out of the tailgate of the truck past his mute companions, at the scorching yellow sands bisected by the rough road. A heat shimmer distorted the horizon and there was no clearly defined line between the realm of man and the heavens, in whose fantastic blueness shone the unrelenting midday sun. God it was hot! Peter had never known heat like it. The meagre shade of the truck's canvas cover gave paltry respite to its occupants. His khaki shirt was soaked in sweat and every breath seemed to draw in dry, furnace-like heat and a fine talcum powder dust, thrown up from the wheels.

It was, Peter decided, an improvement on being used for target practice by German submarines, or his life at home for that matter. His father was a difficult man possessed by his own experiences from another war. He always seemed to doubt whether Peter would amount to anything and told him as much on the frequent occasions he returned from the pub, drunk and resentful. This resentment had not stopped Peter's dreams of flying. If anything, it nourished them. He was pushed from home as much as he was pulled by the incipient war. He had volunteered for flying duties well before Dunkirk, even before the Phoney War had started in September 1939. He was a man out to prove himself, in a service that offered the opportunity to be whatever he aspired to be.

The truck pulled up outside a dusty collection of fly-blown tents on the RAF aerodrome. Peter heard the cab door slam and the driver appeared at the rear.

'XXI Squadron dispersal area,' he shouted, before wandering off. Peter climbed out alone, and dropped down onto the dirt. Someone handed him his canvas bag and suitcase and the lorry drove off, leaving Peter in a thick cloud of dust and diesel exhaust. His new home was not salubrious, the few sagging tents pitched haphazardly about a large central marquee. Washing hung from crude lines strung between them. A painted sign was the only clue that this was home to a fighting squadron. Beyond the tents, he could make out the large distinctive tail fins of a handful of Bristol Blenheims, the bomber that Peter had been assigned to fly as one of XXI's pilots.

Ducking under the flaps of the marquee into its stifling warmth, Peter entered the private world of his new squadron. He took in the sparse furnishings: trestle tables; a gramophone propped up on some old books; a solid Welsh dresser at one end; and some beaten up old leather chairs. Everything sat on a dust-covered canvas groundsheet that had, in the dim past, been painted in a white and black chequer pattern. The gramophone played a record that Peter recognised from before the war, *Little White Lies* by Annette Hanshaw. Some smiling fresh-faced young men were sat in the chairs; they did not immediately register his entrance because they were in an animated discussion about county cricket. It was not a conversation to which Peter could offer anything useful, and he was considering whether he should make an exit when one of them noticed him.

'Hullo, are you a new boy? Don't hang about in the doorway, you'll block the airflow.'

This was met with some guffaws from the seated group. Peter overcame his nerves and stepped forward.

'Hello, I'm Peter Denhay, posted in to XXI Squadron. Is there someone I should report to?'

'You'll want Potty, the Adjutant,' a chubby Flight Lieutenant said, rolling his eyes, 'he's a Penguin.' A couple of the others laughed in a way that Peter decided he did not like much.

'A Penguin?'

'Yes,' he replied, anticipating the question, 'he's a flightless bird.'

There was more laughter, which ended abruptly.

'If you're looking for the Adjutant, you've found him,' said a voice from behind Peter. He looked about to see a man whose countenance so strongly resembled a horse that Peter was actually surprised when he did not whinny. He had entered unobtrusively and stood with his arms crossed and head bowed under the canvas.

'I'm Brian Potterne,' he said kindly, flashing an equine grin and shaking Peter's hand with a firm grip. Brian stood at least 6 foot tall and was skinny with it. He was dressed in khakis, worn thin with age. His stick-thin legs protruded from tattered grey socks and suede desert boots. He was like a ghost of the pre-war air force that had somehow become stranded in the canvas purgatory of Helwan.

'I see you've met some of the other crews,' Brian glanced at the seated group of officers with a knowing look, 'I'm afraid things are quite dull around here with the main squadron flying operations against the Italians out in the desert.'

Peter felt disappointed, he had expected to be on operations immediately. His frustration was palpable when he spoke.

'I've not flown for months now. Any chance I can get some time on Blenheims?'

Someone guffawed behind him. Peter's cheeks burned at what he suspected was a veiled criticism of his zealousness. If Brian noticed Peter's embarrassment, he did not acknowledge it. He looked thoughtfully at Peter.

'I'm sure we can find a spare kite for you. How many hours have you got?'

'I've got 30 logged.'

'On Blenheims?'

'On the Avro Anson,' Peter said with a downcast look. The Anson was a training aircraft, Peter had 30 hours on twin-engine aircraft in total. Brian pursed his lips.

'They're really pushing you lot out of the training system quickly now, aren't they?'

Peter said nothing. Brian sighed.

'I'll tell you what, I'll find someone to run you about station to sort out briefings and your flying kit. Then, tomorrow, we'll talk about sending you off somewhere for a flight.'

Peter followed Brian to one of the tents where he dropped off his belongings. As they walked Brian explained that the main body of the squadron was flying operations from a desert landing strip called El Daba, where they had been since the Italians crossed the border into Egypt a few weeks before. They were due back within a week for a period of rest and reorganisation.

Brian led him onto another tent, where the boots of a reclining figure showed through the open flaps.

'Kendrick, you lazy ass. Get up, I've someone here you need to meet.'

A Flying Officer with wiry dark hair and an Errol Flynn moustache appeared from the tent. His green eyes stared at Peter in a way that hinted of amusement, although it was unclear whether this was down to having been caught napping or an expectation of what was about to come.

'Peter, this is Charlie Kendrick, one of our navigators. He'll give you a tour of the camp, introduce you to Squadron Leader Operations, and bring you back in time for tea. Don't listen to any of his rubbish though, he's only about a month ahead of you and still not crewed up yet.' Brian laughed, and walked away, leaving them to it. Peter felt Charlie was sizing him up. He held out his hand and Charlie shook it, a firm grip.

'Alright then, first stop is a briefing with the Squadron Leader in charge of operations. Then we need to sort out kit. Did you bring any from England?' Charlie asked, wiping sweat from his neck.

'Just uniform and boots,' Peter said. He found himself unconsciously emphasising his 't's and foreshortening his vowel sounds, to conceal the natural West Country burr in his accent. He had, he reflected, done this since flying training. Most of his fellow trainees spoke with the clipped accent common to public or grammar schools, and he felt his natural accent betrayed that he had attended neither.

It was a hot walk to Station Headquarters down a dusty temporary road. Occasionally a truck or car rattled by, but no-one stopped to offer a lift. Peter felt thirsty and dehydrated, but Charlie seemed to be acclimatised, and just nattered on about all manner of things; the Italians, other members of the squadron, the likelihood of seeing combat. Charlie told him that the invasion of Egypt by Mussolini's forces had bogged down in the Western Desert, around a strategic position called *Sidi Barrani*, a town on the coast road just shy of the Libyan border. Although he was unsure how, Peter formed an opinion that Charlie came from a wealthy family. He certainly sounded well educated, but he was also cynical and hardly plagued with self-doubt. He decided to move the conversation away from Charlie's opinions for a moment.

'Why do they call Brian, 'Potty'?'

'Well, his name's Potterne of course. But that's only half the joke. He don't fly, you see, and that's odd for a pilot. So the others call him Potty. Behind his back, of course,' Charlie added, with a hint of disapproval.

'Is there a story behind that then? Brian not flying, I mean.' Peter asked. He could not decide whether he liked Charlie or not. He seemed friendly enough, but he was conscious that their backgrounds were quite different. In truthfulness, he felt somewhat intimidated by him.

'Oh, I expect so, there usually is in my experience. The chaps can be so terribly dull about anyone who's different. Here we are,' Charlie pointed at a long brick bungalow, which sat in the centre of the main camp. It was here that the sinews of the station's command structure came together. They entered the building and travelled down a long, gloomy corridor. Passing signs that read *Station Warrant Officer* and *Cipher Room,* they stopped at a door marked *SLOps.* Charlie knocked firmly and a stern voice within beckoned. Charlie gave Peter a nod to enter. Inside, Peter was met with a staring, red-faced man with close-cropped grey hair and a dark moustache. He wore the General Service Medal and India General Service Medal ribbons on his smart tunic beneath a set of pilot's wings that were faded nearly beyond recognition.

'Come in. Don't stand in the door like that, I don't bite,' he barked. The Squadron Leader did not invite Peter to sit down. Neither did the Squadron Leader sit himself. As Peter realised, there were no chairs in the room.

The Squadron Leader seemed to read Peter's mind, 'You won't mind if I don't invite you to sit,' he gestured around the room, 'you'll see I don't hold with the practice of sitting. Except for when eating, of course. Terrible thing, sitting. It causes fetid breath, poor stature, and flatulence. Among other things y'know, it's been proven *medically.*' He drew this word out by syllable. Peter sensed a certain unhinged quality to the Squadron Leader and resolved to stay quiet in order to get through the experience as quickly as possible.

What followed was a lengthy and well-rehearsed, if occasionally quite batty, speech about the importance of position-fixing and attention to wind speed and direction when desert flying. He refuted in the strongest possible terms the arguments he had heard in the mess about the importance of prosecuting attacks at low-level and droned on about the need for rigid formation flying, both for navigation and weapon effect purposes.

Just when Peter hoped he was coming to a close with a passage on fuel management, he switched back to desert flying again, having apparently missed out a crucial section concerning astral navigation. Like a locomotive coming to the end of a long and tiring journey, the old man finished with a couple of exhausted puffs on aerodrome discipline, adding somewhat obscurely, '-and I should know, I flew in Pink's War!'

*

As Charlie Kendrick let the door shut behind Peter, he was at a loss for something to do. His normal hunting ground was the personnel office, where he liked to chat up the typists. But he noticed the sign for the post room and, determined to find some use for his visit to station headquarters, he went to check for XXI Squadron's mail. A couple of clerks in short sleeves were sorting out post bags for collection at the back of the room and, after a time, one detached himself to attend to Charlie. There were only a few envelopes for the squadron. Among this handful though were two marked for him and he was scrutinising the handwriting when a W.A.A.F. Section Officer entered the post room. She was carrying a stack of sealed packages.

'These are for the A.O.C.in.C, courier only,' she said to the clerk. While she waited for the clerk to fill out a docket for the packages she glanced at Charlie, who smiled back. She nodded to his letters and spoke in a polite voice.

'News from home?'

'Just eviction notices, I'm afraid,' he grinned.

She laughed and the image was fixed in his mind's eye - dark hair held up in the regulation bun, hazel eyes, a hint of freckles. But there was something else there too. He found it hard to place immediately, a sense of sadness perhaps, or of loss. Before the impression was fully formed in his mind, the clerk handed her a completed receipt and she turned to go.

'That's the problem with fly boys, they spend so much time in the desert they end up behaving like hobos,' she said with a wink, and was gone.

Charlie stood in silence, listening to the sound of her footsteps die away down the corridor. He suddenly recalled the two letters and opened the first, which was from his bank. It thanked him for writing, but under the current circumstances it would be quite impossible to extend any further credit. It added that he should settle his account within the month, or they would be forced to close it.

The second letter was addressed to him in Anne's spidery scrawl. She asked after his health and apologised again for how she had broken off their engagement. She told him that she felt she had behaved terribly with Frank Thornley. He should know Frank was a good man, he had volunteered as an Air Raid Warden after all, and Charlie should not hate him for what she had done. She hoped one day he would forgive her, and that he would not take unnecessary risks. Charlie pondered this for a moment. He knew he was not the first man on earth to be jilted by a woman, and probably not the only one to receive the news at the Church itself. He felt he ought to forgive Anne for starting the chain of events that brought him here, he could be dead within a few weeks after all. But on balance, Charlie still burned with the shame of it, and even the kindness of his friends in the wake of being stood up was more than he could bear. He dropped both notes into the bin and headed off to collect Peter.

*

Peter made it back to the squadron's dispersal just as the sun was setting. The temperature had drained away since the height of the day and all that remained was a muggy warmth. The smell of the Nile was carried to him on the light evening wind. On the walk over, Charlie had kindly permitted him to carry all of the equipment he had been issued with at their various stops around the station. The bundle of gear weighed a ton. As they walked Charlie expounded on his theory about why he was yet to be crewed up.

'You see, crew selection is a science. You don't want to put the wrong characters in a crew, because when they have to work together it all falls apart.'

'Are you the only navigator without a crew?'

'Yes. And that's my point, all the other skippers are drips, Peter. They don't want to listen to a master of the craft; they want it all their own way,' Charlie said, shaking his head.

'*You're* a master of the craft? The craft of navigation?'

Peter heard the incredulity in his own voice and tried to change the inflection halfway through to avoid being impolite. He failed.

'At the risk of sounding a touch egotistical, yes I am. You'd need to see me in action to believe it Peter, but I think I have a gift.'

Peter stopped in his tracks. He had heard some tall tales in the past, but this was a classic. He overcame his natural reserve, 'I have to say, Charlie, that sounds like horse shit. Are you sure the reason you're not crewed up yet is because no-one wants to work with you?'

Charlie scowled, the jab had gone home.

'I don't need to explain anything to you. You'd kill for a navigator like me.'

At the dispersal, they ran into Brian who was waiting outside the tent with a cup of tea.

'Ah, there you are Peter. You've kept your end of the bargain and I've kept mine. You're off flying tomorrow, first thing after breakfast. *And*,' he added an emphasis on the last word, 'I've had a think about crewing you up.'

Peter wanted to chuck the bundle of gear at Brian, he knew what was coming. A voice in his head screamed *not Charlie Kendrick*.

'With Charlie?' he said out loud.

'Exactly. I thought a little cross-country jaunt tomorrow would settle you both in. You'll both be on operations before long, so it's a great opportunity to get to know one another.'

Charlie folded his arms, 'I'm not sure that's a great idea, Brian,' Charlie said quietly. 'I'm looking for a pilot with a bit more chat - Peter's the quiet, unassuming type.'

'I'm bloody not-'

'Right,' Brian said firmly, 'that's quite enough from both of you. You'll fly together tomorrow like I said, and you'll get along. The rest of us have to do the same.'

Peter realised the discussion was over. He was incredibly tired and his head pounded from exertion in the hot weather. He nodded and headed wearily back to his tent, which he eventually found after poking his head into several identical tents. He threw the gear next to the empty bed and laid down on the lumpy, uncomfortable mattress. He could not care less. He was so tired it felt like a bed in a luxury hotel.

A thousand thoughts crowded his mind, but chief amongst them now were the reservations he had over flying with Charlie Kendrick. He had known when he was assigned to bombers, that he would not face the lonely cockpit inhabited by the fighter pilot. But it had never really occurred to him he might end up working with someone in a bomber crew that he disliked. With his cynicism and yet strongly held opinions, Kendrick reminded him of his father. Perhaps this was one of the reasons he was struggling to find any redeeming qualities in his soon-to-be navigator. The question was still unresolved in his mind five minutes later when his eyelids became heavy and he dropped into an uneasy sleep.

Chapter 2

Charlie Kendrick entered the mess tent for breakfast. Although the sun was only just creeping above the horizon, the air inside the tent was already close and stuffy. Irritability dominated Charlie's mood, not because of the heat, but because he was still dwelling on the fact that he had been scheduled to fly with the squadron's new boy. The smell of fried eggs and bully beef reached him as he walked in, as it had on all of other 35-days he had spent at Helwan. The warm air combined with the smell of cooking fat as usual brought a sickly feeling in his stomach. This barely registered today though, because his mind was occupied with thoughts of getting out. He was pondering the merits of a transfer, away from the squadron. He felt isolated and overlooked. It had been a familiar feeling throughout much of his life, but here he had never managed to build a rapport with the other newly-arrived aircrew. Not for want of trying, he thought bitterly.

They were all there; Milne, King, Elvington, even 'Fatty' Taylor. The new men, he thought, ironically. If he could have avoided them, he would have. But he was committed now and pulled up a chair at the end of the long breakfast table. He ordered tea and toast from the mess steward. Peter entered shortly after and, hesitantly, took a seat opposite him. Charlie wondered if he deliberately avoided his gaze, tucking into his egg sandwich. The omnipresent flies hovered above the table, waiting for their chance to pounce on the food. Everyone learned to eat with one hand at Helwan and use the other to ward off the wildlife.

The chat centred around the bombing underway in England. The Blitz, as it had been termed, was alien to these men who had left England even before the fall of France. Their tiresome conversation bored Charlie, and his gaze shifted again to Peter who was leafing through the pilot's notes for the Blenheim. This sight caused him to roll his eyes unconsciously. He was unsure of what it was that made Peter Denhay such an unattractive prospect to him. Perhaps, he thought, it was because he seemed an identikit of the men they were breakfasting with. With their dull talk about sport, the weather, and their sweethearts at home. They were fighting a global war for survival, he fumed - bloody Little Englanders.

Milne at the top of the table called down to Peter.

'You must have seen some bombing before you left England, Denhay?'

Peter looked up from the notes and shook his head.

'Not really, I'm afraid. I know as much as you do,' Peter said, before returning to the manual.

Charlie took a sip of tea and, leaning back in his chair, he decided to speak.

'It's the working-class factory workers I feel sorry for, they're the ones who'll suffer the most from city bombing. They live next to the targets. For so-called 'national socialists', the Krauts ought to hang their box-heads in shame,' he said.

Fatty Taylor made a face and replied drily.

'Nazi. Communist. They're all the same to me. But, as far as terror bombing goes, don't forget we started it, Kendrick - we bombed Berlin first.'

'Oh really? Then how do you explain Guernica? You reap what you sow, brother.'

Taylor looked irritated but said nothing, jamming another slice of buttered toast in his greasy maw. Charlie guessed that, if Taylor was even remotely familiar with Guernica, he had decided to forget Germany's indiscriminate bombing of the Republican stronghold during the Spanish Civil War. Charlie knew a great deal about it because, despite his middle-class upbringing, he had until recently been a member of the Communist Party. He wondered what Taylor would say if he knew he was sharing a breakfast table with someone who had unashamedly sung the Internationale. He thought back to the meetings of the left-wing intelligentsia, held in the dingy backrooms of houses in Whitechapel that he'd regularly attended and smiled inwardly. His train of thought was broken by Fatty Taylor speaking again.

'I've heard a rumour that some of us are going to get thinned out,' he said in his weaselly, conspiratorial voice, 'Brian says the horrible old transport squadrons are crying out for crews and he's been asked to trade some bodies over to them.'

Charlie caught the glance Taylor flicked towards him and Peter. the implication was clear. On one hand, he felt this was the answer to all his problems, but on the other there was shame in being culled from a squadron before he was even operational. His ego and natural sense of pride chafed at the accusation he was not good enough for light bombers. It made him loathe Fatty Taylor even more. He felt Peter's expectant gaze, his breakfast plate empty.

'We're due to crew-in shortly. Brian's waiting for us,' Peter said.

Charlie drained his tea slowly and deliberately. It was lukewarm now and oddly refreshing in the heat of the morning.

'Come on then, Biggles,' he growled at Peter.

*

The short walk across the dispersal to where their aircraft was parked nearly did for Peter. The sun was so strong that it baked the sandy earth and radiated back in his face in punishing waves. The heat was draining, and he pulled his peak cap down to shield his eyes from the piercing brightness of the day. Charlie lagged behind seemingly disinterested, which he found odd since today surely was an opportunity to showcase his alleged impressive navigation skills. Peter was weighed down with parachute, flying helmet, oxygen mask, and his chart pack. He was, therefore, very glad to see Brian stood beside one of the large earthen pens that provided protection for their aircraft. It was built from empty oil drums, wired together with sand piled up against the side. Inside the pen was something that attracted all of Peter's attention.

The Bristol Blenheim was a distinctive aircraft. Its oversized tail fin was joined to the large wing section by a thin fuselage. In the middle of that fuselage the designer had placed a gun-turret that carried a pair of machine guns. It looked like an afterthought. Peter thought it would be a terribly cramped experience for the poor soul who had to operate the guns and the wireless equipment at the same time. The next thing he noticed were the large engine nacelles that housed the Mercury motors. From the cockpit it would be difficult to see over the tops of those engines, meaning visibility would be problematic. There was a nod to this further forward where the pointed glass canopy of the nose was scooped out on the pilot's side to permit an improved view forward. The whole contraption sat on a pair of large main wheels, which folded up inside the wing when airborne.

Peter surveyed the aircraft with the eyes of, if not a lover, then certainly a distant admirer. He had first seen one during flying training when it had diverted into his airfield with engine trouble and was instantly impressed by the sleek lines and precocious speed. With its sand and brown upper camouflage pattern and dirty duck-egg blue belly, the bomber was a brute. But a handsome one. Its aircraft serial number was picked out in an aggressive red, this one was UT-Q, or *Queenie* in RAF speak.

'Chuck your gear in Peter, then I'll talk you through the exercise,' Brian smiled then, looking over to where Charlie stood talking to the engineers, he shouted, 'Kendrick, are you joining us?'

Peter dropped his parachute on the wing and watched Charlie stroll over at a leisurely pace. He found himself fretting, not for the first time that morning, that he was about to go flying with a navigator he did not trust.

'Today's job is a simple navigation exercise,' Brian continued, 'get airborne, fly to Ismailia, report in, and then come back again. It's just a gentle introduction to flying the aircraft.'

Peter nodded.

'So, no aerobatics, no buggering about. There and back - do I make myself clear, Peter?'

'Crystal clear, Brian. And I can hardly get lost with Charlie on board,' Peter smiled, wondering if Charlie would pick up his faint sarcastic tone.

'Have you marked up your map, Charlie?' Brian asked.

Charlie looked up at the sky, which was typically free of clouds, and shrugged.

'I can if you like Brian. But visibility is unlimited and its one bearing out and the reciprocal on the homeward leg. A 30-minute flying time; it's a cake walk!'

'Yes, Charlie,' Brian said slowly with a little exasperation, 'I want you to mark up your map.' They watched Charlie disappear off to find some shade in which to work. Shaking his head, Brian motioned for Peter to climb up to the cockpit.

Heaving himself up onto the wing, he slid the perspex canopy hood back to its furthest position. Peter sat down on the edge of the hatch, swung his legs over and dropped into the pilot's seat. The cockpit smelt of hot metal, rubber, and there was a faint whiff of gasoline about it too. He placed his feet on the rudder pedals and moved the control column in a circular motion to check for full and free movement. Another man might have felt claustrophobic, or perhaps overwhelmed by the number of gauges, switches, levers and handles. But as he sat there crammed up against the instrument panel and the control column, Peter was excited. He felt, perhaps for the first time since arriving in Egypt, entirely at home.

Brian's head appeared at the hatch above his head.

'All settled then?'

Without waiting for a reply Brian went on.

'Good! Just a few things to run through and we'll have you on your way. "See one, do one, teach one" is what I always say,' he snorted.

'The cockpit of this aircraft was designed by a lunatic; there's switches and levers all over the place,' Peter shook his head. Too often manufacturers permitted engineers to design aircraft with little or no thought to crew management. The Blenheim's cockpit might have made sense on a drawing board, but in practice it would be a nightmare to find a way around it under pressure, perhaps in smoke or darkness, or with the canopy shot out and dead men on board.

Brian pointed out the principal features that a pilot unfamiliar with the type should know - the brakes, the firing button for the single forward-facing gun in the wing, and the unusual cockpit layout with some controls mounted behind him. This arrangement forced a pilot to be extremely dexterous when operating, for example, the variable pitch lever for propeller blades.

'Just be careful when you reach behind you to adjust the pitch,' Brian warned, 'the pitch levers are the exact same shape as your carburettor cut-out levers and they're in almost the same place.' He mimicked the action of flicking the lever off.

The carburettor cut out levers have a spring-loaded guard on them, but it's easy to confuse the two and accidentally shut off the fuel supply to the engines.'

Brian paused for a moment to let that revelation sink in and continued.

'On start-up you need to select electrical power, fuel, and pneumatic power 'on' first. The ground crew will turn the propellers to prime the engines, left hand first. You just need to signal when you're ready and they'll get out of the way. Then it's magnetos to 'on', crack the throttle, hit the starter switch and Bob's your uncle.'

'Righto.'

'Leave it idling and then repeat for the right-hand engine.'

Brian stood up for a moment and stretched off his back, then leaned over him again.

'Couple more things to remember: first, don't forget to shut the cowling gills using this wheel before you start your take-off roll.' He pointed to a wheel on the right of Peter's seat. 'If you forget to close the gills, the engines won't develop sufficient power to generate lift and you'll never get off the ground.' Brian gave him a significant look.

'Second, as soon as you're airborne, get the gear up. There's no pumping a lever like in the Anson. The undercarriage is hydraulic and there's an indicator on the port side that tells you whether the gear is up or down.'

Green is down, red is up?'

'Quite. Got it?'

'Everything can kill you; clear as mud,' Peter laughed. Brian ignored him.

'Right. I'll chase down your navigator and you take a quick look around the aircraft to check she's fit for flight.' Brian's head disappeared.

Climbing out, Peter strode over to the party of engineers who were preparing for the aircraft's departure. A tall, suntanned Sergeant detached himself from the group and met him halfway.

'Alright, sir? I'm Sergeant Mellish. Me and the boys here look after the kite. Do you need a hand getting away?'

Peter was just about to tell Mellish that he would appreciate that, when he heard an aircraft in the circuit overhead. Several aircraft from the sound of it. Looking up, he held a hand up to the sun to get a better look, but the outline was not one he could place. Not a British aircraft anyway, he thought.

There was a spectacular explosion about 600 yards away, which sent great clods of earth into the air. Everyone instinctively dropped to the ground. Peter found himself looking directly into Mellish's sweating, startled face as they both tried to hug the dirt. Another bomb slammed into a parked Lysander in front of the main hanger and detonated, blowing it apart and starting a raging fire as its gasoline tanks ruptured. Shrapnel from the explosion whistled over their heads and some struck the walls of the pen, sounding bizarrely like gravel thrown against a wall. Thick, black smoke rose up from the burning wreckage, it seemed to blot out the sun as it climbed up in oily coils like a great black serpent. Peter suddenly glimpsed Charlie appear from around the side of the pen, running like a mad man towards him. He was yelling as he sprinted.

'Come on, Peter. Don't just lie about there like a great clot. Let's get it up.'

Peter took one glance beyond the pen where Italian bombs were falling onto the airfield and realised their options were to run the gauntlet or be killed where they lay. He decided he was not going to lay cowering on the ground waiting for uncertain death today.

'Mellish,' he shouted, 'start her up!'

As Peter turned away to ascend to the cockpit, he heard Mellish cursing to himself. If standing next to several hundred gallons of 100-Octane gasoline was not his preference, Peter thought ruefully, imagine being sat on top of it! Sliding into his seat once more, Peter saw that Charlie was already strapped into the folding seat next to him and connected to the intercom. With the electrics off Peter could only just see his mouth moving, but he could tell what he was saying; Charlie was strongly encouraging Peter to hurry up.

Peter looked at the instruments again. It was only the second time he had set eyes on them before, but he had read the pilot's notes and felt reasonably confident that he could get airborne without killing them. He ran through the checks as quickly as possible, feeling angry with himself that his fingers would not move as fast as his mind. He turned on the electrics and Charlie's voice echoed in his ears.

'-king move on.'

A bomb went off nearby. Peter felt the shock wave reverberate through his body. Sand and dust blew across the top of the aircraft and, for a moment, nothing could be seen through the cockpit windows. A fine, talcum powder dust hung in the air inside the cockpit. It smelled like old paper or a fusty attic and was tinged with cordite. As it cleared, Peter gave the signal for the engineers to clear the propellers. This was somewhat optimistic, he realised, because they had already scarpered.

He pushed the starter button and after a couple of cracks the pistons fired, smoke drifted in a cloud away from the exhaust and the propeller spun up to 700 rpm.

'Starboard engine clear,' Charlie shouted.

He repeated the procedure for the starboard engine and glanced at the instrument panel. With no small satisfaction, he noted that oil temperature and pressures had risen to the correct levels and were holding steady. He reached behind and located the variable pitch levers, adjusting the pitch of the propellers from coarse to fine, removed the brake and advanced the throttles. *Queenie* leapt forwards out of the pen and moved ahead at what Peter gauged was running pace.

'You won't make it to the threshold,' Charlie said, peering over the nose, 'Just pick some clear dirt and go for it.'

Peter could see that Charlie was correct, the first wave of Italian bombers had scattered their bomb loads across the aerodrome, cratering the surface and closing the active runway. If they were to make it into the air, Peter realised, he must make a bid for it now.

'Strap in, here we go,' Peter said into the intercom.

Peter pulled his straps tight and placed his left hand on the throttles. Neutralising the pedals, he pushed the throttles forward to take-off RPM and felt the aircraft surge forward. A utility truck appeared out of a cloud of dust off to Peter's right and raced in front of the aircraft as it picked up speed. They missed it by a matter of feet. Peter aimed for a gap in front where he could see an uninterrupted stretch of ground just long enough for a take-off. His heart thumped and he fought the image in his mind of their bomber flying directly into a bomb blast. He was surprised at how quickly the nose dropped and found himself looking at the flat expanse in front, with bombs detonating off to one side as a second wave of Italians attacked the field.

Charlie counted the airspeed off for Peter as they raced along.

'150, 180, 200 miles per hour,' he spoke the numbers clearly, sharing the workload with Peter whilst gripping on tightly to the fuselage with one hand. Peter noticed a slight willingness on the part of the aircraft to pull to the right. He guessed that a very slight adjustment with the rudder would correct this. With only a touch of rudder the aircraft straightened up and it suddenly dawned on him why the designers at Bristol had insisted on such a large tail fin. The ground rushed by beneath and he a felt a bounce as the machine tried to leave the ground. He pushed the control column forward slightly to maintain airspeed and then they were up, up, climbing gently away from the fire and explosions below.

'Strewth,' Charlie said, craning his head to look back at the airfield, 'you can barely see the airfield with all that smoke. Those poor bastards down there.'

'What about these poor bastards up here? What do we do now?'

Peter remembered to flick the undercarriage selector switch and felt the rumble as the wheels retracted into their bays. Looking back to the instrument panel he saw the altimeter rising through 900 feet and levelling off at 1000 feet. *Queenie* was a fast climber, they had barely blinked in that time. Charlie pointed out the window, where the Italian bombers were turning away westward to begin their homeward flight - they were unmolested by RAF fighters.

'Let's follow them, and see where they go,' Charlie said.

Peter glanced at the fuel gauge. It read full. There was no reason why they could not track the Italians, they had more than eight hours' flying time. Whether they *should,* was a different matter. Brian had given no instructions about what to do if they were attacked during their exercise. This was, Peter decided, something of a grey area.

'You know we've no ammunition, what are we going to if we catch them?'

'We don't have to catch them, just tail them long enough to work out where their airfield is. I bet the lazy Eyeties fly directly home - we can work out where they're based and let Brian know. If he's still alive, that is.'

Peter looked sideways at Charlie. He found himself surprised that he agreed with him so readily. In fact, he was starting to ponder whether his initial appraisal was not altogether too rash.

They crept along at 1, 000 feet, shadowing the returning Italian bombers from their blind spots below them. The bombers passed south of Cairo and made a course adjustment over the Nile, settling on a heading of 280 degrees. Peter kept an eye on the fuel gauge, he was conscious of the recklessness of saving the aeroplane, only to lose it in the desert through lack of fuel. He could see Charlie hunched over the navigator's table in the nose. He was at work, measuring drift and airspeed. Drawing lines on his map. After 40-minutes he crawled back to his seat next to Peter and plugged into the intercom again.

'Ok. We've got them. You can head back now, turn onto 120 degrees.'

Peter glimpsed briefly at the chart held by Charlie and saw that he had marked a line representing the bomber's course away from Helwan. This was cut at intervals with range annotations that Charlie had converted to percentages of confidence. The 90% confidence line was sat in northern Libya, near a spot named *Marawah.*

'How did you work that out?'

Peter could see Charlie smiling above his oxygen mask.

'We've got their heading and we know their target was Helwan. All we need to know is their operating range and we can take a stab at working out the location of their base,' Charlie said, folding the map away into his boot. Peter thought he looked quite pleased with himself.

By the time they returned to Helwan, some form of order had been re-established. Even from their approach altitude, Peter could see that fire engines had been employed on the burning wrecks and the blazes were mainly put out. Small parties of airmen around the airfield were busy filling craters in the runway. Taxiing back to the dispersal, they passed a lorry where a handful of engineers were busy loading the bed. A second glance revealed that the forms were wrapped in grey RAF blankets, some of which blew away in their propeller wash to reveal human remains. Peter was fixed by the grim scene as they passed. An airman turned around to stare at them. Pain and grief were etched deeply on his young face. He looked to Peter like he had seen enough of war today to last an eternity.

The engines clattered to a standstill as the carburettors were cut and there was a moment of silence before Peter tore off his flying helmet and ran a hand through his sweat-soaked hair. By the time he and Charlie clambered out of the cockpit onto the wing, their ground crew reached the aircraft and Brian was at their head. He looked like he had been in the wars himself, his arm was in a sling and there was a raw and bloody welt across his cheek.

'I have to admit,' Brian shouted up at them, 'I was beginning to wonder where you'd got to.'

Peter opened his mouth to reply, but Charlie beat him to it.

'We just flew circles around the sky until it looked safe enough to land,' Charlie said. Peter looked sideways at him, surprised by the blatant lie. But Charlie just flicked a look at Peter for a moment, seemingly daring him to break their confidence

'That's right,' Peter said, to his own amazement, 'we needed to burn off fuel before we could land.'

21

Chapter 3

'What the hell happened there,' Peter asked angrily, ducking under the flaps of Charlie's tent, 'why did you lie to Brian?'

He could barely make Charlie out in the darkness of the tent, bent over trying to light an oil lamp. A struck match illuminated Charlie face for a moment, before he turned away to find the wick.

After landing they had joined in with the clean-up of the aerodrome. Recuperation, Brian called it, and it was everyone's job. An arduous, dangerous job it was too, as far as Peter was concerned. An astonishing number of unexploded bombs lay out on the field, waiting for brave men to go out and destroy them. They finished filling sandbags and removing the last of the wreckage as the sun dipped towards the horizon, and it was dark by the time they returned wearily to their tents. A thin strip of light blue surmounted the purple sky, the only evidence that day had ever existed there at all. The air had cooled a little but the desert retained its heat.

The oil lamp took. Charlie hung it up, where its meagre light caressed the sagging canvas of the tent. He turned to face Peter with a tired look.

'Peter, I know I've done nothing to earn your trust. I might even have acted a bit like a prat to you. But, like it or not, we have to rely on each other - I'm asking you to trust me.'

Peter mastered his surprise, he had not expected this.

'Trust you how? What are you planning?'

'The rest of the squadron will be back soon, and then the C.O. and Brian will decide who's being tossed out,' Charlie said, folding his arms, 'We need leverage in case it's us.'

'We put our necks on the line in the middle of an air raid. What more can we do to prove we're worth keeping?'

'We're the odd ones out. The deck's stacked against us. Saving that aircraft counts for nothing unless we can show we're better than all the others. And we've got just that - a plan to have a crack at the Italians where they least expect it,' Charlie said, his face illuminated.

'You can't really believe they'll swallow that? We've barely got any certainty that your location is accurate. What if they changed course after we left them?'

'They never changed course because they couldn't change course. They got around our fighters somehow on the way in, I'll wager they had to do the same to get out.'

'Why don't we discuss this with Brian,' Peter said, 'he seems like a decent bloke. He can give us some advice on how to play it?'

Charlie shook his head.

'We've already concealed this from him. If he doesn't like the plan, then we're right back to square one again. It's a good plan, Peter, so I'm going to find a way to propose it to the C.O. Just say you'll support me when I do?'

Peter considered his options. Both of them. The easiest course of action, he thought, was to stop this nonsense right here. Brian would be incensed when he heard about their deceit. If he sold Charlie out, Peter might just be able to keep a place on the squadron. But that was not his style. Even though he owed Charlie nothing, he longed to have a crack at the Italians and he had already committed to it now by backing up Charlie's story.

'Ok. You're on. But no more lies.'

*

Squadron Leader Johnny Corbett was the Commanding Officer, or C.O., of XXI Squadron. Charlie heard he had a reputation for being a talented, aggressive flyer, although he had not met him personally. The Squadron had arrived at Helwan a couple of days after the Italian raid, roaring over the airfield in a full nine-aircraft formation, before splitting off to land individually. Charlie sought out the C.O. and eventually found him inside the tent that served as a squadron office, in conversation with Brian.

Charlie wandered up and down outside the tent long enough to hear him tell Brian what he thought of the Italian raid.

'It's just maddening, Brian. To hear they slipped through our fighter screen and got as far Cairo. Two of our Blenheims destroyed on the ground for not a single Italian loss. The whole thing stinks - I don't wonder it's those leaky bastards at Middle East Headquarters.'

'Is that you loitering out there, Kendrick?'

Charlie heard Brian call from within.

He ducked under the flaps and stood to attention. The inside of the tent, apart from being baking hot, was covered in sand thrown up during the bombing raid. It was a total mess. Brian stood in one corner next to a jagged tear in the canvas, through which sunlight entered, the C.O. sat at a desk. He had reddish blond hair and a fierce look about it him. A Cranwell man through and through, thought Charlie, an untouchable.

'Who's this?'

'Flying Officer Kendrick is one of our new boys, sir,' Brian said, pointing to a stack of files on the desk, 'I jotted some notes about the orders we've got to send some of them to fly transports.'

The C.O. found the appropriate file, blew sand off it, and opened it up. Charlie noticed the C.O.'s expression change to one of faint disapproval as he read the file.

'Your training record is excellent,' the C.O. said, looking up from the file, 'but thereafter it is, ah, mixed.'

Charlie licked his lips but said nothing.

'This is not Flying Officer Kendrick's first squadron, he was originally posted to 230 Squadron, but was moved on to us because they were fully crewed,' Brian added. Charlie knew there was more to it than that, and silently thanked Brian for giving the abridged version.

The C.O. shot Charlie a dissatisfied look.

'Kendrick, it would be easy for me to wash you out to another unit. Why should I hang onto you?'

Brian leaned forward to address the C.O., but Charlie took a deep breath and spoke first.

'Sir, my skipper and I got one of the kites away during the bombing raid. We were able to track the Italians and get a location for their base in Libya.'

The C.O. looked at him wordlessly for a moment before speaking.

'The hell you say,' he turned to Brian, 'I thought he wasn't crewed up?'

Charlie felt Brian studying at him. His stare betrayed nothing, but he felt a mounting regret at not telling Brian first. That was a mistake, he reflected.

'They're *not* crewed up. His pilot, Peter Denhay, only arrived a few days ago and I was sending them off on a navigation sortie when the Italians struck,' Brian said.

When the C.O. looked back, Charlie felt something had changed in his face. He thought he might have made out a gleam in the C.O.'s eye.

'Tell me your plan, Kendrick. You've got three minutes.'

Charlie explained how he had come to the conclusion that the Italians had used a break in the fighter cover to slip through to Helwan. He showed the C.O. and Brian the chart and his calculations marked in pencil in the margin. Then he described how they could send an attack into Libya early the next morning, before the Italians launched their first wave, and avenge their attack on Helwan. As he spoke, Charlie noticed how the C.O. looked thoughtfully at the map. Even Brian looked halfway impressed.

'You'll not have nine aircraft for a raid like this, half the machines need maintenance,' Brian said, folding his arms, 'I might be able to scrape together three aircraft.'

'We won't need more than three, if we have the advantage of surprise,' the C.O. replied, 'I'll lead it, with Venner as my number two and-'

Charlie cleared his throat pointedly. The C.O. treated him to a withering stare.

'Alright. Denhay and Kendrick can fly number three, it was your hard work I suppose.'

'Marcus Venner has requested a leave pass, sir,' Brian chipped in.

'Has he, again? Fine. Gus Sinclair then.'

'We'll need to find Denhay and Kendrick an air gunner too.'

'That shouldn't be a problem, look who's back.'

Charlie followed the C.O.'s gaze through the tent opening. He saw a dishevelled Sergeant standing outside between two service policemen in white caps.

'He's yours now, Kendrick,' Brian said, nodding to the Sergeant, 'you can sort him out. Off you go. Oh, and you might as well go and introduce yourself to Flight Lieutenant Venner too - you'll all be part of his flight, if you stay with us.'

Charlie came to attention once more, turned about and left the C.O. and Brian to plan the detail of the raid. He was feeling pretty pleased with how the interview had gone. Although no promises were made, he believed that he had given the C.O. cause to think twice about ditching them.

Emerging back out into the sunshine he called over to the RAF policemen. Charlie had met a few service policemen in his short career and found them to be universally unlikeable. His sense of fellow-feeling for the prisoner was not inconsiderable.

'Hello, Corporal,' Charlie said to the policeman, 'is this one of ours?'

'Sir! Sergeant E876541 Miller, Patrick. Handed over to your custody, pending sentencing,' the policeman replied in a terse voice.

'Sergeant Miller, I'm Flying Officer Kendrick. It looks like we'll be crewed up together. Fancy telling me what happened?'

Miller's eyes swivelled towards Charlie, though he continued to face the front. Those eyes were red-rimmed and bloodshot, Charlie noticed, the bruising about his left eye threatened to close it and he stunk of liquor. Not too difficult to guess what had happened, but a story worth hearing, he thought to himself.

'Fighting, sir. And being out of bounds,' Miller said, proudly.

'-And resisting arrest, which is a charge in itself. And soliciting,' added the Corporal.

Charlie whistled. That was a charge sheet, alright.

'Well, a fat lot of good you're going to be to us with only one working eye. You better cut away to see if you can find something to reduce that swelling. Off you go.'

Miller smiled and went to walk away, but Charlie called to him.

'Sergeant Miller?'

He stopped and turned back to Charlie.

'I hope you're better at shooting Wops than you are at fighting the Old Bill,' Charlie said, in a neutral tone.

'Oh don't you worry, sir,' Miller smiled, 'I'm the best.'

*

Peter heard about the interview with the C.O. and their new air gunner over lunch, and then walked with Charlie to meet Marcus Venner. They found him in his tent, where he was packing a suitcase. Peter saw that he was tall and athletic, handsome but immediately not particularly engaging. He chose not to turn away from the small shaving mirror he was gazing into as he brushed and oiled his dark hair, greeting them over his shoulder. They introduced themselves and stood awkwardly just inside the tent as Venner talked at them.

'Brian said you might pop round to see me. He thinks you'd be good for my flight.'

'We certainly hope so,' Charlie smiled, with a wink at Peter.

'Well I disagree. You might think you've won the C.O. over with your little plan to go and bomb the Italians, but I'm not impressed. We underestimate them all the time and do so at our peril. They're quite capable of mounting a surprise raid and misleading you into thinking you know where their base is. I wouldn't be surprised if you found a whole squadron of fighters waiting for you,' Venner said, shaking his head.

Peter stood silently, he had nothing to say to that.

'I told Brian as much, but he's as taken with your damn fool plan as the C.O. is. In any event, I'm not letting it get in the way of my leave. We've been on continuous operations for nearly six weeks now and I need a drink.'

Venner turned around to attach his wristwatch, a gold Rolex with a leather strap. He stared at Peter for a brief moment, and then at Charlie. He had fierce blue eyes and a roman nose. His face wore a look of barely disguised dislike. Placing his hairbrushes in the suitcase, he shut it before pulling on his tunic.

'I don't like either of you,' Venner stated baldly, 'you don't fit in around here and you, Kendrick, you shouldn't even be a commissioned officer, in my opinion. When I get back from leave, I'm going to do my utmost to get you both shifted off elsewhere. As far from me as possible.'

He barged past them and stalked off in the direction of a waiting motorcar.

'I feel that went well,' Charlie said.

'What did he mean about not fitting in here - and you not being suitable for a commission?'

Charlie considered this for moment then shrugged.

'There were some things before I got here. Some stupid stuff, nothing more serious than that.

*

The opal blue sky, clear of cloud as far as the eye could see, was empty save for the three aircraft crossing high above the shimmering, grey desert floor. They flew in a standard 'V' formation with the leader in the centre and the others to either side, trailing a little way behind. Despite his inexperience in formation flying, Peter found it came naturally to him. Once they had left the comparatively lush Nile delta behind, the landscape they flew across was largely devoid of features, a moonscape of dunes swept away to the south in a vast empty sea.

Peter thought back to the mission briefing at Helwan, just before dawn that morning. The nine men of the three bomber crews grouped around a trestle table in the dispersal tent to inspect a large-scale aviation map. It depicted most of the Western Desert theatre of operations from the Nile to Benghazi. Markings on the chart in blue and red pencil indicated all the major airfields and likely concentrations of both friendly and enemy forces. The brief was lit by spirit lamps hanging from a pole suspended between the tent posts. Most of the men were standing and there was a strong smell of cigarette smoke and sweat.

The C.O. had explained that the Italians had crossed the Egyptian border at Sollum and were now about 60 miles inside Egypt, near a place called *Sidi Barrani*. So far, attacking the Italian's airforce had been difficult, because the location of their bomber's forward bases was unknown. Until now. Peter listened carefully to the plan that the C.O. outlined. There was no time to gather aerial reconnaissance photographs of the target and the only map they had showed a fort and nothing else at *Marawah*. They would drop down to low-level as they crossed the border, to avoid Italian fighters, and then head to *Marawah* where they would conduct an attack from alternating directions to keep the ground defences occupied.

At 10,000 feet, the heat of the day was less of an issue, and Peter found himself quite comfortable with the cockpit vent cracked open. He could make out Charlie's back in the navigator's position in the nose of the Blenheim, where he was bent over the map table. Charlie had just announced that they were crossing into Libya when Miller came up on the intercom.

'Message from Tinker Leader, Skipper: "descending to low-level now, adopt line-astern formation"'.

'Acknowledge,' Peter replied.

The C.O. began a gentle descent and Peter eased the throttles back to permit Gus Sinclair's aircraft to slip into the number two position. It was some time before they levelled off at 500 feet and Peter was surprised at how the terrain had changed from the flat emptiness of the Egyptian desert to a far more undulating pattern of hillocks crisscrossed by many small valleys.

Peter felt that flying at low-level, even at 500 feet, was far more demanding for a pilot, whose attention was absorbed by keeping station within the formation, avoiding terrain, and flying the aeroplane all at once. The ground flicked past beneath them at over 200 mph and at one point, when cresting a low hill, they noticed a goat herder and his animals gathered in the lee of the hillside. He glanced up, and Peter looked into his bewildered face for less than a second before he disappeared below and behind them. If Charlie was right about the Italian bombers, Peter thought, then they could expect to see a fairly large aerodrome in front of them shortly. If he was wrong, however, they would continue to fly over this type of terrain until the C.O. called an end to it and led them back to their base. Back to an ignominious departure from operational flying.

'How long to the target, Charlie?'

'15 minutes,' Charlie reported. He was leaning over the Mk IX bombsight, positioned in the perspex window at the front of the nose, to enter settings correct for their height and speed. Looking back up through the canopy in front, Peter could see Sinclair's aircraft in perfect silhouette, as if on an aircraft recognition chart, and beyond it the smaller shape of the C.O. They rose and fell gently with the undulations of the ground, like the tail of a kite in a strong wind.

'Initial Point ahead,' Charlie called, and then in a louder voice, 'look at that.'

Peter saw the fort a few miles away and slightly to the left of the nose, a distinct white walled building with motor vehicles parked nearby. But beyond it was what had excited Charlie's attention. The flattened space of the aerodrome sat in a shallow valley. On the field sat no less than two dozen bombers, and most parked almost wingtip-to-wingtip as if waiting for an inspection rather than an air raid. Better still, a pair of aircraft were at the end of the airfield preparing for take-off, and another two were turning onto the field behind them. They were unmistakably *Sparvienos,* that much was evident from their three engines and prominent hump behind the cockpit containing a defensive machine-gun. It was also clear that they had been caught with their pants down.

The C.O. made a tight left turn to put the aerodrome on the starboard wing, this would carry them directly over the fort. As they flew overhead, Peter glanced down and saw within the walls a collection of tents, a military truck loaded with stores, and figures with faces upturned towards him. He braced himself for the airfield defences to open up on them at any minute, they must have anti-aircraft guns waiting for us, he thought. But no fire greeted them, it appeared as if the Italians were as surprised to see him as he was to have found them all the way out here. In front, Sinclair's aircraft rolled violently and peeled off to starboard, hammering in towards the parked aircraft.

'Break, now,' Charlie shouted over the intercom. Peter hauled the aircraft over onto its new course straight down the runway towards the *Sparvienos*. The Italians recognised the danger far too late. They were at their most vulnerable here with full bomb bays and fuel tanks. Their only escape would be to get off the ground before the RAF bombers struck. Peter found himself thinking how brave the leader of the first pair must be to think it was a gamble worth taking, forgetting he and Charlie had done the same a few days before. The Italian set off down the airstrip; his wingman followed a touch behind and to one side to avoid the cloud of dust blown up by his leader.

Charlie passed him course adjustments over the intercom and Peter tried to respond to each one with a gentle touch on the rudder or stick. He heard an almighty explosion off to their right somewhere and guessed it was Sinclair's bombs going off. The escaping Italians were accelerating towards him along the runway but had not yet left the ground. Soon it would be too late, they would escape and-.

'Bombs gone, bombs gone' The Blenheim lurched slightly with the release of its payload of four 250lbs bombs. The first three bombs in the stick landed harmlessly behind the two escaping Italians, cratering the surface of the strip but causing no real permanent damage. The fourth bomb, however, landed squarely between the two *Sparvienos* and detonated. The blast sheared the tail off the leader and tore the port wing off the other, before setting off the bombs and petrol in a tremendous sympathetic explosion that engulfed both aircraft and tore them to flaming shreds.

Peter felt the shockwave from the explosion pass through them even after they had left the bombers well behind. He rolled the aircraft over in a half-turn to starboard to confound any anti-aircraft gunners that might have been aiming for them and, looking back through the canopy, surveyed the scene of absolute devastation they had caused. Aside from the burning mass on the airfield, from which thick black smoke was now issuing up to an impressive height, Sinclair's bombs had also found their target. Most of them had exploded either on or around the packed aircraft on the far side of the airfield causing severe damage and starting a conflagration that would be very troublesome to contain.

As he watched, the C.O.'s aircraft appeared through the smoke screen heading towards the second pair of *Sparvienos* in the act of bomb release. Debris littered the airfield and made it impossible for either of the Italian aircraft to get airborne. This had dawned on the Italians too because men could be seen running from one of the grounded aircraft. The other crew must have been frozen to the spot. Peter thought the C.O. was very low, probably less than 200 feet, and running in at maximum speed. The result was inevitable; there was no escape. He gazed open-mouthed, as the bombs struck squarely on the enemy aircraft and exploded, rending them apart. Pieces of aircraft fuselage and bodies were thrown into the air in an obscene fireworks display. He felt sure that the bomb blast must have caught the C.O. and was amazed to see his machine turn and climb gently away from the smoke and flame, disappearing behind their wing apparently unharmed. There were people running on the airfield now, but the *Sparvieno* crews were past helping.

'They didn't even fire back,' Charlie said into the intercom, 'Not a single shot', he was bewildered. Peter said nothing, but quietly reformed on the C.O.'s wing as the three Blenheims climbed away from the burning pyre they had left at *Marawah* and turned for home.

*

They landed at Helwan in the early afternoon, after a total of eight hours flying. The debrief was short and sweet, the C.O. told them how pleased he was as they stood around smoking and then wandered off to telephone their results through to Group. Normally, Charlie would have celebrated with a drink, but he felt completely shattered from his first operational sortie and his body demanded sleep. He bid the others goodbye and walked off to his tent, running into Fatty Taylor and Kilvington who were leaving the squadron in their service dress uniforms, presumably off on leave, he guessed. He nodded a hello, but Taylor stopped and barred his path.

'So that's it then, Kendrick. They've decided we're off to fly transports. You win, although I'll never guess how it's us leaving and not you.'

Charlie was not a vindictive man and he felt gloating was ungentlemanly, so he just smiled at him.

'You snide bastard,' Taylor growled, 'you'll get yours, Kendrick, just you wait and see. It's going to be a long war and you'll get yours, *mate*.'

Chapter 4

The mess tent was packed for the dining-in night and had been decorated in the best possible taste, despite the demands the war had placed on luxury goods. The tables were laid out with white linen and, though the cutlery was not silver, nor the plates china, the catering officer had worked miracles with the fare. The services of a commis chef from the Hotel Cecil had even been secured for the evening. Candles burned brightly between the diners and the meagre quantity of silver the squadron possessed was laid out so it could be admired by all.

The sides of the tent were folded back to admit some slightly cooler air, as well as the music of the station volunteer band. Mess stewards in white jackets stood waiting to re-charge wine glasses that were emptying quickly in the heat of the evening.

From his position seated at the bottom of the centre leg, Peter surveyed the dinner in its entirety. Along the top table the C.O. and Brian sat either side of a bearded civilian. Venner was in the corner, making polite conversation with an officer Peter did not know. As the most junior member of the mess, Peter was performing the role of Mr Vice for the evening. This meant he had responsibility for announcing the loyal toast. He was flanked by two trusted souls who could be relied upon not to get him blind drunk.

On his right was the squadron's Engineer Officer, a short choleric man, and opposite him the Station Padre, Flight Lieutenant The Reverend Ogilvy, who was widely regarded as a thumping bore. He was boring them now with a lecture on some ecumenical matter. The Engineer Officer looked like he found this unbearable and applied himself vigorously to the wine. His face was flushed even before the fish, and this was a four-course meal. He looked around moodily, trying to catch the eye of one of the mess stewards.

Beyond Peter's immediate neighbours were a group of subalterns from a light cavalry regiment, guests of the Air Liaison Officer, a soldier attached to the squadron. They were engaged in animated discussion. The subject of which was hard to discern, for they were all roaring drunk and throwing bread at each other. The squadron's crews sat mainly down the long legs of the table. Dotted about in ones or twos amongst them were their guests, a mixture of uniforms, frocks, and men in evening dress. Their chatter and laughter bubbled gently, only just audible over the band's music. Peter noticed that Charlie had managed to find a seat next to a pretty-looking woman in a blue evening gown. *Lucky sod*, he thought.

*

Charlie also considered himself lucky, as it had been quite by accident that he was seated next to Margot Dacre, the officer he had met on his last visit to station headquarters. Charlie was half-cut, but knew he was at his best in this state.

Margot was excellent company. Quite unlike the silly girls that Charlie had known in London, she was funny, engaging, and cultured. They discovered a shared love for Gilbert & Sullivan's Savoy Operas. She sang the Major General's song from *Pirates of Penzance* in her sweet voice flawlessly, to rowdy applause around the table. Throughout, she focused her attention in the middle distance, which made her look charmingly cross-eyed.

Save for a brief moment at the start of the meal when they had greeted their neighbours, Charlie and Margot spoke only to each other. This was not lost on the frowning red-haired Flying Officer opposite them, waiting for pause in the conversation to say something witty. Charlie was not ignorant of his determined stare, but he did not give in to it. The opportunity came, however, as MacNeish was regaling the table with the story of how he had secured the services of the Cecil's commis chef on behalf of the catering officer. It was a gambit that led to a well-rehearsed joke about catering in the RAF and MacNeish was bringing it artfully to its climax.

'-And we all know the catering course is the hardest course in the RAF-,' when his neighbour, Wardle, robbed him of his punchline, *because no-one has ever passed it*.

It was an old joke, repeated often, but the audience was in high spirits and the table erupted in peals of laughter. It startled the Padre, who spilt his wine across the table. The better part of it landed, somewhat predictably, in the Engineer Officer's lap.

Wardle was wiping a tear from his eye and giggling at MacNeish, who responded with a smile and a shrug. In the lull that followed, the red-haired Flying Officer leaned forward to speak to Margot, but was beaten to it again by MacNeish, who called across the table to her.

'I suppose you've heard that one before?'

'The old ones are the best ones, aren't they?'

'Oh, for God's sake.' The red-haired Flying Officer muttered under his breath with arms folded in frustration.

MacNeish launched into another story about a belly dancer that he had seen in a nightclub in Cairo, but he was in turn interrupted by the band coming to the conclusion of *Midnight, the Stars and You*. There was polite applause, which the bandmaster acknowledged with a tilt of his head, and without taking more than a breath, the band were straight into *Goodnight, Sweet Dream.*

Margot turned back to Charlie, who was discretely admiring her beauty in the candlelight.

'I absolutely adore this song,' she sighed, 'Who's your friend over there? The one you keep looking over at.'

'Who, Peter? That's Peter Denhay, he's my pilot.'

'*Your* pilot?' She asked mischievously, 'I thought pilots captained the aircraft?'

'Well, they do,' Charlie thought quickly, 'but I tell him where to go, so who's working for who I ask you?'

Margot laughed, covering her mouth unconsciously.

'Is he a good pilot?'

'The best I've flown with,' Charlie paused to fill her wine glass, 'also the first I've flown with.'

She laughed again.

'The truth is,' Charlie went on, 'he's very straight-laced. But we seem to rub along just fine. We flew our first sortie a few days ago and that was a coup.'

'Sounds intriguing, will you tell me about it?'

'Well, really I shouldn't. But you work in intelligence so I dare say that you're safe.'

Charlie explained how they had come up with the plan to strike the Italians, following a hunch about the whereabouts of their forward operating base. And he described the low-level attack in accurate detail, with only a few exaggerations here and there. There may have been a few less bombers, he thought to himself, perhaps the air defences were a little less alert. But he was broadly happy with the result when he came to the conclusion. Margot's expression changed as he recounted the story and Charlie began to wonder if he had made a mis-step somewhere. His impression was that she was alarmed, rather than impressed by his tale. Desperate for some way to restart the conversation, he changed the subject.

'Have you been to many of these dinners before?' He asked, finally.

'A few. When I was with Gordon.'

'Who's Gordon, if you don't mind me asking?'

'Not at all. He was my husband,' she said, looking at him for a moment and then looking away.

Over the course of the meal, Charlie learned that Gordon Dacre had worked for the Foreign Office in Cairo. He had been very well regarded within the Diplomatic Service as a linguist and expert in the Levant.

'How did you meet him?'

'I was very young and impressionable, and I ran into him at a drinks party in Pimlico. He was friends with all sorts of dreadfully clever artists and writers. But he was intelligent and kind, and I suppose I fell for him at once,' Margot said, taking a sip of wine and studying Charlie carefully for his reaction.

'Papa, was dead against it of course, because of the age gap. But I put up such a fuss that he relented in the end. We married in 1937 and I followed Gordon out to Egypt.'

'It must have been very exciting for you; like an adventure.'

'Oh, it was! And I adored it at first, but Gordon fell very ill a year later, and I became his nursemaid. And then he died. It was very sudden. He was only 36.'

'I'm so sorry, Margot.'

'Don't be, it's ancient history now. Poor Gordon was brilliant in every respect, but one. He was appalling at managing money, so I had to find work quickly or risk asking Papa for a handout.'

'I suppose that wasn't easy?'

'The firms here will employ anyone as long as they're public school-educated boys. But I eventually found work as a typist with the Suez Canal Company and then joined the W.A.A.F. as soon as I was able. The odd thing is, Charlie, the whole experience left me feeling-'

'Heartbroken?'

'Free. I went from Papa's house to Gordon's house without ever really knowing what it was like to work for myself, to earn a living and do with it as I please.'

Charlie smiled. Margot was very different indeed, he decided.

'But Charlie, I've bored you enough with my troubles. What about you? How do you come to be here?'

Charlie had been expecting this and took a deep draught from his glass in preparation.

'I was in medical school in 1938, Guy's in London. But I could see how things were going in Europe, and I wanted to go and fight in Spain. But my father threatened to cut me off if I left. So, I became active on the home front instead.'

'Charlie, are you telling me you were a communist?'

Margot's face lit up.

'Ssssssh,' Charlie looked around to see if anyone had heard. Seeing they had not, he went on.

'I moved with a lot of very different people from street sweepers to lords. But they all had something in common, they all hated oppression. I felt entirely at home.'

He paused for moment to collect his thoughts.

'Then there was a girl, and some difficulties with the police. The war was a godsend really. I joined up in August 1939 and volunteered as aircrew. The RAF doesn't frown upon men who drink, and it can even tolerate revolutionary ideas - up to a point.' Charlie flashed her a winning smile.

'You're drunk, Flying Officer Kendrick,' she said, but not unkindly.

'I must be. For a moment I was thinking that perhaps some good can come out of this awful war after all.'

Before he could say any more, he was interrupted by the band playing the national anthem. They all stood and drank off a glass of port in honour to the sovereign. After the loyal toast, the C.O. thanked everyone involved in organising the dinner and gave a short speech. Charlie only half listened to it, his thoughts filled with Margot Dacre. The C.O. closed by saying they had received orders to move to a new airfield not far from *Mersa Matruh*. Their time had come, Charlie knew, they were really off to war now.

There was light applause and the C.O. sat back down. After a time, people began to drift away from their seats to chat to their friends or to move out into the slightly cooler night air. As they left the tent, Margot paused to look across the airfield where the faint outlines of several aircraft were visible in the murky darkness. Charlie followed her gaze and wondered if she was also asking herself how many of those aircraft and young men would survive to return to Helwan again. She turned to Charlie and spoke in a serious tone.

'Charlie, I'm sorry if I seemed distracted when you told me about your bombing raid. You're right, it was a smashing yarn. But something in what you said troubled me.'

Charlie said nothing. He wondered if she knew he had embellished the amount of ground fire in his story.

'You see,' she continued, 'we were concerned that the Italians could read our signals. There were unexplained- difficulties, in our operations in the desert. But an investigation ruled out the possibility that they had cracked our ciphers.'

Charlie was amazed, he had no idea that Margot had access to this kind of information and was stunned to hear about the secret war of intelligence.

'Well if they're not reading our signals, what's the problem?'

'That doesn't mean they don't have access to our secrets. Our working theory is that one of ours is passing intelligence to the Italians,' Margo said in a low voice.

'But why would someone do that? Sell us out to the Italians, I mean,'

Before Margot could answer another voice from behind Charlie interrupted.

'Sell what to the Italians, pray tell?'

It was Venner. Charlie wondered how long he had been standing there. He must be very light-footed, he realised. Venner's jacket was unbuttoned, his blotchy face was a mask of curiosity, and he looked from Margot to Charlie with faint surprise and expectation.

'Oil,' Margot replied, 'It seems the Germans provide oil to the Italians.' Charlie raised an eyebrow at her collusion.

'Most certainly, they can't have access to it from anywhere in their piddling Empire,' Venner smiled.

'I see that you're leaving, Mrs Dacre,' Venner went on, 'Perhaps I can escort you back to your accommodation. It gets awfully dark around camp at night; no place for a woman to be on her own.'

'No, thank you, Marcus. I'm quite happy to walk alone, it's not far and I have the light of the moon to find my way.'

He nodded but looked disappointed.

Goodnight Marcus, goodnight Charlie,' Margot said. Charlie thought she gave him a last lingering look.

Venner looked sideways at Charlie, 'She's a bit out of your league, isn't she? You haven't got a hope in hell of ever capturing her affections.'

'You know it's funny, but I never got the impression that Margot Dacre could really be happy belonging to anyone,' Charlie replied.

'Tell yourself whatever you like. She just wants for a good man, that's all.'

Venner took a deep draught of his wine, turned away and walked off into the murky tent.

*

Peter made his excuses to the Padre and the Engineer Officer and stood to leave. As he did, he bumped into the C.O. saying goodbye to the civilian he sat with at dinner. The C.O. introduced him as 'Jumbo' Sutherland, and Peter shook his hand. Sutherland was a trim, serious man with a deep mahogany tan from years spent in the Middle East.

'Peter is one of my newest pilots. He's green, but he beat up some Italians in Libya the other day and I bet they haven't forgotten about it yet,' the C.O. beamed.

Sutherland spoke with a faint Ulster accent. He asked about the Libyan raid and Peter gave a brief account of the sortie, to which he listened intently, asking intelligent questions at pertinent points. He seemed particularly interested in how they had located the Italians. Conscious that he had talked almost non-stop since they were introduced, Peter changed the subject.

'And what do you do, sir?'

'Well, I suppose officially I work for His Majesty's Government as its representative in these parts.'

'Oh, Foreign Office work?'

'Often quite foreign, yes,' Sutherland replied with a hint of amusement, 'So, are you looking forward to this exciting move to the front?'

'I dare say so, yes. Although there's not much out there beyond camels and sand though.'

'Certainly not, and more than enough sand when the Khamsin blows,' Sutherland winked.

'The Khamsin?'

'Yes. The Khamsin is a hot, dry wind that blows from the south across the desert. It brings sandstorms that can last anything from a few hours up to 50 days. There's an old Arab proverb that says if the Khamsin blows for three days a man has the right to kill his wife, for five his friend, and for seven days, himself.'

Chapter 5

The Khamsin did blow, but not for 50 days. Nevertheless, in six hours it whipped up a storm that covered everything with a fine dust and infiltrated sand particles into every conceivable object. It got everywhere, into sleeping bags and coffee cups, hair and teeth were gritted with it. It was impossible to fly or even stand outside during the sandstorm.

For the men of XXI Squadron it made their new base at *Wadi Begoush* even more miserable than its bleak isolation warranted. No-one knew how the place justified a name. There was absolutely nothing there, save for the indeterminable remains of a building that could have been a fort or a toilet, for what remained to be seen. Aside from a handful of palm trees that grew around what was once an oasis, beyond the aerodrome miles of camel thorn stretched out to the horizon in every direction.

The main party had arrived a few days previously and had set up much of the camp ready to receive the aircraft and crews from Helwan. They had no trouble finding it because it stuck out like a sore thumb in the miles of empty desert that surrounded it. Arriving from their fuelling stop at *Fouka*, they surveyed the expanse of the aerodrome, vehicles scattered around its edge and the ubiquitous canvas of all descriptions - a large marquee for messing and smaller bivouacs for living in.

'What a shit hole,' Miller said over the intercom, summing up everyone's thoughts.

Venner's 'A' Flight arrived first and were waved over to what they took to be their dispersal. Sliding the canopy hatch back, Peter was pleased to see Sergeant Mellish supervising their engineers and he waved hello. Mellish jumped up onto the wing to help him out. He wore shorts and boots with a green pullover; a sign of cooler temperatures coming with the approach of winter.

'I'm pleased to see you, sir. The last few days we ain't stopped,' he jerked his thumb over his shoulder, 'an poor Tom Crawley there got bitten by something and his 'ole arm swelled up like suet pudding.' He laughed. Crawley looked up at Peter from where he was stacking petrol cans next to the wing with a look of mixed embarrassment and resignation. He had almost certainly been the butt of the men's jokes for the last few days for this painful, if temporary, abnormality.

'How do you find it here, Mellish?'

'Well, it's not Cairo, sir. There's nothing to do or see, although that's no problem seeing as we're working so hard. The water's chlorinated, the latrines are a disgrace and you better like bully beef. But there's no reveille and no inspection, so I think we're just about even-stevens.'

Peter was about to reply when he caught a raised voice on the otherwise quiet airfield. It belonged to Venner who was publicly remonstrating with one of the ground crew for the lack of slit trenches or sandbag protection. His victim, Warrant Officer Tyler, faced the admonishment with a stoicism bred from years of service to the Crown.

'The Eyeties could come tearing over right now and bomb this damned place to kingdom come, and where would we be then? Buggered, that's where. And all because you lot have been sat about with your thumbs up your arses for two days,' Venner shouted, before storming off to the aircrew lorry without waiting for a reply.

Peter was mortified by this display of petulance towards the engineers, who had obviously been working hard to prepare for their arrival. He found himself oddly not surprised. Venner had contrived to be elsewhere for most of the period of preparation running up to their move to *Wadi Begoush*. He was also late to their pre-flight briefing that morning and spent most of the flight haranguing the formation over the wireless about their station-keeping. Peter, who ordinarily liked and wished to be liked by everyone he met, felt a growing coldness towards his new flight commander.

Miller helped Charlie unload bags and other gear from the body of the aircraft and now offered to help the engineers with the refuelling. There were no fuel lorries here, so refuelling had to be done by hand using four-gallon petrol cans. It was a time-consuming process. Charlie agreed to stay on too, so Peter found himself sat in the back of the lorry with MacNeish, Wardle, and their crews heading to squadron operations to report in. Venner sat up front with the driver and, relieved of his overbearing presence, the men smoked and talked freely as they were bumped around in the back with the movement of the truck.

Though neither MacNeish nor Wardle spoke about Venner in front of their crews, Peter sensed an uncomfortable atmosphere. He reached for his cigarettes in his shirt pocket. By the time he had lit one and taken a long drag, they arrived at squadron operations, which was a converted truck. Brian sat inside with a wireless operator and some chalk boards. He looked tired but greeted them warmly and recorded their names on his board.

Brian explained that Group had allocated the squadron an operational sortie for tomorrow and, because 'A' Flight had already arrived and was therefore most rested, it would go to them. Venner opened his mouth to say something, but seeing the look on Brian's face, he quickly closed it. Brian said that he would brief them later, once they had settled in and had eaten. He added that it was a two-aircraft operation. Before he could say more the wireless crackled with the voice of 'B' Flight's leader, Gus Sinclair, seeking permission to land and Brian turned away. They tumbled down the steps and headed back to the truck. Venner turned to Peter as they walked.

'Denhay, you'll be flying with me on that sortie tomorrow. Meet me at squadron operations after dinner,' he instructed, then turned away and got back into the cab. As Peter sat down, he was conscious that MacNeish was smiling at him wryly.

'Lucky boy,' MacNeish said, at last.

*

Lunch was Bully Beef, as some wag had predicted in paint on a sign outside the mess that read: 'Today's Menu'. The cookhouse fried it and threw in some onions and canned tomatoes to make a crude stew. The flies were worse here than at Helwan, in Charlie's opinion. He wondered where they came from, all the way out in this emptiness. It was only as they were leaving the mess tent that he noticed the onset of the sandstorm. The wind had been rising since they arrived, but now a dirty yellow smudge appeared on the horizon to the south. Within minutes it arrived with tremendous force. It masked the sun, tinting everything with an odd brown light and blotted out visibility of anything over a couple of feet away.

Common sense dictated that nothing could go aloft in these conditions, and so Charlie led Peter back to the bivouac tent they shared. He groped past the unrecognisable forms of tents and other obstacles, and pulled the flaps tight shut. Their meagre belongings had already accumulated a fine coating of sand that was pointless to remove at this stage. Instead they sat in the semi-darkness and conversed. Charlie immediately launched into a critique of Venner. He believed, even if his views on the necessity of blast protection at *Wadi Bagoush* were correct, his method was wrong.

'Frankly, shouting at a man who cannot reply is mean and contemptible,' Charlie was saying, when Venner's head appeared at the tent door. Neither could be certain how much Venner had overheard, or that his reddened face was not from exertion caused by finding his way through the tents in the face of the storm.

'Sortie's scrubbed for tomorrow. You can stand-down,' he said. The red face withdrew, leaving them in darkness and silence. Peter was first to speak.

'I can't agree with that last part, you know, about giving orders. The entire Service is based on the principle that you can shout at someone, and he cannot reply.'

Charlie frowned at Peter, slightly irritated by being caught out.

'Your trouble is that you're a product of the system. All you know is the hierarchy, so it's common to you.'

'Why? Because I'm not privileged, I suppose?'

Charlie realised that he was on dangerous ground. He had not meant to offend Peter, but this was an awkward situation to extract from.

'No. Because you're institutionalised. We all are. Isn't that what happens when you join up? Your freedom is sacrificed for the freedom of others?'

Peter looked dissatisfied but said nothing.

The sandstorm blew itself out. It departed almost as quickly as it had come, leaving a salmon coloured sky as the sun dipped towards the horizon. Reluctantly, they tidied up their tent. Charlie was just pouring sand out of one of his flying boots when Miller stomped up. He had been woken by Venner's air gunner to tell him that the sortie was back on. The briefing would go ahead for a launch at first light.

*

Peter found himself back at squadron operations in the falling dark, squashed into one corner of the box body while Brian and Venner craned over a chart. Brian explained the local situation. The Italians had advanced east of *Sidi Barrani*, but had stopped short of an all-out offensive on *Mersa Matruh*, which was strongly fortified by the British in anticipation of just that. Their troops were divided into a series of defensive pockets that hinged on the great coastal road and ran roughly south-west into the desert in a fishhook shape.

It was expected that the Italians would renew their offensive in late November or early December. Aerial reconnaissance had identified efforts to build up strength, with line of communication troops building new roads and convoys of trucks heading towards Italian positions at the front from bases across the border in Libya. The British plan was to forestall the enemy offensive, so they were switching from airfield attacks to bombing concentrations of enemy vehicles and equipment.

A convoy of over 50 vehicles had been spotted near *Sidi Barrani*, Brian pointed out the location marked on his map. Their mission was to locate the convoy and bomb it. But if that was impossible, then they should strike targets of opportunity instead.

'What about enemy air defences?' Venner asked.

Brian shrugged, 'Hard to say. The Eyeties have been less active recently. They might be conserving strength for something.' He added that they could expect to find Fiat CR.42 *Falcos* on combat air patrol over the Italian lines. The *Falco* was a single-seat biplane fighter. It was a threat to even a fast light bomber like the Blenheim. Although it was assessed as under-gunned for a fighter, it mounted only two machine-guns.

The two Blenheims took off just before sunrise and headed towards their target area at 4, 000 feet. There was thick cloud cover that extended down to just below their flight level. Venner had briefed the plan was to use the cloud to cloak their approach to the target. He told them that, once they had located the convoy, they would conduct a single attack in line astern formation at 2, 000 feet before turning for home. His parting words to Peter were blunt, 'Stick to me like glue. If you end up alone, it's your own fault.'

At the top of the climb Peter retracted the flaps and switched the hydraulics over to the turret. In the narrow waist, Miller raised the turret into the airflow and swung the guns left and right to check they traversed freely. He scanned the skies all around, expecting to see enemy fighters at any moment. Out of the corner of his eye, Peter saw Charlie next to him, scrutinising the map carefully. Their route took them in a long hook to the south-west before turning north between two of the Italian pockets at *Sofafi* and *Nibeiwa*, where a gap had emerged in the Italian line. Peter thought it was a bit like walking around someone's hedge to enter through their garden gate.

'Bit of a headwind,' Peter grunted into the intercom. Charlie nodded to show that he too had noted it. Approaching the estimated position for the Italian convoy, Venner descended to attack altitude. They dropped beneath the clouds as they descended, finding themselves over a great dun-coloured landscape, flat as a billiard table. Charlie moved forward to the nose to try to get a better view of the ground ahead. About 15 miles in front he could just make out the settlement of *Sidi Barrani*, indistinct in the dusty haze. Off to port he spotted the smaller settlement of *Buq Buq*, sitting astride the great coastal road. Even at this distance it was clear that there was no major convoy at the reported location, nor anywhere near it.

'See anything, Charlie?'

'Not a jot, could be a red herring?'

Venner appeared to be unsure too, because he entered a gentle turn. They circled for a while. Long enough to cause Peter to wonder if it was common sense to hang around like this, when he heard Miller's warning over the intercom.

bandit at eight o'clock Skipper, break to port.'

Peter responded by heaving the aircraft over in a flick roll and jamming the throttles forward. The engines roared in response. He glanced over his shoulder and just caught the silhouette of an aircraft diving down on them from several hundred feet above. It was a single-engine biplane with a fixed undercarriage. Though he appeared out of the cloud above them he must, presumably, have been stalking them since they descended. Without Miller's eagle eyes he would have been on them in a trice. Machine-gun fire sounded, but no hits registered on their aircraft.

'It's a *Falco* Skipper. No, wait, a pair - there's a second one hanging back above his mate.'

He heard Miller give him a couple of blasts from the twin machine-guns and was amazed as the lead aircraft sheered away, avoiding the fire. Peter reversed the turn and saw the *Falco* reappear through the starboard window as he banked. For a fraction of a second, he considered trying for a shot at him with the forward machine-gun, but the *Falco* pilot pulled into a tight spiralling turn and seemed to just drop away out of sight. He was followed by bursts of fire from Miller's machine-guns as he sought in vain to hit the fleeing aircraft. Peter looked about desperately for the second fighter, or for a sign of Venner's aircraft, but could find neither.

The clouds formed a kind of gigantic stadium above them. Its base and ceiling were open, perhaps six or seven thousand feet separated the two. An aeroplane could dive beneath or rise above it without entering the cloud. Its length and breadth Peter guessed at a couple of miles, a lopsided oval, if any shape at all. But the cumulus in between hung there in the late morning heat, barely moving. Higher up again were faint wisps of cirrostratus.

'I'm going to try to take us back up, we'll lose them in the cloud,' Peter said calmly. He selected boost to assist with a rapid climb and turned southwards, away from *Sidi Barrani*. Then he caught sight of the second Italian who was manoeuvring to cut off their escape. With an advantage in both speed and height, he would quickly do so. Peter realised what a precarious position they were in. To dive or climb would place the fighters at an advantage; it would permit them to press an attack. The only option was to seek solace in the surrounding clouds. But the fighters could move quicker than the Blenheim, to bar all the exits.

Charlie called out, 'That first fighter is climbing up again, looks like he's positioning for a belly attack.'

The two Italians were working as a hunting pair, one running interdiction and the other lining up for the *coup de grace*.

Peter tried to think clearly, forcing himself to set aside the anxiety caused by their disadvantageous position. It dawned on him that there was something odd about the way the two Italian pilots were cooperating. Normally pairs operated in a formation, either loose or tight. But these two seemed choreographed, like they were twins or, more likely, one a mentor and the other his student. He didn't need to defeat the pair, just the leader.

'Miller, I'm going to attack one of those Eyeties. I need you to let him have it as we pass by. We can't afford to miss.'

'The guns are jammed,' yelled Miller. Charlie crawled back down the fuselage to give him a hand. To buy time, Peter switched back towards the second fighter, now climbing up behind them. The fighter broke away at seeing the unexpectedly aggressive move by his quarry. Peter knew instinctively they must even the odds, so he pointed the Blenheim's nose back at the first *Falco,* which was attempting to cut them off.

The Italian realised the Blenheim intended to press on towards him and paused, undecided about how to respond, for a fraction too long. The closing speed ruled out a head-on attack and he opted to get back behind the bomber instead, exactly as Peter had planned. The fighter pulled up into a climbing half-roll, aiming to set up for an attack on the Blenheim as it passed below him.

Peter pulled up violently as he passed the fighter and felt himself pressed into his seat, a blackness appearing at the edge of his vision. He rolled the bomber over to port so that the *Falco* seemed to hang momentarily in the air no more than 50 yards away, caught at the apex of its own climb.

'Guns clear, firing now,' Miller shouted.

All too often defensive fire was an insignificant quantity in aerial combat. The chance of hitting one moving target from another moving platform travelling at several hundred miles per hour with deflection angles, range, and wind speed all to be calculated, could never be a certainty. Neither was the calibre of the weapon perfect for causing the sort of damage that would cripple a modern aeroplane. But Miller had two things in his favour on this occasion. The first was that the number of variables had been reduced by the slow speed of the fighter and its close range. The second was that, from this distance, he could not miss.

The guns exploded into action and time seemed to slow down as rounds impacted all along the fuselage and the engine of the fighter. They tore holes in its fabric surfaces, punched their way through aluminium, and slammed into the petrol tank. This erupted with an intense flash, sending flames rushing back from the engine cowling towards the cockpit, where the pilot could be seen tearing furiously at his own straps.

He was some way behind when they heard the resultant explosion rip the aircraft apart. It was not clear to any of *Queenie's* crew whether the pilot had got out or not. Peter could see, however, that the second fighter now thought better of the engagement and was breaking off in the direction of Libya in haste. He reduced the throttle and let the aircraft come back to straight and level flight for a moment. Nothing had been heard from their flight leader since they were bounced by the enemy fighters, but then both fighters had focused on his aircraft and not Venner. As much as he could admit no liking for their flight commander, his crew were good men and the thought of them sitting in the desert waiting to be made prisoners of war - or worse - left him feeling quite uneasy.

Peter considered several courses of action, but now one crystallised and he spoke into the intercom, 'Charlie, give me a heading to take us back through the gap to base, we're going to drop down to low-level to see if we can find any trace of Venner.'

'Is that wise? I mean, it's more dangerous-'

Peter gave him a look over his oxygen mask and Charlie reluctantly scanned the chart for a route home through the desert. He passed the heading to Peter, who put the aircraft into a steep dive, levelling out at 200 feet above the desert floor. The terrain loomed upwards towards them rapidly in the last few hundred feet before levelling off.

Charlie wanted to avoid the possibility of accidentally running over the point on his map marked as *Nibeiwa*, where he knew there was a large Italian fortified camp. At low-level they risked exposure to all sorts of ground fire, including flak and machine-guns that would make things very uncomfortable indeed.

'Settlement ahead,' Peter called out.

Charlie looked down at the map and shook his head.

'That can't be right; I think-' Charlie stammered, 'I think we're off our track.'

'You think? Charlie, I need you to *know*, otherwise-'

Peter paused to slip the aircraft, so they would skirt around the edge of the settlement. As they got nearer, he gasped at the sight.

'Christ, it's an Eyetie supply dump.'

Charlie looked up as they roared over the depot in time to see concentrations of lorries parked together under camouflage netting, piles of wooden boxes with tarpaulins stretched over them, and bunkers dug into the sand. Viewed from altitude, the depot would have been extremely hard if not impossible to identify. But at treetop height they had an oblique view of the ground, and this was obviously a major target of opportunity.

Peter turned to Charlie. They had just buzzed the depot at low-level, alerting everyone to their presence. To go back around for another pass would be to do so in the face of whatever enemy air defences were situated there. On the other hand, they could fly home and report a likely depot at these coordinates, so that medium bombers could bomb it instead. Of course, the Italians would be expecting this and would likely have fighters and more anti-aircraft defences lying in wait for them. This entire thought process took a fraction of a second, Peter knew it would not do. Catching his look, Charlie moved forward wordlessly to the nose.

The aircraft entered gentle turn to starboard. Peter's intention was to loop back over the dump on a similar heading to their first pass. It was such a rich collection of lorries and piles of stores that bombing accuracy was of only secondary importance.

'We're going back around again, Miller. Eyes out for a damage assessment,' Peter said. Miller acknowledged. He could see Charlie leaning over the bombsight.

'There's an ideal target, a big concentration of trucks. Come left slightly,' Charlie said, taking the bomb release button in his hand.

A machine-gun position opened up on them, but it was poorly handled and the gunner's fire sprayed wildly about. It did not register for Peter who gripped the controls tightly to keep the aircraft steady on its course. He saw cluster of trucks at the centre of the compound, and now small, dark figures sprinting away from them.

A black puff of smoke appeared with a crack 100 yards in front and above them, followed by another, closer still. His intuition told him it was a light flak gun, tracking them from below as they flew their straight and level course to the target. If they held their course long enough, it must score a hit. Peter's mouth felt dry, his palms sweaty on the flying controls, the passage of time was unbearable.

'Bombs gone, bombs gone!' Charlie yelled.

Peter threw the aircraft over in a tight turn to port, where he thought the flak gun was positioned, to throw off its aim. As he did so he felt an enormous thump. He was vaguely aware that Miller was shouting.

'Blimey. That's one big blast. And secondaries, too many to count. The stick landed slap bang on top of them. Looks like there's a fire down there too Skipper.'

Peter could take little joy from this because the controls felt spongy and the aircraft had a pronounced tendency to drop the starboard wing. They had been hit, although he discovered the bomber could still be controlled by balancing rudder and power.

It was hard work and nerve-wracking. Then they were flying over clear desert once more and the ground fire had ceased, so he cautiously climbed and turned for home. Miller and Charlie were cheering, clearly ecstatic at having survived a successful raid. Peter remained silent about the damage to their aircraft, there was no need to worry them unnecessarily, he told himself.

Soon they were back above the airstrip at *Wadi Bagoush.* Peter thumped *Queenie* down on the packed sand and taxied onto the dispersal. He shut down and sat for a moment in silence, until Mellish knocked on the window. Peter undid the latch and slid the canopy back. He climbed out onto the wing where he stood unsteadily. In the distance an Austin utility truck raced towards them from squadron operations, raising a cloud of dust behind it. Mellish seemed surprised to see him and was trying to give voice to something. Miller climbed up through the upper fuselage hatch and he heaved himself out onto the wing.

'You won't believe this, Skipper,' he shouted down to Peter, pointing at the starboard wing. As Peter walked around the rear of the aircraft, he saw Tom Crawley and a couple of other technicians stood at the trailing edge of the wing. They gazed with wonder at what remained of the starboard aileron, which had an enormous hole punched in it that had removed much of the fabric covering, leaving a skeletal wreck. The control surface had been effectively destroyed. That explained the problems encountered on the trip home, he thought. Before he could say anything, the Austin pulled up and Brian leapt out.

'Denhay. Good lord, it is you after all. We thought you'd had it.' He shook Peter's hand vigorously.

'Where did you get that idea?'

'Venner said as much,' Brian replied.

Charlie's head appeared in the cockpit hatch at this news.

'Venner made it back?'

'Yes, about 45 minutes before you landed. I'm sorry to say that he reported you all as missing.'

Chapter 6

Peter gazed out onto the parched aerodrome, where the engineers were busy changing a main wheel on the C.O.'s machine. It was roasting hot out there in the sun, hot enough to cook an egg, he thought. Not that he could stomach one, since he had been sick with stomach gripes and fever for several days. He was only now able to get up out of his cot and walk around, a weak and gaunt version of his former self. Even though he sweated in the marquee's shade, he alternately shivered with the illness wracking his body. The Medical Officer had restricted him temporarily from flying duties.

Brian had asked him to lend a hand with various duties while he convalesced. Today's job was to fill out the squadron's operational record. The current record had only been completed up to the point of their deployment to *Wadi Bagoush*. Peter was drafting the entry for their first sortie with Venner, weeks ago now, which read:

Wadi Bagoush 17.10.40. Weather: cloudy. Flying: Two aircraft departed at 0700 to attack supply dump in the vicinity of Nibeiwa. Bombs were observed to burst in target area. One aircraft received damage to starboard aileron, both aircraft returned.

The terse, official language used in the record betrayed very little of the actual events of the sortie. It never mentioned, for example, that the flight leader had left his more junior wingman to fight it out with a pair of fighters, choosing instead to make a run for it at low-level. Though it did acknowledge the battle damage they had suffered in the bomb run over the Italian depot, it did not state that the damage had been caused by an anti-aircraft shell passing through the wing. Or that, had it occurred even a fraction earlier, it would have hit the fuel tank and blown them to smithereens.

Above all, the paragraph did not record the cool manner in which they greeted Venner on their return, when they entered the mess tent and found him casually drinking a cup of tea. Venner had looked quite surprised to see them again. He gave them a nonchalant look and said, 'So, you made it back then? I thought there was no sense hanging around with no sign of the Wops.'

Back in the present, Peter tried to focus on the job at hand. He glanced again at the post-sortie reports and compared them to the operations log. Ordinarily he would not have access to all this information, other than the events he had physically witnessed. As individual incidents they appeared unrelated but when read as a whole, he noticed something curious. A pattern was emerging.

The day after their sortie with Venner, Gus Sinclair led 'B' Flight in an attack on an Italian column near *Bir Sofafi*. They could not find the target and so dropped their bombs on a fortified camp instead. The day after that there was a full squadron operation to *Bardia*. This was a dawn raid on an Italian airfield with nine bombers flown with fighter escort. The Italians had been waiting for them and, though they managed to come away with all nine aircraft, there had been a tough battle over the target and several fighters were seen going down.

He scratched his head and cast about for the most recent post-sortie reports, finding them underneath a half empty teacup. These recorded the results of three more sorties in which Blenheims from their squadron had either failed to find the target, and attacked something else instead, or had been bounced by enemy fighters. A week after that, the Italians bombed their base at *Wadi Bagoush* by night. The bombs fell beyond the airfield boundary but even finding it in the pitch darkness was something of a triumph. It took either great luck or prior intelligence to locate an airstrip at night in the unrelenting blackness of the desert.

Peter tried to set aside the complicating, irrelevant information in the records. The stuff that cluttered his mind and obscured the trend. Details of visits by senior officers, reports on training missions flown, reports on the supply situation, all were peripheral to his interest. Yesterday, the C.O. had come back from a mission to *Sidi Barrani* on one engine and burst a tyre upon landing. His number two landed ahead of him, but the third aircraft failed to return. There was scuttlebutt that they had gone in too low, against the recent direction from Group to avoid low-level attacks. The same flak that had damaged the C.O.'s aircraft had done for the number three. Maybe. The report, written in the C.O.'s hand, described the anti-aircraft fire as 'unusually heavy'. It could be a coincidence, but then you would have to believe in coincidences. The same phrases repeatedly cropped up in the pages, *failed to locate…encountered heavy enemy opposition…fire unexpectedly heavy*. He was just thinking about how low the C.O. had been at *Marawah*, when he had swept down on the two Italian bombers, when Charlie entered the tent.

'Ah, Peter, there you are,' Charlie called.

He pulled his pipe out of his top pocket and plonked himself down in the chair next to him, throwing Peter's notes into disorder and fumbling for his tobacco pouch.

'You're a sight for sore eyes, what's all this bumf?'

Peter primly re-ordered the notes and looked at Charlie, thinking of the right words.

'I've been writing out the operational record, but I've found something really strange.'

'How so?'

Peter explained his concerns about the squadron's post-sortie reports. The pattern of missing targets or being ambushed. Charlie looked through the reports that Peter offered him and made a dissatisfied face.

'Peter, if you're out to prove a conspiracy, you can see anything in these pages. Look here,' he waved a report at Peter, 'photographic recce sortie in Libya, aircraft returned safe. No enemy aircraft encountered: mission accomplished. How do you explain that?'

Peter shrugged.

'I never said it was an overwhelming, but you have to admit that it's remarkable at the very least?'

'I'll give you that we seem to have had a run of bad luck recently. War's like that though, it doesn't always go your way. Even if there *is* a pattern, what's your point? Someone on XXI Squadron is working for-'

Charlie stopped mid-sentence. He looked thoughtful for a moment and then asked, 'who has access to these documents? Besides you and I.'

'Well, Brian completes them normally, and the C.O. signs them off. Why?'

'I suppose I'm just trying to think through why you might look past information like this.'

'You just said yourself that it's a conspiracy theory. Are you saying that the Boss and Brian are in some way culpable in this - that's pretty far-fetched, isn't it?'

'Margot Dacre told me that headquarters believes information is being leaked, and it could be any one of us who's responsible for it.'

'Margot who?'

'Dacre. I sat next to her at dinner, you clot. She works in Intelligence. I mentioned our raid and she told me about the spy,' Charlie said.

'A spy? Can she help us, do you think?'

'It can't hurt to ask. Shall I ask Venner if we can have some leave?'

'You can try, but he's off on leave himself.'

'Again?'

'He went the day before the bombing raid, or the day after - I forget which. Better ask Brian, he's more likely to say yes.'

'Are you fit to fly? You look terrible. No offence.'

'None taken, old chap. And yes, I can swing it with the medics. I'd crawl out of here, for a couple of nights in Cairo.'

'Great, I'll speak to Brian.'

'Charlie, this isn't an elaborate ploy just to go on a date with some beautiful creature you've discovered, is it?'

Charlie looked hurt and made the sign of the cross with his pipe.

'My word is my honour, governor.'

*

They landed at Helwan just before lunch, to Charlie's great relief. In the last 30 minutes of the flight, odd rattling noises emanated from the starboard engine, and the oil temperature crept up to 80 degrees, even though they were cruising. It did not reach the level where shutting the engine down was advisable, but it was noticeably hotter than normal. Peter didn't seem concerned, although Charlie could barely see his face, crammed forward in the nose as he was. They were carrying Mellish, Crawley and a couple of other airmen, squeezed into the fuselage behind Peter. Miller sat in the turret, whistling to himself.

Helwan was wreathed in an early afternoon haze, so they circled for a short time to ensure the airfield was clear. When they taxied onto the dispersal and shut down, the driver sent to collect them witnessed the improbable sight of six men climbing out of the aircraft, where he had only been expecting three. Charlie laughed at his open-mouthed stare. The engineers stayed with the aircraft, so Charlie, Peter and Miller headed to station headquarters to arrange a lift to Cairo.

He left Peter on the telephone and slipped away to the Cipher Room. An RAF policeman sat at a table outside and told him to wait a moment while he stepped inside. With the door open momentarily Charlie got a view of clerks seated at typewriters and a chubby, bespectacled officer looking through some buff files before it closed in his face. When it reopened, he was disappointed to see it was only the policeman again, who sat down wordlessly at his desk and resumed his role as sentinel.

When the door opened again it was Margot, smiling and stepping out into the corridor. Although he had thought of several good opening lines, Charlie now found himself robbed of words. He eventually managed to stammer out, 'Hello there' and felt a prat for saying it. He explained he had a few days of leave and was heading up to Cairo. He asked if she was free for lunch and added that he wanted to talk about a matter concerning intelligence, with a wink.

Margot smiled. She was delighted to join him, and they agreed to meet at Shepheard's Hotel. Back in the corridor he ran into Peter and Miller, who had managed to book them a room at

Talbot House, not far from the central Bab-El-Louk station.

The terrace at Shepheard's Hotel looked out onto a busy street in central Cairo and, even with a war on, it heaved with nationalities of all types. Thin-faced British officers in khakis with stockings pulled up to their knees, loud Australians with their lady-friends, and civilians in cotton suits and Panama hats could all be seen. And all competed for the waiters' attention from the comfort of their wicker chairs. This was long before the Afrika Korps landed in Libya, when Allied troops would joke that the only thing that could hold Rommel up was the queue at Shepheard's bar. On the street itself, the workaday folk of Cairo thronged. Pedestrian, animal, and vehicle squeezed past one another on the busy road.

Charlie arrived early by habit and chanced upon a pair of vacated seats. He settled in and ordered a pot of tea. Dressed carefully in immaculate khakis, shirt and tie, and his blue Service Dress hat, he worried he was sweating profusely into his uniform. He had also forgotten his pipe, discarded on his sponge bag when he bid Denhay and Miller farewell. They were planning to tour the souks and then find somewhere for dinner, but the pair were in no rush to leave Talbot House, where they had showered and slept in a proper bed for the first time in weeks.

He was just thinking about the relative luxury of Cairo compared to their field billets when he noticed someone waving at him from a car, it was Margot. She drove past at the wheel of a dusty, tired old Morris 8. Shouting something intelligible and gesturing, she disappeared around the corner. Charlie wondered if she was saying that she had something else on but dismissed this. She would have telephoned if that was the case. She finally appeared twenty minutes after the agreed time wearing a simple cotton summer dress, buttoned up the front, and slingbacks. She wore her hair down but with a straw hat to keep the sun off her face.

He stood for her as she apologised. Margot was flustered and looked like she had been running. He ordered more tea and she asked him what he had seen of Cairo since he arrived. Charlie admitted that they had seen nothing except a dirty nightclub they visited last night, at which Miller had consumed several pints of Egyptian beer.

He omitted the part where Miller had been involved in a scuffle with a soldier following an angry exchange of words. Miller had told one young lady that, whatever her soldier boyfriend was paying her, he would double it. On the face of it, this was commentary on the disparity between the basic pay of soldiers compared to RAF aircrew. However, it also made a grubby, if not entirely unfair, jibe at the lady's virtue. A jibe that any drunken soldier could not look past. A punch was thrown; the woman screamed. There was a late-night escape from military policemen who were called to break it up. The entire series of events had left Charlie with the impression that, while Sergeant Patrick Miller was a talented Air Gunner/Wireless Operator, he was a terrible drunk.

'You've seen nothing?' Margot exclaimed. 'Oh Charlie, we have so little time. Come, come - I must take you on a tour. Cairo is such a wonderful place.'

Before Charlie could ask her any questions about leaks, the tea arrived. Margot poured it, took a sip and made a face. She stood up and took his hand.

'I'll call us a taxi. No, wait, we'll take the Morris. It's easier.'

Pulled bodily from his seat, Charlie had just enough time to reach into his pocket and scatter a few piastres on the table. Their departure from Shepheard's excited only a little comment from those seated on the terrace. It was hardly the first time a serviceman had been dragged away forcefully by a young lady.

*

Peter left Miller sleeping off his hangover at Talbot House, his ugly bruised faced looking bizarrely peaceful as he snored. He flagged down a taxi with the intention of finding a tour guide. But, unable to communicate with the taxi driver, he found himself dumped outside the Khen el-Khalil Bazaar with his pockets plundered for small change.

It was crammed with people, both off-duty servicemen and Egyptians, many of the latter in their country clothing. The women wore long *abayas* with a veil, the men were in *galibya* robes and little red hats. Here and there went Europeans, by far the minority here. All mixed eclectically beneath the impressive Islamic and Mamluk architecture of the market. The souk itself was crammed with coffee shops, and gold merchants, tiny restaurants, street hawkers, and men with monkeys on their shoulders.

Peter did not have to walk far down one of the many packed alleyways before he found a shoemaker who advertised his wares from a wooden shelf built into the shop front. The heady scent of tanned hide, dust, and sweat met him immediately. Using gestures and holding up an example for reference, Peter asked if he made the suede ankle boots that had become popular amongst officers serving in Egypt. The shoe-maker beckoned Peter to a low bench, where he removed his shoes to measure his feet. A fierce shout brought a small boy to the doorway, but from where, Peter could not tell. The man spoke to the boy at length and he listened, nodding intelligently throughout. Then the boy turned to Peter.

'Captain, he will make your boots today and bring to wherever you choose. You stay where?'

Peter told him and handed over a few notes, which the man accepted without complaint. He had a vague impression that he had just been a victim of daylight robbery. He left the shop eager to eat, but found the market packed with people also in search of refreshment, the hour being just after the midday prayer. He tried to find a short cut to one of the bazaar's many entrances, but he forgot how many left-hand turns he had taken and became hopelessly lost inside the cavernous interior. A man pulled at his uniform, eager to advertise his wares, but Peter shrugged him off and kept walking. He was out of breath, it was so damnably hot and he felt dizzy. He mopped the moisture from his face with his handkerchief, he had to find a place to sit in the shade for a moment to recover his wits. A cooling glass of lemonade would be most welcome.

The cafe he eventually settled upon was located at a junction and leant directly onto the inside wall of the bazaar. It opened on two sides to permit the patrons to watch people passing by down a narrow alley into the market's heart. There was no roof at this point and bright daylight shone down through the gap, illuminating the space before the wooden building. It was Peter's reluctance to expose himself to that fierce light that caused him to pause. That was when he spotted Venner. He faced away from Peter and was deep in conversation with a thin Egyptian in a suit. Peter froze, then slid into the shade at the side of the alleyway.

He was not close enough to overhear their conversation, and was occasionally distracted by peddlers tugging at his elbow. After brushing off one particularly insistent fellow, he turned back to see Venner standing. The two men shook hands and then Venner walked off towards the market's entrance, pushing against the flow of the crowd where he quickly disappeared from sight. Peter couldn't follow him, but instead stepped into the cafe and sat down at a low table.

He tried to get a good look at the Egyptian, to commit his features to memory, but saw very little to differentiate him from any other Egyptian. The man was studying a notebook, in which he scribbled with a pencil. He had a thin moustache and a long nose, Peter guessed he was in his forties or perhaps a little older. Suddenly, the man looked up directly at Peter and for an instant their eyes met. One of his eyes was brown and the other, the right, milky white with a large cataract. Then a waiter appeared at his side, and Peter ordered mint tea. Ghastly stuff, he thought to himself, but all he could think of on the spot. When he looked back, the Egyptian was gone.

*

Margot was so comfortable at the controls of the little Austin that she spent most of the time talking to Charlie and pointing out various historical sights around the city. They had already seen the Citadel and the Alabaster Mosque, and were now on their way to the Egyptian Museum. It looked like this could only end in disaster, once when she nearly ran into the back of a goods van parked diagonally across the road, and again when scattering pedestrians about them during a break-neck turn into the Midan Opera. It was incredible that no-one came to any harm.

They finished their tour in the tea garden of the Gezira Sporting Club, under the shade of a large Acacia tree. Margot was wiping a tear, a happy tear, from her eye as she laughed at Charlie's vibrant description of the fleeing pedestrians in the Midan, and how one man had leapt onto the bonnet of a parked saloon in search of escape.

'You're very cruel Charlie Kendrick, that never happened at all,' Margot said when she stopped laughing. Charlie was enjoying himself so much he had clean forgotten the entire purpose of their meeting. He wondered when he had last spent such a delightful period in anyone's else company. A silence descended on them and he knew that it was coming to a close. Then he remembered his errand.

'Margot, I clean forgot! There was something I wanted to ask you. I've had such a nice time that it slipped my mind.'

'Ask away, Charlie. What's this urgent matter concerning intelligence?' She laughed gently at his sincerity.

'Well, I remembered you told me about suspicions you had about a British officer giving away secrets to the Italians.'

'Yes?'

'Peter has been going back through the operational records. You remember Peter?'

'Yes.'

'And Peter thinks he found a pattern, in the squadron's operations. Odd things, like missed opportunities or unexpected alertness on the part of the enemy. So, I thought you might help put our minds at ease.'

'Let me get this straight, you think that someone on your squadron is feeding the Italians information that will endanger you all?'

'Damn it, Margot, when you say it like that it sounds so stupid. But trust me on this, Peter went back through the books and it seems like more than just a run of bad luck.'

'But why would anyone divulge information that might lead to their own demise? Our theory was that any leak could only come from the headquarters. Someone who had access to classified information and a reason to pass it over to the enemy.'

'Like what?'

'People betray their country for all sorts of reasons,' she glanced away for a second, 'it's the ones you least suspect too. Perhaps they are being manipulated through blackmail, or maybe they have a complicated past, others sympathise with our enemies. Some are just greedy, doing it for the money or the excitement, or both,' Margot shrugged.

'So, you think our idea is ridiculous?' Charlie felt deflated.

'Not necessarily,' Margot said in a softer tone, 'But it's not my area of expertise. I do signals work; you need a counter-intelligence specialist. Let me speak to a friend. I'll get a message to you with anything we turn up.'

She placed a reassuring hand on Charlie's leg, and he felt a moment of exhilaration at her touch.

'Can we do this again?'

Margot said nothing. She must be aware of his feelings, he thought, to expose himself like this and receive no reply was crushing to him. He tried to brush it off, it was not the first time he had misread a situation, nor was it the first time he had acted the fool for a pretty girl. His cheeks burnt momentarily with half a dozen memories of scenes like this.

'Charlie, your squadron is going to be moving elsewhere soon. I can't say much about it here,' she cast a glance around them at the others taking tea in the garden, 'But you'll be recalled tomorrow.'

'How did-'

He answered his own question before the words left his lips, her job was to read the signals traffic. She knew all the key information about operations.

'Come and see me tomorrow, before you go. I'm on duty, but I have something for you.'

*

They cadged a lift back to Helwan with a staff officer whom they met by chance at Talbot House. Crammed into his battered and dust-covered blue RAF staff car they motored back from Cairo. After dropping Charlie off at Station Headquarters, Peter and Miller went to check on their aircraft. They found Sergeant Mellish outside the workshops where was he smoking a cigarette. He looked troubled.

'I'm afraid it's bad news, sir. That starboard engine was shot and they're going to do an engine change for *Queenie*. But that will take a few days with an air test. So we got a new kite to take back to the squadron. She's only got delivery miles on her, an' Tom Crawley is looking over her directly.'

Peter felt conflicted by this. He had logged over 60 hours on Blenheims now, nearly all of which was with *Queenie*. On the other hand, one aircraft was much the same as another, he told himself. He refused to be led by the superstition to which many other pilots fell pray.

'Alright, Mellish, we better go and take a look at her then,' he nodded.

'There's all this as well, sir,' Mellish gestured sheepishly to a pile of boxes and packages behind him, covered with a tarpaulin. Peter knew better than to ask what it was. Mellish would only lie and tell him that it was legitimate aircraft spares and tools. He studied Mellish closely, whose face was a picture of pure innocence in spite of his heavy-set brow, broken nose, and ruddy complexion.

'Very well. But you're carrying that lot, and anything that doesn't fit is going into the desert.'

Charlie made a point of collecting the squadron's mail and filled out a signal form to inform XXI Squadron of their planned departure time. He then went to the Cipher Room, where the stony-faced RAF policeman sat at his table, and again asked for Margot. She appeared holding a brown paper parcel, which she handed him.

'What's this?'

'Just a little something that I found for you. I hope it will make your life in the field just a little more comfortable. Don't open it until you land.'

'It's not an easy chair is it?'

'I don't want you to be *that* comfortable, you know. You're supposed to want to come back to me.' She paused to look at him for a moment and he was struck by her pale beauty and wide eyes. Then she opened the door and was gone.

*

The flight to *Wadi Bagoush* ended just before dusk and was entirely uneventful. Uneventful, save for two aspects. The first was that the aircraft was packed with boxes, sacks and packages, plus the passengers who had flown up with them. Consequently, Peter had to use boost power and nearly the full length of the airstrip to get airborne. The second was that they had been unable to raise XXI Squadron on the wireless, even when they were directly above the aerodrome. This was not unusual, but with the light failing it was not wise to delay a landing.

Peter made a perfect three-point landing, albeit with something of a longer landing roll. They were met at the dispersal by a driver in the utility truck. He told them excitedly that the C.O. was waiting to start a full squadron briefing, and they should drop everything to attend immediately.

At the mess tent they found all ranks of the squadron, some 250 men, either sitting or standing under the canvas. Lamps were already lit, and the C.O. stood in front of the crowd. At their approach, Brian signalled from the corner of the tent and the C.O. began.

'Gentlemen, XXI Squadron has been ordered to Greece.'

The C.O. told them that the Italians had invaded Greece in October. Several RAF squadrons from H.Q. Middle East had been dispatched to support the Hellenic forces. But now an additional bomber squadron was requested by the Prime Minister, no less, and XXI was to be given that honour.

Their immediate orders were to pack up the camp at *Wadi Bagoush* and proceed to RAF Ismailia on the Suez Canal. Here they would be brought up to full war establishment and complete preparations for their move. The ground party and its equipment would then travel to Alexandria to embark on a Royal Navy vessel for transport to Piraeus, with the aircraft following a few days later. He added that Greece in winter would not be like the desert and so they would have to take precautions to ensure they could operate in cold, wet conditions. Charlie took that to mean *including outright theft of government property*.

The C.O. concluded with questions, but Charlie didn't listen. In his hands was Margot's parcel. He tore the paper off under the yellow light of the oil lamps. Inside was a thick woollen jumper and wrapped within it was a heavy object. He gripped it and felt cold metal, Margot's gift was a Webley .38 revolver.

Greece, November 1940

Chapter 7

The Blenheim formation threaded its way through the cloudy winter sky at 10, 000 feet. Above them was an azure blue canopy, when it could occasionally be seen between the towering clouds. Beneath, they glimpsed an angry ocean flecked with white. Their route took them over Alexandria and Crete. This was to reduce the amount of flight over water, in case any of the crews had engine trouble and were forced to ditch. For safety, the crew aboard *Y-Yorker* wore their regulation Mae Wests, painted yellow with aircraft dope, and all the warm clothing they possessed.

Charlie sat at the little chart table in the nose and studied the map laid out in front of him. He reflected on how difficult it had been to find modern maps of Greece. This one was marked 1913, but he reassured himself with the thought that all the mountains would be in the same places, even if the borders were not. Through the nose windows the cloud was thinning. Wisps rushed by beneath them, and between them he saw the Cretan coastline and grey sea that divided it from Greece. He could make out a naval convoy heading to Souda Bay by their wakes stretching out behind them.

'They'll be relieved to make shelter on a day like this,' he said over the intercom. No one replied. Charlie stretched his leg out, it threatened to cramp up after so long squeezed into the small crew compartment. His pistol holster dug into his hip, the sidearm was an uncomfortable nuisance inside the aircraft. As he gazed down at the ground below, he thought of Margot. He was unable to see her during the few short weeks that passed before they left Egypt and now he tried to remember the details of their time in Cairo, her smile, her eyes, her laugh. *She touched your leg*, he told himself. Surely that was a sign she felt something for him.

He had written to her. A long rambling letter in his clum
hand that seemed to go on forever without saying anything. He
tore up three attempts and almost lost the desire to continue.
When he did, the result was lacklustre and devoid of the
emotion that threatened to bubble up within him at every
thought of her. To the dreary text he added a line about his
concerns about Marcus Venner, hinting of the suspicious
behaviour Peter had witnessed in Cairo. He prevaricated,
changed his mind; sent the letter anyway. What the hell.

Miller's voice rattled over the intercom with a new course and
arrival time at *Menidi*, their new home near *Athens*. Landfall
was made just south-east of the city, passing the Acropolis to
port and some way distant. The weather was better than he had
expected in Greece and they descended steadily down to 4, 000
feet once they were over land. The airfield was easy to find, not
far south of the Royal Palace at *Tatoi*. It was a long, grass strip
with hangars and other airfield buildings along one side, hinting
at its former life as *Athens* Airport. In the east the massive
Mount Pentelikon rose up from the plain and overlooked the
airfield, dominating the land for miles in all directions. With its
snow-topped cap, Charlie felt that he would always be able to
find home if he could find that.

As the aircraft lined up for a final approach, Charlie moved
back next to Peter. He had sat silently at the controls for hours,
occasionally adjusting their speed to keep station within the
formation. He looked tired now. Over the nose he got a better
view of *Menidi*. There was not much too see, a handful of
scattered white-walled villages nearby. Fields and rough ground
predominated. The airfield sported a mixture of Blenheims and
Gladiator fighters, and the circuit above was crammed with
circling aircraft.

On landing they followed a motorcycle rider to the southern
side of the airfield, where their engineers waited to receive
them. They shut down and clambered out for a cigarette while
awaiting a lorry to take them away. Charlie was crammed in the
back with the others as they arrived at their new mess, a large
hotel requisition for their accommodation. Brian stood outside
waiting for them with his arms crossed.

'Bloody hell,' Brian exclaimed, 'it's Fred Karno's Army!'

He referred to the well-known and much loved music hall performer. Charlie could see what he meant too, for in Egypt the crews had acquired cold weather clothing of sorts. Many had pulled out their blue Service Dress uniforms, but an assortment of other gear could be seen. That included sheepskin flying jackets, khaki trousers and overalls, army battledress jackets, and woollen jumpers. Miller had even acquired a Sidcot Suit, a set of baggy overalls with a wide sheepskin collar, of which he was immensely proud. No two men dressed the same, and all came with a variety of bags, cases, and packages that constituted their worldly possessions. If *Menidi* had possessed a Station Warrant Officer, he would have had a fit, Charlie laughed to himself.

Brian ushered them inside where plates of bully beef sandwiches and mugs of tea were laid out. As Charlie walked in, Brian stopped him and gestured to his holstered Webley.

'You better watch where you point that. You don't want it going off in someone's face,' he said with a wink.

*

That night the squadron was welcomed by the Air Officer Commanding the RAF in Greece. The temperature was much colder than in Egypt. Charlie wore the thick jumper Margot had given him under his uniform tunic, and a woollen scarf over that. Still he shivered as he stood inside the hangar in the orange glare of the floodlights, waiting for the great man to arrive, his breath misting in front of his face.

The A.O.C was a sharp-looking, round headed man with a small moustache and piercing grey eyes. He arrived by car from *Athens* with an unknown Wing Commander and Squadron Leader in tow. After greeting the C.O., he went straight into his talk. He welcomed everybody to Greece and hoped that they liked their new home. Charlie glimpsed the faces of the engineers whose new home was the freezing hangar they stood in. They did not look much like they were pleased with it.

'The Greeks have been kind hosts, but they've been caught out by the Italians,' the A.O.C. said, 'The invasion really galvanised them into mobilising for war, and they're doing a handsome job in the north now. RAF units in Greece now number three bomber and two fighter squadrons - our strength is building all the time.'

Charlie had heard that there were insufficient airfields available for RAF use. Therefore, there would be no more additional squadrons until the weather dried out the other aerodromes.

'Most of our bomber force is concentrated at bases around *Athens*, here at *Menidi* and also *Eleusis*, to the south-west. We have no radar, nor a coordinated system of air defence. Just some spotters on hills to report enemy movements in the north. Consequently, I am compelled to place the fighters as close to the front line as possible,' the A.O.C. spoke in a harsh, formal tone. It echoed badly inside the hangar, making it even harder to hear.

The A.O.C. looked around at the young men of the squadron, Charlie got a sense that he was building up to a climax.

'Now, I have discussed operational policy with the Prime Minister and the Commander-in-Chief, and I am pleased to say that they agree entirely with my views on how our air power should be directed. The bombers will attack the Italians at their points of concentration in Albania. You will bomb their marshalling yards and ports of disembarkation, and their supply dumps. You will wreck their ability to build up their force and slow their progress into Greece.'

Almost every man in the hangar was familiar with the geography of the Balkans, and those who were not had it explained to them in whispers by their friends. Charlie knew immediately that the A.O.C. was really telling them the bombers faced a 600-mile round trip over mountainous terrain, in the face of enemy fighters and bad weather. Someone behind him gave a sharp, humourless laugh. The A.O.C. let the news sink in and waited for the chatter to recede.

'Under these circumstances it will be difficult to arrange fighter escort for you. You will need to make best use of cloud cover and terrain to avoid enemy air defences. The Greeks will render us every support, as we in turn support them.'

Charlie considered himself an intelligent man, he recognised that the A.O.C.'s closing words were a half truth. He had read the papers and knew that the Greeks wanted, above all, material support from the British. But they got military support instead. General Metaxas, the Greek Prime Minister, was a Germanophile and his politics were not necessarily so far apart from those of the Germans either. So, while he accepted British support, he walked a fine line between receiving Mr Churchill's assistance and earning Mr Hitler's displeasure. Charlie wondered why the A.O.C. had not said anything about the Germans. He must be aware that to bring the Germans into the war in Greece was to lose the war in Greece.

Then the A.O.C. cleared his throat.

'Well then, I am sure you have preparations to make that I do not intend to delay. I know that in whatever struggle is to come you will do your utmost to prevail, in keeping with the best traditions of your squadron and the Service to which you belong. Goodbye and good luck.'

The A.O.C. took one last look around the room, turned and left. Charlie saw him say a few words to the C.O. and the unknown Wing Commander before he stepped into his staff car and motored away. The C.O. turned to speak to Brian and the Engineer Officer, who stood next to him. As the meeting broke up, MacNeish appeared through the crowd and grabbed Charlie's arm.

'Venner wants a word with all the 'A' Flight crews. He's waiting now.'

He was stood in the corner of the hangar at the centre of a circle of men, seeing Charlie and MacNeish approach he started to speak.

'The C.O. wants to put on a show tomorrow, a nine aircraft job to show the Eyeties we've arrived. I'll post the crew list tonight. Now, on to a more serious matter.'

Charlie mused to himself whether anything could be more serious than flying an operational sortie, in an unknown country, after barely any sleep.

'I'm afraid that all of you will have to submit your letters to me for censorship in future,' Venner said, bluntly. This was met with surprise and some grumbling from the back of the crowd.

'Officers don't have to submit letters for censorship. You know that Marcus,' MacNeish replied, clearly angry at the thought of Venner reading his correspondence and knowing his private thoughts.

'Well, this order's come right from the top. It's from the head shed, so don't bellyache to me about it, old boy. It seems there's concerns about secrets being leaked to the enemy and we need to shut it down,' Venner glanced at Charlie for a moment and then looked away.

Charlie felt his face flush. If someone had censored his letter to Margot they would know what he had written about Venner. Perhaps the censor told Venner about it, or maybe Venner censored it himself. *Jesus*, he thought to himself, *if he found out that he and Peter were digging around in his business he'll be furious*. He looked over at Peter who had no idea they could be blown.

*

The full squadron show never happened because the weather turned bad and they were unable to find the target. The entire formation turned back before the Albanian border. It was an inauspicious start. The weather was bad the day after too, and the day after that Venner led them on a raid to Sarande Harbour, where Italian troops were disembarking. He insisted on bombing the target from over 10, 000 feet and they returned to hear him report near misses on the target. Peter began to wonder if he had got Venner wrong, he never shied away from action, but it never seemed to work out entirely to plan either.

Squadron scuttlebutt held that the C.O. had given Venner a dressing down in private for this operation, which it was thought he regarded as a waste of bombs and a lost opportunity to impact the Italian invasion. At the end of the week they stood-to for another full squadron show of nine aircraft, but again it was weathered out. The same bad luck that the squadron had experienced in Egypt continued to dog them.

Peter sat inside the dispersal tent with the side flaps down and listened to the drumming of the rain on the canvas. He was playing chess with Charlie, who seemed distracted. It was either that or he was an appalling chess player, he decided. A brace of Charlie's pawns, a knight, and a bishop had fallen. Not a hopeless position but neither was it one Peter would wish to find himself in after only nine moves. Peter gazed out of the open door across the airfield where one of the squadron's Blenheims was being rolled back into the hangar. It felt like a metaphor to him, and he reflected on the news that they had received that morning of the successful attack by the Royal Navy's Fleet Air Arm on the Italian Grand Fleet at *Taranto*.

Flying off their aircraft carrier, HMS Illustrious, torpedo bombers braved heavy enemy defences to wreak havoc on Italian battleships moored in their home port. The courage and unexpected success of this raid only heightened the disappointment felt by everyone over their inaction. It irritated Peter that the greatest share of the glory should go to the Navy and not the RAF; he was desperate for an operation.

'What's on your mind?'

Charlie looked startled. His expression told Peter that whatever lie he was about to give voice to had died in his throat.

'God, Peter. I've been working up the courage to speak to you about this for days. You remember Venner's orders about censoring the letters?'

'I do. Not something that bothers me. I've nothing to write home about.'

Peter inwardly regretted the reference to his past. There was a lack of honesty there too, he knew. He really meant that he had no-one he wanted to write to at home.

'Well, I wrote to Margot and I mentioned what you told me about Venner's meeting with the odd-looking Egyptian-,'

'Yes,' Peter said, with a sinking feeling.

'-and our concerns about his odd behaviour, and I think he might have read it.'

Peter put a hand to his head, he closed his eyes. After a moment's thought, he spoke through gritted teeth, 'How? And why did you write it in a letter to your girlfriend?'

'She's not my girlfriend. She just offered to help. I thought she ought to know the truth, in case it was useful.'

'Charlie, all we know for certain is that the squadron has had a run of bad luck. You said that yourself. Venner's a martinet. But we can't say for certain that he's the leak, or even that there's a leak at all,' Peter said in a low voice, for there were others present in the damp tent. His mind raced with the unforeseen eventualities of Charlie's admission.

'I don't know for certain that he saw the letter. It was just that he gave the order for mail censoring so soon after I sent it. And I thought he gave me a significant look. It might be a coincidence still.'

'Ok, let's think about damage limitation,' Peter sat up in his chair and leaned forward to speak in a hushed tone, 'Let's say Venner read your letter and now he thinks we're spying on him. But he's not a traitor and just finds the whole thing odd.'

'Best case scenario?'

'No, the best case scenario is he didn't read your letter and there isn't a leak at all.'

Charlie shook his head.

'Margot said there was. She thought it was someone in headquarters, but she couldn't be sure.'

'Fine. Then there's the scenario in which he actually is a traitor, and he goes out of his way to put us out of the picture,' Peter said.

'Do you think he'd do something like that?'

'Of course. It's got to be a possibility, Charlie - if he's working for the Wops.'

'What do we do about it?'

'You've got that pistol, haven't you?'

Charlie looked at him wide-eyed. Peter was able to keep a straight face only so long, before breaking into a fit of laughter. Charlie pursed his lips.

'You tit. I thought you were serious just then.'

'Look, if it is someone on the squadron then the censoring of mail should stop their game. I really don't think we need to worry about this.'

Charlie nodded thoughtfully and went back to looking at the board in hope of deliverance. He found none and flicked over his king.

'The king is dead,' he said with a wry smile.

Chapter 8

The next morning the weather was dry and crisp. The air smelt of pines and above the airfield the sky was an unremitting blue, preceding a pale winter sun. As they rattled along in their truck to the dispersal for briefing, Charlie yawned and scratched himself unconsciously. It was certain that the mission was on today, and he felt a growing unease in the pit of his stomach. He effected nonchalance by placing his empty pipe in his mouth, it stopped him biting his lip. Margot drifted into his mind again, she was never far away from it. No letters yet, nothing.

It was a simple brief. The C.O. outlined the route to the target, the port of *Valona*, and the route home. He pointed out the obvious navigational hazards, specifically the high Pindus Mountains over which they would cross to get into Albania and gave the location of emergency landing grounds. Charlie got the impression that the C.O. was excited about the prospect of going into action, and a full nine aircraft mission was a sight to behold. As 'A' Flight, they would lead, Venner in front and MacNeish flying number two.

The C.O. was succeeded by the Air Liaison Officer, with some blown-up aerial photographs of the objective. He pointed out the harbour, power station, port buildings, and a military barracks. These were all legitimate military targets and he stressed the attack direction was to be from south to north, to ensure that civilian casualties were minimised. There were no questions, and the crews traipsed out to their waiting machines.

They crossed the Pindus at 10, 000 feet in scattered cloud and descended to 2,000 feet as they neared the coast near *Dukat*, ready for the final run-in to the target. This took them down a steep-sided valley. In the nose, Charlie watched the green sides of the Dukat Valley reaching up as if to embrace them on either side. With the terrain funnelling them, they dropped into single file to fly down the valley. The steep hillsides gave way to a patchwork of fields and a small village of white-washed houses marked the coast. Then they were over water again, the waves glinted silvery in the morning sun. There was *Valona* emerging in the corner of the wide bay beyond, its two jetties poked out into the blue Aegean like a pair of white horns. In the harbour two, no three, transports alongside. One of which was making steam. The sky over *Valona* was alarmingly free from cloud and it was easy to make out the town and the principal features thereabouts.

'Hello Tinker formation, hello Tinker formation. Target ahead, tally ho!'

Venner's voice, oddly distorted through his oxygen mask, rang out over the wireless. In the nose Charlie bent over the bombsight, set the airspeed and adjusted it for the estimated drift. He had decided to drop their stick of bombs on the northernmost jetty, where he could see equipment being unloaded and two of the transports moored up alongside.

'Left a touch skipper, a little more. Hold it, hold it there - dead on!'

He lifted his head away from the sight for a moment, just in time to see bursts of flak appear above and ahead of the leader with a crack. Each burst sent thousands of jagged metallic shards flying in all directions. He instinctively ducked away from it, powerless as he was to do anything to protect himself. The shells burst orange for an instant and left a black puff of smoke in the air. It was not thick, there were probably no more than a handful of light flak guns positioned around the harbour, he guessed. Nevertheless, he could feel the buffet as the shells went off around them.

Ahead of them a stick of bombs dropped from Venner's aircraft and he peeled away in a tight turn to starboard, putting as much distance as possible between himself and the flak. MacNeish dropped shortly after. It seemed like the bomb release point was drifting back away from the ships into the sea, and Charlie realised that he would have to delay release to correct this. There were warehouses beyond the ships that he could target instead. He observed Venner's bombs hit the water alongside the transport ships, sending great geysers of white water up into the air. All misses.

The warehouses appeared in his bombsight. Charlie squeezed the bomb release trigger, feeling the jolt as the four bombs were released from their cradles. A flak burst went off close by and he recoiled from it, then the engines roared and they were pulling around to starboard to follow Venner. He took one last look at *Valona* and saw that someone had scored hits on the harbour, there were fires on the jetty and the innermost ship was smoking badly. Behind them came the next formation of bombers, hurrying to add their load of explosives to the damage below.

Venner was yelling on the wireless again.

'Come on Tinker formation, reform on me now.'

His voice sounded like it was tinged with hysteria. He was panicking. Charlie decided he could not sit and listen to Venner lose his head, so he pulled his intercom lead out. As he did so he heard the sound of machine-gun fire overhead. He looked up through the canopy in time to see three enemy fighters swoop down on them from above. Rounds flew past the nose, missing them by feet. They had the unmistakable shape of *Sparvos*. How they had got there was a mystery. His best guess was that they had caught sight of the bombers as they descended out of the clouds in the moments prior to the attack, then positioned themselves for an interception.

Their ragged bomber formation made it hard for the air gunners to cooperate, but easy for the fighters to try and pick them off. When he plugged his headset back in he heard Miller cursing as he tried to get a bead on the Italians. Charlie could not help but wonder at the ambush the Italians had arranged. They had everything right, timing, positioning, speed, *everything*. But still they had blown it. A wise fighter leader should have circled around for a pass from below, where the gunners' fire would not reach them. But these clowns looked to be trying for a tail-on attack.

'Watch out, Miller,' Charlie said, looking out of the starboard side window, 'bandit, six o'clock.'

A burst of fire went over the top of the cockpit, then Miller returned fired fire. Charlie felt reassured by sound of the twin machine-guns answering back, their rapid metallic din echoed through the aircraft in short bursts, *rat-at-tat-tat*. He looked around at the surrounding terrain, the wide, blue bay, the dark mountains rising up in front. There was nowhere to go but back up into the clouds.

The aircraft shook as another burst from the lead fighter punched into the port wing. Then Miller was shouting, 'Got him! I got the Wop bastard.'

The lead *Sparvo* entered a tight spin. Belching black smoke from its engine, it plummeted towards the earth. It its death spiral, the fighter grew smaller as it dropped away from him until it struck the mountainside and exploded in a fierce fireball. There was no parachute. Their leader gone, the two remaining fighters hesitated to renew the attack. They rolled away in the direction of *Valona*. There was silence aboard the Blenheim for a moment, broken suddenly with Venner's shouted order to close up again.

Peter spoke over the intercom, his voice comparatively calm and authoritative compared to Venner's insistent nagging.

'Our port engine's playing up. Oil temperature's in the red, so I'm going to throttle back to keep it going for as long as we can.'

Charlie knew that was bad news for several reasons, mainly because two engines were better than one, but also because the hydraulics were all powered off a pump in the port engine. Without the port engine there were no flaps, no brakes, and no gun turret.

'Miller, you better tell Tinker Leader that we're falling out of formation,' Peter instructed.

'I'm sure he'll be thrilled,' Charlie said, but without keying his microphone.

'Can you find somewhere to land closer than *Menidi*, in case we can't make it?'

Charlie unfolded the map. Airfields did not abound in Greece, particularly at this time of year. *Araxos* could work, he thought, but it would mean flying down the coast rather than going overland. It also meant crossing the Gulf of Patras, a flight over water with a bad engine.

'Message from Tinker Leader, Skipper,' Miller said, 'Acknowledged.'

Venner was a cold fish, thought Charlie, not even a *good luck* or *cheerio* to send them on their way. He showed Peter the map.

'Here's *Araxos*, but you'll need to hug the coastline. It's still 200 miles away, want to try for it?'

Peter glanced at the port engine and nodded.

'Ok. We'll head for *Araxos*. Miller, raise Tinker Leader again, tell him we're diverting to *Araxos*,' Peter said, turning south onto their new course. There was no response from Venner this time; they were on their own.

Their southerly course placed the cloud-wreathed mountains firmly behind them. Charlie kept his eyes glued on the instruments to help Peter, only glancing at the map from time to time to confirm they were on course. To the left of the nose, the dark hills and mountains of Greece disappeared into cloud. On the right, the blue waters of the Mediterranean rippled in the sun.

After an hour or so, the troublesome port engine started to cough and splutter. Charlie checked and rechecked the fuel system, but found nothing unusual.

'I think the engine must have been hit, I can't work out what's wrong with it,' Peter told them.

The lone Blenheim continued on its path, its crew lost in their individual thoughts. Charlie barely registered the Island of Corfu slipping by to starboard, or *Preveza* on its enormous inland sea directly below them. It was not long after this that the faulty engine gave up completely and, with a terrific whine, the propeller seized. This forced Peter to throttle back on the remaining motor. He dropped the nose to pick up airspeed and used the rudder to keep the aircraft from slipping into a spin.

Charlie quickly switched the fuel feed over to both tanks, in case there was a problem with the feed to the remaining engine.

'It's hard work to keep the aircraft in balance. How long before we reach *Araxos*, Charlie?'

'Ten minutes.'

'Let's get the gear down.'

Their altitude was diminishing steadily, just over 1, 000 feet remained when they eventually crossed over the deep blue waters of the Gulf of Patras. They sighted the airfield on a headland on the far side and almost directly in line with their flight path. It was a rough grass strip with some wooden huts and little else. They did not respond to Miller's wireless call and Charlie pumped the undercarriage extension lever furiously as Peter set up for a flapless approach and landing. It was going to be close.

They touched down on the strip main wheels first, bounced a couple of times because their airspeed was too high, even with only one engine, and then rolled almost to the end of the strip. Pressing the brake lever hard to bring the aircraft to a stop, Peter looked exhausted.

'Not my best landing,' he said.

'Any one you can walk away from,' Charlie laughed, delighted that they were alive.

They turned about and taxied back to the huts, shutting down next to a couple of Royal Hellenic Air Force trainers. As he climbed out, Charlie was mobbed by Greek pilots and ground staff who were curious to know why they were here and wanted to look at the aeroplane. Peter insisted on first calling back to *Menidi* to let them know they were safe. So, he pushed through the curious crowd and was shown to a telephone in one of the buildings. After a couple of attempts, he was frustrated to find that he could not get a line to *Menidi*. Eventually, he managed to get through to a staff officer at Headquarters in the Hotel Grand Bretagne in *Athens*, who agreed to pass the message on. By the time he returned to the huddle around the aeroplane, Charlie was holding several bottles of Retsina and, with no imminent prospect of rescue, they opened the wine and poured out a few glasses. Their new friends sat with them and raised their glasses.

'Yamas,' Charlie said. *Yamas, yamas*, they replied.

*

Peter awoke the next morning with a staggering headache and a copper taste in his mouth. With some difficulty he rose and stepped outside the little hut he shared with Charlie and Miller into the fresh air. It was clear and sunny, the salt smell of the sea carried to him on the light breeze. Despite the hangover, he was in good spirits, joyful at the promise of another day after their narrow escape from *Valona*. Those fighters had been so perfectly positioned, he remembered, it was amazing that they had not knocked out an engine. Or hit a fuel tank for that matter. His mind drifted back to Venner, Cairo, and Charlie's letter. He tried to shake it away, it was becoming like an obsession for him now. Like the way he flew: determined and intuitive. He barely had to think about moving the controls, it was so natural to him. He had learned to trust his instincts - Egypt had taught him that. And his instincts told him that something was wrong.

Aircraft noise intruded upon his thoughts. It sounded like a small twin-engine aeroplane and then it appeared overhead. It circled once and dropped gracefully onto the field, taxiing right up alongside the Blenheim and shutting down its engines as it rolled to a stop. He saw that it was a *Percival Q6,* a passenger aircraft, but it did not wear a RAF paint scheme. Peter was surprised when the door at the rear swung open and Sergeant Mellish's grinning head appeared in the opening.

'Alright, sir?' Mellish yelled from the doorway. He jumped down and stared about him for a moment, blinking in the morning sun.

'We heard you had difficulties and we've come to fix you up.'

He was followed by Crawley and a couple of other airmen who stood staring, waiting for orders.

'Mellish, you're a sight for sore eyes. The port engine packed in and we had to divert here. I was worried the squadron didn't receive my message.'

'Oh, we heard alright, sir, and Mr Potterne told us to come out first thing to sort you out.'

Mellish continued, gesturing at Crawley.

'In any event, Tom Crawley needs a break from chasing tarts in *Athens*, so we fair jumped at the chance to come and collect you.' Crawley blushed and turned back to the *Percival* to unload their equipment.

Before long the engineers had the panels off the port engine and were probing around to find the problem. The Percival's pilot wandered over to where Peter stood next to his Blenheim. He was in RAF uniform and, when he removed his Mae West, wore the rank of Wing Commander on the shoulders of his light blue shirt. He looked up at the port wing where there were several bullet holes in the metal nacelle. He did not introduce himself and spoke to Peter in a clipped voice.

'Looks like you had a lucky escape there, how far did you have to take her?'

'We managed to do about 200 miles, but I think it was only about 50 or so on the one engine. We landed flapless because all the hydraulics were out,' Peter said, trying to avoid a bragging tone.

'You don't say? Damn me.'

He whistled and looked impressed.

'I'm Cranmer. I look after intelligence matters in *Athens*.'

Peter shook his hand and introduced himself.

'So, is this your aircraft, sir? You're not worried about flying about without any identification then?'

'Yes, she's my gal. I brought her over from Egypt when I was attached to the staff here,' Cranmer replied. Before going on he paused for a moment with a thoughtful look.

'I suppose that the other side *could* argue that it is somewhat perfidious, and they would know, the saucy devils. But I prefer to think of it as a legitimate *ruse de guerre*.'

Mellish stood up on the wing, wiping his hand on a dirty rag and called down to them.

'Looks like we found the problem, sir. One o' these 'ere bullets nicked the oil feed to the cylinders and the pistons are blown.'

'Can you fix it?' Peter asked.

'Bless you no, sir. She's fucked.'

*

They returned to *Menidi* at midday, still feeling the effects of their hangovers. Mellish and his team remained with *Yorker* to prepare for the engine change, which was necessary to render it serviceable again. They needed to fly a spare engine and equipment out to *Araxos*. It would be a few days before they could find a transport aircraft capable of lifting the equipment, and nobody wanted to try to recover the aircraft by road. So, it seemed sensible that Peter, Charlie and Miller should leave with Cranmer.

Once past his initial reserve, Cranmer chatted nonstop to Peter, who he had generously permitted a turn at the dual controls, about flying around Greece and some of the small strips he had visited in his travels about the country. Peter was surprised at all the small airfields Cranmer knew about. He wondered why Cranmer did so much flying when his job was connected with intelligence, but he felt that it would be rude to ask too many questions.

Cranmer did not hang about. The minute they were clear of the aircraft he spun around, taxied back to the airstrip and took off, climbing away to the north towards *Larissa*.

Brian stood outside squadron operations puffing away on his pipe and he greeted them warmly.

'Ah, the wanderers return! How was your time with the Greeks, did they bear gifts?'

Charlie wondered if he referred to their somewhat shabby appearance, unquestionably down to the Retsina.

Brian told them that the attack on *Valona* had been a success. The post-mission aerial reconnaissance revealed considerable devastation, with one transport ship lying half submerged against the jetty, warehouses burnt out, and several buildings damaged or destroyed. To capitalise on their success, at that exact moment the C.O. was leading the squadron on another circus operation over *Tepelene*. Brian nodded at the departing Percival.

'I see that Lord Aberdair brought you back. He's a delightful chap, isn't he?'

Peter frowned.

'That was Wing Commander Cranmer, he's in intelligence,' he stated, beginning to feel a little stupid. Brian explained that Wing Commander David Cranmer was actually a peer, the 9th Earl of Aberdair.

'How do you think he can afford to fly his own personal aeroplane around like that?' Brian laughed, though not unkindly.

They decided to wait around for the squadron to return before heading back to the mess. It was inside the damp-smelling dispersal tent that they chose to pass their time. The mail aircraft had arrived that morning and parcels and letters were spread across the wooden trestle tables in the back. Peter sunk into one of the battered leather chairs in the corner and dozed. Miller simply lay down on the floor and passed out. Charlie picked through the letters, brown paper packages and boxes. There was nothing for him. He had hoped for a word from Margot, just to give him some hope that he did not pine for her in vain.

Engineers were finishing work on two Blenheims parked a way off in the distance. As they walked off towards their billets as a group, their talk and laughter carried back to him. Others were beginning to appear from tents and airfield buildings, looking at their watches and then skyward again. There was anticipation, but the airfield lay silent. The light was fading early, as it did at this time of year. He lit his pipe and thought about Margot and the uncertainty of a future together. The war seemed like a great and wonderful adventure at one point, but now he had tasted it and found it was bitter. He was beginning to question whether he would even survive. The minutes ticked by and he strained to listen for a sign of the returning aircraft. Finally, he caught the faint sound of aero engines echoing over the hills. It grew louder as they approached, the unmistakable buzz of many engines. The squadron was coming home.

*

The dispersal tent heaved with crews chatting and laughing, their relief at having survived another sortie was palpable. Of the nine crews launched on the operation, eight had returned to *Menidi*. There was hope that Cruishank's crew had managed to put down at an emergency landing ground somewhere. Peter was pleased to be back amongst the others, although he felt a touch of chagrin at having missed out on a big show. The squadron had attacked a concentration of Italian trucks and vehicles that were parked in a depot to the north of *Tepelene*, and Wardle described to him how their bombs dropped on top of and around the parked vehicles.

'It was bang on,' he cried, 'I would say nearly every stick fell inside or within 100 yards of the depot. One lorry got thrown in nd there were explosions all over the shop. I suppose one of them was carrying ammunition or something. It was like Bonfire Night. The Eyeties won't forget that in a hurry.'

Peter was sick with jealousy but forced himself to ask polite questions of Wardle. Out of the corner of his eye, he spotted Brian entering the tent with a stony face. He signalled to Peter.

'I need a word with you for a moment.'

'Something up?'

'You could say that,' Brian replied, cryptically.

Peter found Charlie standing outside and led him to squadron operations. Venner was just leaving and scowled at them in passing.

'Sitting another mission out? Good work if you can get it.'

Peter boiled over with rage at the implication they were skiving. He balled his fists up and spun on his heels. Charlie caught his arm. Peter felt him grip and turned to look at his friend, who shook his head. Venner walked away without a glance back at them. Inside the caravan the C.O. and the Air Liaison Officer poured over a chart. The C.O. looked up as he entered, the smell of paraffin lamps and cigarette smoke filled his nostrils.

'Ah, Denhay and Kendrick,' he said warmly, 'there's a special operation that H.Q. wants us to run. It looks like it could be quite hazardous. You've been selected for it.'

Peter nodded instinctively. It was only fair that they took this one after the rest of the squadron had flown two operations in a row. The C.O. slid the chart towards them. It was folded open in such a way that *Salonika* lay at the bottom and a red pencil mark indicated a target some way to the north near Lake Doiran. This was going to be a long trip, he thought to himself.

'The mark indicates a temporary landing strip, from which you will collect a passenger,' the Air Liaison Officer said.

'The plan is to take off from here and fly to *Larissa* to take on fuel. Then proceed to the landing ground that we have codenamed "Pall Mall",' the C.O. added.

'I'm sorry sir,' Peter interrupted, 'I thought we were forbidden to fly in the area directly to the north of *Salonika*. It was an Air Staff directive. And why refuel when we can get there and back with fuel to spare?'

The C.O. smiled patiently and in a gentle tone said, 'The Greeks don't know that we're flying this sortie, Denhay, and we need to keep it that way. And you'll need to refuel at *Larissa* because the landing ground is only 250 yards long.'

Peter blinked a couple of times and heard Charlie whisper *bloody hell* under his breath. The normal landing roll for a Bristol Blenheim was 300 yards, but this was when landing into wind and on a dry surface. Neither of which could be guaranteed.

'We'll need to lighten your aircraft as much as possible. You'll fly with minimum fuel and no air gunner. I've asked Brian to help you practice short field landings and take-offs, so it will be second nature.'

The C.O. turned to Charlie.

'You'll have to fly at low-level to avoid attracting any interest from the Greeks. As I said, they're concerned about the Germans coming into the war through Bulgaria. if they get word that we've been flying around on the border they will be, quite understandably, furious. You'll need to know the route like the back of your hand.'

'How long have we got to practice?' Charlie folded his arms as he spoke, he looked unconvinced.

'A day or two. I think,' the Air Liaison Officer replied. The C.O. slid the chart to one side and spoke to them both.

'I recognise it's a lot to ask of a crew. To find your way across nearly 200 miles of Grecian mountains to land in a farmer's field in the middle of nowhere and come away with a passenger. But I have complete faith in you both.'

The Air Liaison Officer produced a crude sketch map from his attaché case and laid it on the table on top of the air navigation chart.

'This was provided by Air Intelligence. It shows the principal marks to locate Pall Mall. You will note Lake Doiran; this village to the north of it marked *Poroia*, and the long straight road leading to the north east that rises gently and ends on a small plateau. There is a ruined farmhouse that marks the landing field itself.'

'But north of Lake Doiran is across the border. That's *inside* Bulgaria,' Charlie said, sounding alarmed. The C.O. waved his hand across the map with a dismissive gesture.

'These maps are over 20 years old, Kendrick. The borders have changed in that time. In any event, Air Intelligence assures me that Pall Mall is in Greece. Not Bulgaria.' His tone was firm.

'Who's the chap that we're to collect? He must be important if we're risking lives to haul him out.'

Peter meant *their* lives. He knew his question could not be answered, at least not sincerely. The C.O. gave them a look that conveyed the gravity of the situation.

'Strict need-to-know only, I'm afraid. But I can tell you that your passenger's mission is of utmost importance to the course of the war in the Mediterranean. You must make every endeavour to bring him home safe.'

By the time the left the caravan, it was twilight. Peter felt a growing pride that they had been picked for this auspicious mission and wondered what it meant for his promotion prospects. He had no wish to remain a Pilot Officer forever. But a look at Charlie as they walked away told him the feeling was not mutual.

'Why've we been picked for this job? We're the new boys,' Charlie said.

'What? I think we're as good as anyone else,' Peter said, trying not to sound hurt, 'If not us, then who else could do it?'

'Anyone else! That's what I'm trying to tell you, Peter. MacNeish, Wardle, Milne, even Venner. Although he'd gripe like a good 'un about doing it.'

'Like you are?'

'I'm not griping. I'll do my duty, but as a matter of fact the boss said nothing about us being any good. He just said that we'd been selected.'

'That endorsement's good enough for me,' Peter replied.

Charlie stopped and turned to Peter. Even in the moonlight Peter could tell his expression betrayed anxiety.

'We get called to operations out of the blue and discover that we're off on a really dangerous job. Any of the people involved in this might want us out of the way. Don't you think there's a lot of coincidences there?

Peter said nothing. His own mind had been clouded with prestige at being personally selected for a difficult job. Now he reflected on Charlie's words, they made sense. Who was to say they might not slam into a hillside at low-level, or run into an enemy fighter patrol.

'We don't have the option to turn it down,' Peter said flatly.

'I know,' Charlie said, choosing his next words carefully, 'we just need to decide who we can trust from here on in.'

Chapter 9

Training began the next day. Charlie double-checked the calculations and scribbled annotations on his map. He looked for turning points with vertical elevation, the third dimension of route planning. In practice this meant planning waypoints over geological features, so that they were easy to recognise. At low-level, this was close to impossible.

Miller, who was crestfallen to learn he would not play a role in the mission, volunteered gamely to help arrange things on the ground. He took responsibility for laying out an accurate representation of the landing field. Pacing out the distance in parallel to the strip at *Menidi*, he marked the start of Pall Mall with a length of canvas begged from stores. Then he paced out 200 yards and hammered another piece of canvas in the ground at that point.

'The landing ground is 250 yards long, not 200,' Peter protested to Brian, who smiled and explained that it would be no use practising to stop in 250 yards, if that meant ending up on your belly over a stone wall. If they had 250 yards to land in, they needed to be capable of stopping in 200. Brian drew out on a piece of paper the profile of an aircraft landing on an airstrip. He indicated steeper and shallower approaches above and below this line with a dotted pencil mark.

'You'll recognise a classic engine-assisted approach to an airfield, in which you fly down the glide path using power to keep you at a constant airspeed of about 75 miles per hour.' He gestured to the standard landing technique with his pencil.

'But to land in a short space, you need to use every technique to keep the airspeed low and bring you to halt as quickly as possible. The good news is that the Blenheim has an excellent short-field performance. The large wing flaps give you a nose-down attitude and low stalling speed. It also has those undercarriage doors that sit in the airflow and generate lots of drag when the gear is lowered; they help keep your airspeed down too. The key is going to be flying the steepest possible approach to the airstrip aiming to undershoot, without stalling, to a perfect three-point landing and then getting on the brakes immediately to slow the landing roll.'

'But if I stall, I'll have no height to recover,' Peter stated flatly.

'None at all. So, if you don't want to end up pancaked on the airfield you will need to keep your airspeed between 60-65 miles per hour and pop the engines at the last minute to send you over the line. I warn you though, if you spool up the engines too violently, you'll flood the carburettors and risk losing one or both of them. I don't need to tell you that this would be fatal.'

'You know an awful lot about this, Brian.' Peter considered his words carefully. He didn't want to offend Brian, but he felt he had to ask the burning question.

'Why don't you fly? We could do with a flight commander like you.'

Brian stared at Peter for a moment and then looked away and put down in his pencil. He reached for his pipe.

'I haven't flown since France, Peter. I led a flight of Fairey Battles in an attack against some temporary bridges that the Krauts had thrown across the Meuse at *Sedan*. We were trying to stop a German armoured formation from crossing. But the Germans had fortified the bridgeheads with flak emplacements, and they had fighter cover above and in front of those. We lost many good men trying to hit those bridges and both of my wingmen were knocked down. My aircraft got hit on the way home and we ended up crash-landing in a field.'

Peter had seen the photographs of crashed aircraft around Sedan. He visualised the crippled Battle smoking in a field under a summer sun.

'I managed to get free. But the aircraft was on fire and both the observer and air gunner were killed, despite my attempts to get them out.'

Peter saw the faraway look in Brian's eyes, he looked like he was reliving every painful moment of that crash again. He had no idea what that must be like, he thought to himself, to be trapped in a burning wreck with flames licking up your legs. He shuddered.

'I'm afraid that after that I lost my senses a little and I must have wandered around for a bit, getting caught up with refugees heading away from the fighting. I eventually got picked up by some army gunners, who looked after me, and I ended up being shipped out of Dunkirk.'

'How did you end up here?'

'Well, the RAF thought I'd been knocked about a bit, so they sent me to hospital. I suppose I had a breakdown or something. In any event, the squadron didn't want me back and I got shuffled off to the Middle East when things started to warm up there. I couldn't bear flying, but I could do the admin for those who could. So ended up as an Adjutant.'

Peter said nothing. He knew he needed Brian's help, although his natural instinct was to resist asking for it.

'Brian, I've never flown anything like this before, and I need someone in Charlie's seat to ensure the weight is realistic. Won't you get back in the cockpit and show me the ropes?'

Brian had countless hours on different types of aircraft; what he didn't know about parking an aircraft in someone's back yard was not worth knowing.

'Oh, my nerves have gone, I'd be no use to you. I think you might have to do this one alone,' Brian said, shaking his head.

'You don't need to touch the controls, Brian. Just sit in the navigator's seat and talk me through it. I'm asking for your help.'

Brian said nothing.

'Look Brian, Charlie and I look up to you. I know you've been given a hard time, and I know what some of the others call you behind your back. But I also know that's all bollocks. Just because you needed to sit one out doesn't mean that you're spoilt goods. Here's your opportunity to prove it. Show them that they're wrong.'

A short time passed before Brian cleared his throat and looked back at Peter. With a crooked smile he spoke at last.

'Alright, Peter, I'll do it.'

Peter grinned and shook his hand.

'And after the war,' Brian said, 'you can run for Parliament.'

*

They circled the airfield, Brian's long frame crammed in an ungainly manner into the observer's seat next to Peter. Below them a crowd gathered on the apron in the mild warmth of the midday sun to watch the spectacle. The mission remained a closely guarded secret known only to a select group, but it could not be concealed that something was afoot. Few could resist the urge to watch a pilot practising tricky manoeuvres, and the presence of spectators lent the affair the feel of an air show at Hendon.

Peter lined up on the canvas markers, beginning his approach from 1, 000 feet. At this height the length of the strip seemed appallingly inadequate, and Peter was so focused on trying to land on the first marker that he forgot to reduce his airspeed. He touched down with the main wheels, but tail-high, and was still rolling past the 200-yard marker, even though the brakes were on full. When they eventually stopped, Brian turned to him and spoke in a voice that betrayed much dissatisfaction.

'Airspeed. Do it again.'

On the second attempt Peter dropped the wing flaps and gear early and eased back on the throttles. The engines burbled as the RPM fell to idle. The nose dropped and he found that he could control the airspeed more easily with the column pulled back towards him. The airspeed indicator needle trickled back from 80, 75, 70, to 65 miles per hour and Peter felt the signs of the incipient stall, the hooter went off and he panicked. Pushing the throttles forward at the same time as the control column and raising the gear, he decided to go around for another attempt. He could feel sweat running down his back even in the comparative coolness of the cockpit. He couldn't make out Brian's expression behind his oxygen mask, but heard him speak softly.

'That's alright, that was good. Just control the airspeed and don't be afraid to play with the power settings.'

On the ground one of the watching airmen whistled to himself and said aloud, 'Strewth, another one like that and we'll be picking pieces of them out of the airfield for weeks.'

Miller turned around and gave him a filthy look.

'If you can't shut your trap, we'll be picking pieces of *you* out of the airfield and all, mate,' he growled.

Peter set up for landing again: gear; pitch; flaps; and throttles, he told himself. He watched the airspeed trickling back and lined up on the markers. An early entry to the turn and a little rudder to straighten up, his stomach tightened as the marker approached. Such was his focus, he saw nothing more than the two strips of canvas and the airspeed indicator's needle flickering behind its glass in the instrument panel. The airspeed dipped to 60 mph, the hooter went off, and Peter gently nudged the nose forward. The needle held firm. Then he was in the final 200 feet above the airstrip and heading to land short of the first marker. He reached out to the throttles just as Brian shouted.

'Now Peter!'

He only had to move the throttles a touch to encourage the engines to pick up and the aircraft surged forward to a perfect three-point landing with the tail wheel kissing the centre of the canvas. Peter pulled the brake lever hard and brought the throttles right back to idle. The tail threatened to leave the ground once more, but he instinctively released the brakes and pulled hard again. The second marker raced towards them, the aircraft slipped along the grass and then finally slowed and came to a rest. Brian loosened his straps and craned his neck around to look behind them.

'You're about one aircraft length over the marker,' he said into the intercom. Peter shook his head and cursed, he felt angry with himself that this was so difficult. He flushed bright red behind his mask. Seeing this, Brian sighed and pulled off his mask.

'Why don't we take a break? Let's have a cup of tea and have a think about this logically.'

Over tea and a bowl of unrecognisable stew from the cookhouse, Peter felt a little better and was able to think more clearly about the problem. They sat on the grass next to the aircraft, Peter, Charlie, Brian and Miller, and talked about the practicalities of the landing. Charlie added to the pressure by explaining that, in the event of a cross-wind landing on wet r a downward slope, they would probably carry even ....ner than they were now.

Miller stirred the remains of his stew thoughtfully, muttering, 'Fatty meat this. Bloomin' cooks could trim it more.'

'It's the fat that gives it the flavour-' Brian said, stopping abruptly. Then he jumped to his feet, startling everyone.

'My God,' he cried, 'of course!'

Brian shouted over to Warrant Officer Tyler who was chatting with a group of engineers nearby, 'Mr Tyler? Mr Tyler. Can I have a word with you please, for just one moment?'

As Tyler hurried over, he turned back to them excitedly.

'We've not been thinking straight about this. Peter has been flying the best possible approach he can fly, but if the aircraft's weight is constant then we will only ever be able to stop one length over 200 yards. We need to trim the aircraft weight back.'

'We're already flying with a reduced fuel load and no gunner, what else can we lose?' Charlie asked, sounding incredulous.

'Well perhaps nothing really heavy, but if we take off enough of the lighter items, then it might just make the difference.'

Warrant Officer Tyler appeared at Brian's elbow.

'Mr Tyler, what else can we strip off the aircraft? Can we take out the wireless sets and remove the guns?'

Tyler nodded and looked thoughtful.

'Perhaps,' Tyler said, 'perhaps, we can take off the bomb bay doors and the life raft. We could remove the observer's table, the seat in the nose, and the wing-mounted machine-gun?'

'Not the forward-firing gun,' Peter interjected, 'it's our only protection if we run into anything. The gun has to stay.'

'Very well then, let's get to it.' Brian grinned with satisfaction.

Within an hour the engineers had swarmed all over the aircraft and removed the unnecessary articles, which they laid in the back of the utility truck on a tarpaulin. The Engineer Officer appeared at one point, fretting about his components, but Brian shooed him away, telling him to mind to his own business. The poor devil scuttled off to the hangar looking dreadfully sorry for himself.

The result of their labour was an abomination. Peter thought the aircraft, *J-Johnnie*, looked like a half-completed model aeroplane with its bomb bay doors off. Brian climbed up onto the wing and looked up as three of the squadron's aircraft roared overhead into the circuit, having returned from a bombing sortie. Peter joined him and they both dropped down into the cockpit. As Peter switched on the power he saw Brian plug in to the intercom.

'It's now or never, Peter. Good luck my boy.'

They taxied out to the start of their little strip, completing take-off checks as they went, and swung around into wind. Peter applied the parking brake as he had practised, then lowered the flaps slightly and advanced the throttles to take-off RPM. The engines roared to life and he felt the airframe straining, threatening to drag it forward across the grass airfield. He released the parking brake and the aircraft leapt forward, quickly gaining speed, and with boost selected the tail jumped into the air.

Peter held the control column forward to collect speed and at 120 miles per hour, he pulled back and selected gear-up, the aircraft was airborne by the time it passed the second marker and Peter initiated a slow turning climb to port to bring them around for an approach. Neither noticed the little crowd of onlookers cheering as they cleared the marker. In the circuit he found that the bomber was noticeably lighter on the controls than it had been before. Some of that, he guessed, was fuel consumed from the morning's flying, but that could not account for all the change in handling.

At the top of the descent he set the aircraft up for a steep glide and kept the airspeed sitting just above 60 miles per hour all the way down to 200 feet above the deck. When it looked like he was going to undershoot he again gave the throttles a quick blip and pulled back on the control column. The aircraft touched down gracefully on the first canvas marker, main and tail wheels at the same time. Even before they were down, he chopped the throttles, felt the aircraft settle and pulled the brake lever, holding it tight. The aircraft bumped and skidded across the turf with the wheels complaining, but Peter did not let go of the lever or let the column go forward from its position pulled tight into his guts. They stopped rolling and Brian leaned over to look where the markers where.

'You're right on top,' he said with a grin behind his oxygen mask, '200 feet dead-on Peter - well done. Oh, well done.' He shook Peter's hand forcefully, the delight evident in his eyes.

*

As the propellers slowed to a halt, Charlie and Miller came running up to help them out. Peter could see that they shared his relief at learning the thing could at least be done. Brian pulled off his oxygen mask, his face was shiny and he looked fatigued. He stepped out of the cockpit like a man who had flown far more than the 56 minutes Peter knew he had logged today. Peter helped him out of the hatch where Brian stepped onto the wing and slid down to stand unsteadily on the ground with one hand on the fuselage.

'Are you ok, Brian? Peter's landings aren't that bad,' Charlie said with a laugh.

Peter gave him a disapproving look and dropped down next to them. Brian placed his hands on his temples.

'It'll pass, I just need a moment,' he said, then looking around at the three men, 'I need to say something to you, before you fly this sortie.'

'God, you sound awful serious,' Peter replied.

'We take pride in training and rehearsal in the RAF. But too often we overlook the all-important factor that makes the real difference when the chips are down and there's difficult work to be done.'

'I don't follow you,' Charlie said.

'At its very best, all of this preparation is just a rehearsal. You see? It's impossible to know what conditions you'll find on the day. The number of variables is enormous and any one of them might throw the others out of balance. This is the point at which your training ends and your character begins.'

Peter studied Brian's face. Brian spoke pointedly.

'This is the tipping point, the crucible. Where we really tell the difference between men. Those who blunder, those who run and hide, and those who are stout of heart,' Brian thumped his chest to reinforce his point, 'because when everything appears lost, when the chaff has fallen away, it's character that counts above all else.'

'I understand, Brian,' Peter replied.

'Do you, Peter? I hope you do. Because you ought to know that it wasn't fancy flying or even your little trick with tracking the Eyetie bombers into Libya that earned you a place on this squadron.'

The three men listened intently.

'In your own way, the three of you could not be more different to the other crews, ' Brian smiled, 'As individuals, you'd have always been the outsiders. But the C.O. and I had a wager, and I bet putting you together would be a triumph - I knew we would end making an outstanding team or killing the three of you in the process.'

'I wouldn't count your chickens just yet,' Charlie said.

'Oh, I don't know Charlie,' Brian grinned, 'the odds look pretty good from where I'm standing.'

'Is that why we were selected for this job? Because of your wager with the C.O.,' Peter asked, suddenly feeling like his ego was somewhat bruised.

'Eh? No, that's got nothing to do with it. We asked Venner to nominate one of his crews and he picked you.'

Chapter 10

The Greek mountains received a light dusting of snow early in that December. They seemed unnaturally still and silent beneath the grey sky. The crisp morning air was rent violently by the Blenheim, zipping along at just above treetop height. Its crew sat determinedly at the controls, in the knowledge that a slip up at this height would be fatal.

They surprised the resident fighter squadron at *Larissa* by popping down onto the airstrip without so much as a wireless call. Someone at *Menidi* had the forethought to warn of their arrival by field telephone, and a party of airmen was waiting with petrol cans when they taxied in.

Peter surveyed the airfield as they refuelled, it was one of the better ones in Greece with modern hangars and airfield buildings. The ground was dry and hard, and he could see some dispersed Gloucester Gladiator fighters and Greek aircraft in the distance. Apart from its size, which made it visible from miles away, he thought *Larissa* looked like a very comfortable base indeed.

He went back over the notes he had taken from the briefing that morning. The C.O., Brian, and the Air Liaison Officer had sat in the dispersal tent as they rehearsed route again. Peter visualised it: north-west at low-level as far as *Lamia* before swinging direct north to *Larissa*. The second leg skirted the coast to the east of Mount Olympus then turned north again, keeping *Salonika* well to the east of them. It was almost due north again from this point, whereupon they would pick up Lake Doiran quite easily and follow the marks to Pall Mall from that point. The C.O. nodded, satisfied that they could find the place. The Air Liaison Officer added some additional instructions.

'The rendezvous time is set for 1100 hours, but we've agreed a window of plus or minus two hours. Your passenger's authentication word is "Players", the reply is "Camels". If you arrive at the landing ground to find that it's occupied, you are not to land. If the passenger does not arrive on time, do not wait. You are to return here as quickly as possible and report to me.'

Peter recalled that, as he paused for a moment, his eye seemed to twitch involuntarily.

'One final thing, and I really cannot stress enough how important this is. In the event that you have to force land in an isolated position or end up stranded somewhere, you must destroy the aircraft and any documents before making your way back to friendly lines. Any questions?' There had been none.

Taking off from *Larissa*, Peter turned over the implications of the mission in his mind. He found himself questioning why the Greeks had not been made aware of their mission, and why this level of secrecy was necessary. It seemed odd that their allies should be kept in the dark.

The ground beneath them passed by in a blur, occasionally it was low hills and valleys, sometimes a patchwork of fields, and then the sea, looking dark and troublesome today. It was fringed with a strip of white sand and they followed this for a time. They saw no other aircraft, not unusual with a cloud base at around 2, 000 feet, although Peter knew there were Greek airfields in the immediate vicinity.

The terrain changed remarkably as Salonika passed away off to the right. It became flatter and apparently dryer. Brown and olive hues were more evident in the fields below them than they were around *Menidi*, or even *Larissa*. There were rolling forested hills on the horizon and, at one point, Peter had to pull up sharply to avoid a stand of tall Poplar trees that appeared, unexpectedly, to bar the way. Having cleared them, he took the opportunity to rub sweat off his brow with his glove. The practice of low-level flying demanded absolute concentration, and to do so for hours at a time was physically exhausting. Charlie's voice rang in his ear.

'That was close,' he said, without looking up from his map.

The ground rose slightly, they crested a long, low ridgeline and caught sight of snow-covered mountains far beyond that they knew marked the border between Greece and Bulgaria. Much closer, Lake Doiran glinted in the sparse sunlight with its crescent of steep hills to one side. Peter brought the aircraft into a climb over the lake to give Charlie a better chance of identifying the marks.

'See it yet?'

Peter was conscious that their fuel load had been calculated on the minimum safe quantity to fly the 200-odd miles from *Larissa* to Pall Mall and back again. They had a small allowance for a maximum power take-off and a reasonable headwind, but could not afford to fly circles above Lake Doiran forever. Charlie shot him a sideways look.

'I can make out half a dozen small settlements above the lake, but this sketch map only has one: *Poroia*. And these roads are difficult to make out. They're really no more than dirt tracks.'

Charlie flicked the map with his hand, 'Swing north of the lake and circle there.'

Peter banked the aircraft over to starboard and held it in a long lazy turn whilst Charlie looked down through the canopy glass. As they neared the lakeshore, Peter noticed that one of the villages was larger than the others and had a road leading northward, which climbed up a steep-sided valley running roughly north-west away from the village.

'Looks promising, just off the nose,' Peter said.

'That's *Poroia*, I know it. Follow that road,' Charlie replied firmly. The road ran up the valley for three or four miles, climbing gently but steadily. To one side of the road ran a series of thin fields demarcated by low stone walls, many of which had tumbled over. The fields were empty and fallow, other than the long grass, bushes and small trees that sprouted at random. The same bushes and trees covered the slopes of the valley in uneven clumps. It looked like quite some time had passed since the land had been worked.

The valley opened out onto a small plateau near its top, it was about the length of two and half football fields. A low stone wall enclosed the space, but there was a gap in one corner where the track terminated. The gate, posts, and wall had all fallen in an untidy mound here, creating an obstacle to entry. In the opposite corner to the gate were the remains of a single-story house with an outbuilding. The roofs had fallen in on both buildings. But the clearest indication that this was Pall Mall was the long, straight strip cut diagonally across the field. It had been done crudely and looked slightly narrower than the distance between the wingtips of a Blenheim, the cutting exposed rough, uneven ground beneath the shorter grass.

A quick pass over the field told him three things. The first was that there was no-one waiting for them, in fact there was no sign of life whatsoever. Second, the field was not level, it had a slight but noticeable gradient of perhaps a couple of yards over its entire length. The lowest point was at the end next to the ruined house and highest next to the pile of debris where the gate once stood. This was a good thing because it would help slow the landing run. Finally, from the movement of the trees below, the wind was blowing directly across the airstrip, meaning that it would be a negligible factor in both landing and subsequent take-off. Not great, Peter thought, because he had practised predominantly into wind.

Peter keyed the intercom button.

'I'm going for it. I'll make an approach from the east to land-on at the end near to the buildings. If the picture doesn't look good at 200 feet, I'll apply power and go around again. If we lose an engine, I'll attempt to land ahead with the gear down. Ready?'

Charlie tightened his lap belt and folded the map away.

'Ready.'

Landing checks complete, Peter set the aircraft up for the approach. On his first attempt, he fixated on the proximity of the surrounding slopes and came in too fast. The instruments backed up his conclusion that they would not stop in the space available. Inwardly, he told himself to relax; there was no rush. He went around again, rather than risk landing mid-field where they would, like as not, end up rolling through the stone wall at the end of the strip.

The second go was more promising. Peter focused on trying to land on a point 20 yards short of the strip and flew the aircraft down a glide path towards that aiming mark. The airspeed hooter went off in the last 200 feet, but he nudged the throttle levers forward to prevent a stall and carry the aircraft over the last yards to the field. The engines burbled but responded to his request for more power and they sailed over the stone boundary with feet to spare. There was a loud brushing noise like a thousand hands caressing the aircraft, and then the silence of anticipation. The ground rose up to meet them.

They landed with a thump. Peter heard Charlie gasp as the wind was knocked out of him, but he immediately braked and drew the throttles back to idle. The brakes squealed and the aircraft skidded, so he released and quickly reapplied them. The wingtips extended above the long grass but not into it, and he saw there was room for the propeller blades to turn freely. They slowed and eventually came to stop a couple of aircraft lengths from the stone wall. Peter turned to his navigator, whose face showed ashen grey above his oxygen mask, and smiled.

'Piece of cake.'

*

Turning the aircraft was made trickier by the long grass and the potential to hit rocks or roots lurking within it. Charlie climbed out and checked the clearances all round, signalling back to Peter that he was free to spin the bomber about. They positioned the aircraft at the start of the strip and shut down. Charlie walked around the aircraft to check for damage and was relieved to find that there was nothing more serious than some vegetation trapped in the undercarriage doors. This mystified him, until he reached the rear of the aircraft and looked back at their approach path. Just above the low stone wall that marked the field was a tall hedge formed of large clumps of thick bushes. Cut in the top of this hedge were two perfect indentations caused by their main wheels passing through it.

Beset by the sudden urge to ease his bladder, Charlie set off in the direction of the ruined buildings, pulling out his revolver as he went. Approaching the ruined house, Charlie held the revolver out in front of him like a character in a Western. He decided that, though he had never been trained to use the weapon properly, it couldn't be too difficult to wield if the need arose. Out of curiosity, he stuck his head into the house but found that the collapsed rafters and roof tiles had buried whatever might have been left there. There was no trace of any recent occupation.

He crossed the open yard in front of the house to the outbuilding. This too was roofless, but it did not look like it had collapsed. On closer inspection the upper parts of the walls and the insides were blackened, probably from a fire. He chose to urinate inside the outbuilding and not the house, subconsciously telling himself it was more polite to piss inside someone's barn rather than their kitchen.

Placing the pistol back in its holster, he unzipped his heavy sheepskin flying jacket and unbuttoned the khaki trousers he had scrounged before leaving Egypt. Then he heard a rustling in the grass behind. He whipped around, pulling the pistol out at the same time in one fluid movement. His trousers dropped around his ankles and he found himself staring at a cat. A common feral cat had rounded the corner and now stared at her fellow intruder with a bored, indifferent look.

'Oh, bugger off.'

When he returned to the aircraft, he found Peter sat against the port side main wheel reading a battered copy of *A Tale of Two Cities.*

'You know Peter, I don't think I've ever seen you read anything before. Do you like Dickens?'

'What rot,' Peter said, looking up, 'I read all the time, it's the only break I ever get from you. And yes, I do like Dickens, he's a natural observer and his turn of phrase is sublime.'

'Did you hear someone else say that?'

'No,' Peter said, with a smile that indicated he probably had.

'If you say so. I think he's too sentimental. Although I'll admit that *David Copperfield* is quite good,' Charlie grunted. He paused for a moment and then asked, 'What do we do now then?'

Peter's eyes did not leave the page when he replied.

'We wait, Charlie. We sit here and we wait until 1100 hours and then, if our man hasn't turned up, we wait for another two hours. Then we leave. Those,' he said drily, 'were our orders.'

Charlie slumped down onto the grass and stared up at the sky. The sun was coming out and an occasional wispy cloud flitted by above them. It took something of the edge off the otherwise chilly day. A silence passed that seemed an age to Charlie but was actually less than two minutes.

'Doesn't it trouble you Peter, how much time we spend sitting around just waiting for things to happen?'

Peter lowered his book and shot him a look of mild irritation. Seeing that he had an audience, Charlie went on.

'When I joined, I thought life in the RAF would be one great party,' he continued, 'that would be filled with action and adventure. And music and beautiful women.'

'I don't see how a damp field in northern Greece fails to meet with your expectations,' Peter laughed.

'Bulgaria,' Charlie corrected him, 'But it's not at all like that. In fact, it's mostly sitting around in dingy tents waiting for somebody to make a decision. Or to countermand a decision and send us back from whence we came. And for the short periods that it's not like that, it's completely bloody terrifying.'

'You could always go back to medical school,' Peter replied.

Charlie smiled in spite of himself. Of course, he could not go back to medical school, war or no war, he had firmly burnt that bridge. He wondered whether he could tell Peter that story. He felt he should be open with him, they were friends after all - more than that, in fact, they were a crew. He had told Margot about it and he barely knew her. But beneath his revolutionary zeal and his idealism, Charlie knew there was a deeply English soul. A character that believed in fairness and sincerity, and playing the game for the sake of the game. It was one of the reasons, he realised, why he hated fascism - it respected none of these things. The English were also terrible at talking about the things that mattered, he mused. Even thinking about speaking to Peter about his past made him squirm and he looked for an opportunity to switch the topic of conversation. Remembering Brian's words to them the day before, he seized on this.

'I was surprised that we were picked for this,' Charlie said after a pause.

Peter put his book down.

'By Venner?'

'Yes.'

'He didn't let on that he'd volunteered us for the mission,' Peter shrugged, 'He tried to pass it off as favouritism or something.'

'Do you suppose he expected us to fail?'

'I don't know what I think about Venner. He's an odd sod, I think it's easy to confuse the way he is with deeper suspicions. I do think we need some help in this - have you heard anything from Margot?'

'Nothing at all, it's been weeks too.'

Peter thought for a moment.

'Perhaps we should bring Brian into this, he could get the service police to investigate,' Peter said.

'I think that would be a bad idea,' Charlie said hurriedly, the last thing he wanted was the service police digging about, 'What if I ask Brian for a weekend leave pass to visit Margot, I can jump on the mail plane and be there and back in 72-hours.'

'Without calling ahead? Are you sure she'll be free?'

'I'm sure she'd enjoy the surprise - everyone likes surprises, right?'

Peter opened his mouth to speak, then stopped. A crackling noise carried to them on the wind. Charlie cocked his head to one side and then stood up.

'Can you hear that?'

'I think I can make something out,' Peter replied. The sound grew louder, it echoed up the valley towards them. Peter's eyes widened and he turned to Charlie.

It's gunfire by god.'

'Get the kite warmed up, we're leaving,'

*

Peter scrambled to his feet and shouted to Charlie, 'Open the gunner's hatch.'

'Why?'

'Because if they're not shooting at us, they must be shooting at our passenger,' he yelled over his shoulder as he jumped up on the wing. He slithered neatly down into the pilot's seat to run through the start-up checks.

'Come on, come on,' Peter muttered. Charlie appeared in front of the nose, holding a thumbs up to signal he was clear to start up. Peter hit the engine starter and the port engine coughed into life. He let it idle and started the starboard, which spluttered and then ran smooth, to his great relief. Peter sat waiting as Charlie jogged further up the field, presumably to get a better look down the road. He needn't have bothered, because a motorcyclist shot into view on the track travelling at full pelt towards them.

The motorcyclist took the corner into the field without slowing and hit the pile of debris at full tilt. Both machine and rider were flipped into the field, disappearing into the long grass at the edge of the strip. Peter was stunned, he must certainly have broken his neck in that crash. But the rider was up and running towards Charlie in an instant. Peter could see that he wore a leather motorcycle helmet with goggles pulled down over his face, a jacket with a leather jerkin over it, and dark corduroy trousers tucked into leather boots. He sprinted unsteadily, like he was hurt.

Charlie waved to him and ran around behind the wing, but the motorcyclist fell over again and lay sprawled on the ground unmoving. Peter removed his straps and stood on his seat to wave Charlie back to the fallen figure. Time was running out, he knew, whoever was chasing the motorcyclist would be coming up that road shortly. As Charlie dragged him around to the wing root, Peter left the cockpit and clambered out onto the wing to help lift the passenger aboard.

Peter was just reaching down to grab the unconscious figure under the armpits, when the motorcyclist's head lolled back and the leather helmet slipped off. It revealed long, dark curly hair and a pale face. A face that was unmistakably feminine, and perhaps the most beautiful woman Peter had ever seen.

'It's a girl,' Charlie shouted. Between the two of them they lowered her gently into the gunner's hatch. Charlie climbed in after her as Peter returned to the cockpit to strap in. He spooled the engines up to take-off RPM, felt the aircraft tugging insistently, and released the parking brake.

The aircraft leapt forward, but its acceleration seemed dreadfully sluggish, even as it was halfway down the airstrip. Peter hit the boost, let the airspeed creep up until the last possible safe moment and pulled back on the control column. The aircraft shuddered, but lifted into the air, the wheels knocking the stones off the top of the wall as it passed over.

The gear rattled as it came up, but Peter barely noticed as he looked down the valley and spotted the reason for the girl's hurry. Not a half-mile distant on the long valley road a dark limousine threw up a cloud of dust as it raced along, followed by a grey, canvas-covered lorry. The limousine slowed at the sight of the aeroplane's sudden appearance. It was the worst decision to make under the circumstances.

Peter pushed the nose down and kicked the rudder over so that the aircraft slewed left until it pointed directly at the small convoy. As it appeared in his sights, he pressed the gun button and the wing-mounted machine-gun barked into life. Bullets stitched the ground in front of the limousine and then smashed into the bonnet, windshield, and the occupants of the car. The car sheared off the road into a ditch, but the deadly trail of bullets carried on into the engine block of the lorry and they ripped through the driver and into the bed of the truck, causing carnage.

Peter did not see much of this because they quickly swept over the wrecked vehicles and broken men and left the otherwise empty valley in Bulgaria. They climbed away and headed for home.

Chapter 11

'…And so we flew towards *Larissa* with the intent of offloading our passenger there. But it occurred to us that we had no orders that covered actions to be taken in case the agent was injured. It was also clear that a modern hospital could be found closer to *Athens*. So, I took the decision to head home without delay, in the belief that we had sufficient fuel to make it back without endangering the aircraft.'

Peter looked around at his audience, the C.O., Brian, and the Air Liaison Officer. The latter stared at him with an expression of blunt scepticism.

'We'll come to that shortly,' he said stiffly, 'tell me about this convoy you spotted on the road to the landing ground?'

'As we lifted off the airstrip, I observed a car and lorry heading towards us. I formed a strong belief that they were in pursuit of our passenger and presented a threat to our safety. Therefore, I took steps to protect us.'

'What does that mean?'

'I machine-gunned them.'

The Air Liaison Officer put his hand to his face, but the C.O. physically sat up at this news, clearly delighted.

'You've blown the bloody mission!' The Air Liaison Officer groaned and, in the silence that followed, Brian cleared his throat and spoke.

'I might suggest that the mission had been blown when the agent found herself chased across the border by a group of heavies. To whom does she belong anyway?'

Brian skilfully redirected attention towards the secretive nature of the mission. No-one had yet appeared to retrieve the girl and she remained under the care of the squadron's medical officer.

'I've asked Air Intelligence, but they don't know. They took the job on as a favour to another body,' the Air Liaison Officer admitted.

'Which one?'

'They wouldn't say.'

The C.O. looked displeased at this revelation. He glowered at the Air Liaison Officer.

'I was led to believe that this operation had been authorised at the highest level within headquarters. Am I now to understand that this was just a favour to an unnamed third party?'

The Air Liaison Officer gazed mutely at the C.O.; Peter could feel the moral high ground slipping away from the poor chap. The C.O. continued, 'Hadn't you better find out then, preferably before she dies in my medical tent.'

Peter was surprised to hear this. He had chatted with Charlie often during the return flight, and he had done all within his limited capacity to keep their passenger warm and comfortable. But he had not been present when Charlie and the others loaded her into the ambulance. No-one had mentioned until now that her condition was fragile. The Air Liaison Officer took the hint and he made himself scarce. And now the C.O. turned to Peter with a frustrated look.

'You can go. I think I've heard enough.'

Peter replaced his forage cap, saluted smartly and turned to head out of the tent. As he did so the C.O. said, 'Oh, Denhay?'

Peter stopped and turned to face him.

'Well done. That was one hell of a job to pick her up out of nowhere, especially under that pressure.'

'Thank you, sir,' Peter smiled, saluting again.

The sun was beginning to dip below the horizon as he emerged into the light and he could feel the dew falling with the approach of night. Charlie waited for him, keen to know the outcome of the inquisition. Peter told him how the meeting had gone, then he asked Charlie about the girl. He tried to sound casual as he asked the question.

'She's with the Doc, you better ask him. She looked a right state to me,' Charlie said, 'I'm going to head back to the mess shortly, I need a drink.'

I'll catch you up later. I think I'll look in on our passenger first.'

It was a short walk to the medical tent on the northern side of the airfield, near their maintenance hangar. He found the doctor and a medical orderly playing Gin Rummy in the back of an ambulance, with the cards laid out on an upturned ammunition crate. The medical officer greeted him warmly and asked if he had come for the VD clinic. Peter looked offended but ignored the impertinent question.

'I don't want to monopolise your time, but I wanted to look in on your patient,' Peter said earnestly.

'No trouble at all, old boy. She'd be glad of a visitor and it makes a change from sorting out Corporal Crawley's pubic lice,' he laughed at his own joke and led the way to another tent with six beds, three a side. It smelt of a mixture of things, chiefly damp canvas, paraffin and carbolic soap. All the beds were empty save one, in which the girl lay sleeping. Her otherwise pale face was discoloured by a nasty purple and yellow bruise around her left cheek and eye. Her dark curls were concealed beneath a wide cotton bandage and she was wrapped in several layers of grey woollen blankets to keep out the cold. In spite of her injuries, Peter thought she looked beautiful. Another medical orderly was sat in the middle of the room reading a book and, in response to a look from the medical officer, he left.

'Will she pull through, Doc?'

'She ought to. As far as I can make out there's nothing broken, but I understand that she took a tumble,' the doctor shrugged.

'I'd say so, she came off a motorbike and landed in a field,' Peter explained. The medical officer gave an impressed whistle.

'Is it normal for her to sleep like this?'

'It's not uncommon, they're funny things head injuries. I once treated a fellow who'd fallen off a Polo pony at Cowdray. He got back on and played the remaining two chukkas, but dropped down quite dead over luncheon afterwards. Tragic really.'

The doctor made a face. Peter thought it was a tasteless anecdote to share at this moment.

'Why don't you sit with her for a bit? You never know when she'll come round. I'll ask Davidson to step through in a jiffy with a cup of tea.'

Peter thanked him and sat down in a folding chair next to her bed. In the warm silence of the medical tent he listened to her gentle breathing and wondered who the hell she was. When they brought her aboard the aircraft, Charlie had said she'd not a single possession to identify her or indicate where she had come from. That could have been a coincidence, but it was curious that she had nothing on her at all. No train ticket stubs, no money, no passport, no letter from a parent or a lover. Not a thing. Charlie thought she might be Greek, she certainly had dark hair, but her skin was pale, not at all like the Greek women he had seen.

He remembered how she had been thrown over the handlebars of the motorcycle and then reappeared shortly after, running through the long grass towards them. She certainly had some courage, of that there was no doubt. Beauty *and* courage, he smiled to himself, traits he personally valued. He felt his eyelids growing unaccountably heavy, his mind wandered and in a half-dreaming state he imagined himself walking hand-in-hand with the girl.

The duty medical orderly popped in shortly after he had been asked him to bring a cup of tea to the Pilot Officer in the tent. The water was heavily chlorinated, and the tea leaves were a negligible quantity, but at least they had fresh milk. As he entered, he saw that the Pilot Officer was firmly asleep in the chair with his head tilted forward. The orderly placed the tea down on the bedside table and used a blanket from another bed to cover the young man, who was snoring lightly. Then he quietly tip-toed out.

*

Charlie's driver dropped him outside the large house in the village that served as the Officers' Mess. The officers slept here two or three to a room, taking their meals downstairs in a space that was both canteen and bar.

He glanced up at the moon and saw that it was completely clouded over. A light rain was falling, and he knew that any operation planned for tomorrow would be scrubbed because of the weather. He felt dog-tired and had decided to head straight off to bed, when he noticed the large, boisterous crowd in the bar and decided to look in for a quick nightcap.

Brian and Milne were talking with Wardle and a couple of the new boys in a knot at the end of the bar. There were several

...ᴗ he recognised who said hello back and he spotted Venner in a corner, drinking alone. He looked a miserable sight and Charlie suspected that he might already be drunk from his red face and staring eyes. It was unusual to see him in the mess at all, he rarely sought the company of others.

Charlie pushed through the crowd to join Brian and the others. They handed him a pint and filled him in on all the news of the past couple of days. The aircraft missing after the raid on *Tepelene* had been confirmed as Failed To Return. It was a euphemism that barely hinted at the actual fate of the crew. Tommy Cruikshank, the skipper, either got disorientated in low cloud or his Navigator had made an error, but the outcome was much the same. News had reached them, through headquarters, that the Greeks had found their blackened remains at the Blenheim's crash site on the side of a mountain. They buried the three flyers in a local churchyard.

Tradition dictated that the bar books of the dead men were opened for the night for everyone to drink on, before the squadron paid off their debts in the morning. They had been a green crew, barely known to the established squadron members. Their loss was not felt as keenly as it might have been. Indeed, the presence of two squadrons in the bar in significant numbers lent the place the perverse character of a university club drinking competition. These men lived with the threat of death daily; familiarity brought a more upbeat mood than might otherwise have been. Or perhaps, Charlie wondered, everyone just thinks it can't happen to them.

The news of their special mission had got around the squadron and they were all keen to get the details that Brian had not already divulged. Charlie recounted the story for them, noticing a few newcomers join the group to hear him speak. Though he retold it with an appropriate amount of artistic license, the outline was broadly true. When he got to the part where Peter had fired on the convoy, a tall thin Australian fighter pilot from 84 Squadron spoke up.

'Pull the other one mate, you can't hit a shithouse from 10 yards with that gun.' This triggered an immense argument over the relative merits of the Blenheim's wing-mounted .303

machine-gun. Someone claimed to have witnessed a Blenheim shoot down a Messerschmitt Me109 in France, which was greeted with widespread derision. The conversation quickly turned to the need for heavier calibre weapons, and Milne bemoaned the drawbacks of the armament on the current crop of fighter aircraft and light bombers. Charlie drained his pint, slipped out of the room and headed upstairs to bed.

When Charlie reached the room he shared with Peter, he found the door ajar. He stopped to consider this, forcing his weary mind to remember when they had left the mess that morning. He was uncertain who had been last out. No-one had keys for the rooms either. Charlie quietly pushed the door open. The room was barren, save for the beds and their few possessions, as it had been earlier. He relaxed, deciding that the fatigue was getting to him, and slumped on his bed.

The nagging feeling that something was out of place kept returning, however. He was not too tired to notice the chest of drawers had been pulled out and not put back quite right, leaving marks on the floorboards. He sat bolt upright and reached under his bed to pull out his trunk.

Someone had opened it and then clumsily tried to do up the leather straps again. Charlie always left these undone. When he opened it, it was clear that it had been rifled by an inexpert hand. Nothing was missing. Whoever had turned over the room had been looking for something, but they had not found it.

Charlie stood, his mind racing. There was only one person on the squadron who could have done this, he was convinced of it. The temper that he worked so hard to control normally, bubbled up. Rage consumed him. He stormed from the room and returned to the bar where Milne tried to offer him a pint. Charlie stepped wordlessly around him and strode to where Venner sat alone at the corner table. He stood over Venner and snarled.

'Looking for something, were we?'

Venner looked up at Charlie through the red-rimmed, unfocused eyes of a determined drunk. A crooked grin split his face and he slurred out a reply.

'Oh, here they come, the golden boys. Kendrick and Denhay, back from another sweet little mission as the rest of us brave everything the Wops can throw at us. But where's your chum, eh, you've not been keeping tabs on *him*, I see.'

'Stand up and say that,' Charlie said, balling his fists.

The crowd in the bar fell silent as they witnessed the scene unfold. Seeing there was a real prospect of a fight, Milne shouted, 'Let him alone, Kendrick. He's not worth it.'

Brian appeared at his elbow, doubtless positioning himself where he could intervene when the time came.

But Venner did not stand. Whether he intended to respond to the challenge at all was questionable, he looked far too drunk. He gazed at Charlie through half-closed eyes, with an open sneer, and said nothing. Charlie realised he was not going to get the fair fight he craved. Venner was goading him, in a packed bar with dozens of witnesses. Charlie was better than that, he knew there would be a reckoning and soon. He picked up the half glass of wine on the table and dashed the contents into Venner's face. A ragged cheer sounded at the back of the bar, but Venner still did not respond to the insult.

'If you ever go through my belongings or my mail again,' Charlie snarled, 'you'll be getting more than a drink in your smug face, you arsehole.'

Charlie turned and left the bar without a look behind him.

*

The morning brought low cloud and heavy rain. Flying was impossible and the C.O. cancelled the planned operation against *Valona*. The engineers drew back the hangar doors to admit aircraft for maintenance, the hiatus in flying was an opportunity to catch up. Underfoot, the airfield became boggy and a cold wind blew from the north. There was faint thunder and it was either this or the drumming of the rain on the canvas above his head that woke Peter. He was unsure of how long he had been asleep, his back hurt and his mouth felt like sandpaper.

'Good morning,' the girl said, 'I was wondering when you were going to wake up.'

Peter flashed her his best smile.

'That's my line isn't it? Does the Doctor know that you're up?'

'He does, he was in here this morning to remove my bandages. He told me that I have you to thank for my rescue.'

She smiled sweetly despite her appallingly bruised face. Her dark locks cascaded down to her shoulders in long curls. She was a lithe creature with blue eyes, high cheekbones, and a delicate nose. Her face seemed at home with a smile on it.

'I was really just doing my duty. Although I should tell you that motorcycling should be avoided at all costs. It really isn't good for your health, you know?'

'I won't take the advice of a man who expects to sleep with a woman without even taking her for drinks first,' she laughed.

Peter was speechless for a moment.

'I'm Peter Denhay,' he said, eventually.

'Evelyn Moore, pleased to make your acquaintance.'

'How are you feeling?'

'Awful. Like I was hit by a train. I must say that I was surprised to see you, I honestly thought that there would be a much smaller aeroplane waiting for me. Did you have any trouble landing on that tiny field?'

'Not much,' he said modestly, 'once we found it.'

'It was rather isolated, wasn't it?'

She quickly changed the subject. Peter sensed that she was steering the conversation away from the mission. They chatted for some time about the squadron, about Greece, and about life at *Menidi*. Peter talked for much of it, and Evelyn listened. He was not normally a talkative fellow, at least not in his own estimation, but he found her very easy company. The few questions she asked him kept the onus on Peter to respond. It was a very gentle interrogation.

'It's very kind of you to look in on me, Peter. I'm not keeping you from anything am I?' She seemed suddenly offhand, and Peter wondered if this was a hint he should go. He was quite innocent where women were concerned and struggled to read whatever signal she was sending. He pointed upwards at the roof of the tent.

'I think we're scrubbed for the day. It's really difficult to fly in this muck.'

117

'I'm relieved, I was worried that you should be away bombing the Italians instead?'

'I dare say so, on any normal day,' he shrugged, 'that's what we've been doing ever since we left North Africa.'

'North Africa? Oh, how romantic, Peter,' she said excitedly, 'have you ever crossed the Sahara on a camel?'

She did her best imitation of Amanda from *Private Lives*. Peter recognised the line from Noel Coward's popular play and laughed.

'I'll fetch the doctor, you're quite delirious,' he chuckled.

'The doctor is already here.' Peter turned in surprise to see the medical officer had crept in unannounced.

'I'm afraid that I have to break up the party, Denhay. I need to examine the patient now she's awake.'

'It was lovely to meet you, Evelyn,' Peter said, rising from his seat awkwardly.

'Likewise, Peter. Please call me Eve. And thank you again for the lift,' she winked.

Emerging into the grey morning rain, Peter headed to the cookhouse feeling ravenous with hunger suddenly. His heart felt strangely light despite the rotten weather. It was only as he tucked into a fried egg sandwich that he realised he had not asked Eve what she was doing in Bulgaria at all.

Chapter 12

The C.O. scrutinised Charlie's leave application in the cold, dank tent with a dissatisfied expression. The sun was yet to rise, although the sky had lightened enough to reveal aeroplanes were being readied for that day's sortie. Charlie thought the C.O. looked as if he expected to find something in the application at any moment to justify screwing it up and dropping it in the wastepaper basket. The C.O. cleared his throat and fixed Charlie with a penetrating look.

'I've been hearing things about you and Flight Lieutenant Venner. Disquieting things.'

'Really, sir? I can't think where from,' Charlie replied, adopting a shocked expression. The C.O. leaned back in his seat.

'It won't surprise you to hear that Marcus said the same thing. As did about half a dozen other officers who were in the bar last night.'

Charlie said nothing.

'Kendrick,' the C.O. went on, 'you might think that after 10 years in the RAF, this is the first time I've experienced a feud on my squadron. But it isn't. After long years of service together, men will quarrel over just about anything. Usually it's women or money, but frankly I could believe it was anything with you. An ongoing row between two officers is like a cancer - it poisons everything around it. In my experience the only way to deal with it is to cut it out. Post both men to new units and bring in others to replace them.'

'I don't want to leave the squadron, sir,' Charlie said, suddenly alarmed.

'Then whatever issues you've got with Venner, I suggest you bury them. Fast.'

'Sir.'

'Now, about this pass. Who is it that you want to visit?'

'My aunt, sir.'

'Your *aunt?*' The C.O.'s tone of complete disbelief was evident in his voice.

'Yessir, my maiden aunt has lived in Cairo for some time now. It looks like she's quite unwell. I just need to go back and take care of the estate. 72 hours should be enough.'

The C.O. was wavering, Charlie could see it in his eyes. He was doubtful, as Charlie knew he would be when he first looked through Kings Regulations for the Royal Air Force. He'd read the passage that covered the allowances for the granting of exceptional leave and knew it by rote. Peter helped him rehearse the script the night before and his answers to the obvious questions.

'You realise how easy it is for me to check your claim?'

Charlie nodded; he did not.

'Fine. You can fly the *Durazzo* raid today and go to Cairo with the mail run tomorrow. They fly back on Monday so that gives you three days to take care of your aunt's affairs. Is that acceptable?'

'Very much sir, and can I say how generous this is.'

The C.O.'s eyes flicked up at him in surprise, he was clearly wondering whether Charlie was making game of him.

'Don't take the piss, Kendrick. Give my regards to your Aunt Jemima.'

*

Durazzo was a long and difficult flight from *Menidi*, and one that threatened danger at every turn. It was just about the furthest the Blenheims of XXI Squadron could fly with diversion fuel. Poor weather across the Greek mountains, coupled with the number of losses of inexperienced crews, forced a change of procedures. No longer would they brave the direct route into Albania across the hills. Instead they were to route westwards along the Gulf of Corinth towards the coast, and then fly north. This had the singular merit of being predominantly free of low cloud, but it was longer and the lack of cloud cover exposed them to enemy fighters and flak.

The round trip was nearly 800 miles, and it took over 5 hours to fly. With maintenance, refuelling, and re-arming, it meant that crews were only capable of flying one sortie a day. It had also become clear that the RAF attacks on the Italian rear areas were now considered more than just a nuisance. The Italians concentrated anti-aircraft defences around the obvious targets and had reorganised their fighter cover to protect the likely avenues of ingress to Albania. More worrying still, they brought across large numbers of a more modern fighter aircraft, the Fiat G.50 *Freccia*, a low-wing monoplane with twin machine-guns. Whenever possible, the squadron's bombers would be escorted, but this was difficult to organise with the shorter range of the RAF's fighters and the locations of their airfields in central Greece.

Today's operation enjoyed no fighter support, but that did not bother Charlie much. The C.O. was leading it, and everyone had total faith in his ability to bring his crews through this ordeal. In any event, Charlie was far more worried about his lack of contact with Margot, and the sense of foreboding this filled him with. He was thrilled to get leave, but he hated to think it could be a waste of time.

MacNeish had told him about how one of the engineers had received an anonymous letter to inform him that his wife was carrying on with the local butcher. The man had requested permission from the C.O. for an absence of leave, so he could go home to Kilmarnock and divorce her. Of course, this was impossible under the circumstances and, when he was told, the poor fellow broke down and wept openly until his sergeant took him away, saying kindly to him, *Come on chum, there's worse things happen at sea.* Women could be very cruel, Charlie thought.

He was still thinking of MacNeish's story as they swept down the Aegean, with Corfu ahead and the purple hills of the mainland on their right. The weather was clear and bright here and Corfu was a lush green mass, standing out of the dark blue waters that surrounded it. They flew over the western tip and in a flash saw a crop of little white villages, a harbour with fishing boats, and the clear waters on which they bobbed. They were number two in their flight, on their leader's starboard wing. All three flights of three aircraft each were in a box formation. This was formed by the leading aircraft in a 'V', the next three behind and stepped-down just below, and the final flight lower again. This was designed to offer some mutual protection for the Blenheim's vulnerable underbellies.

From his position in the Observer's seat, Charlie could look upwards through the canopy at the number two in the lead formation. Its belly was a dirty blue colour with exhaust marks running back from the leading edge of the wing. Peter sat at the controls whistling *Looking on the Bright Side of Life* into the intercom. They were flying *Johnnie* because *Yorker* was still at *Araxos*. Though the C.O. had insisted on a full show on *Durazzo*, this was particularly challenging because of losses. All the squadron's nine remaining aircraft had to be made serviceable, a minor engineering miracle. There was a range of problems to be fixed from cracked landing carriage oleo struts, resulting from a heavy landing, to standard patch repairs from bullet holes and flying shell fragments. The engineers had worked like navvies through the previous day and much of the night to pull it off; all the aircraft were ready at 0700 hours for take-off.

The raid was opportunistic. Wellington bombers returning from a mission had reported a large Italian cargo ship in the harbour, along with several smaller vessels including lighters and tugs. Air Intelligence assessed that this vessel was disembarking equipment for an Italian division. They recommended it was attacked as a priority. The plan was to attack in tight formation in order to deliver the maximum amount of explosive force in the greatest concentration.

They turned north-north-east off *Valona*, to make their final run-in towards the target. The town of *Durazzo* appeared at the northern end of a long, crescent-shaped bay. The mainland was still heavily beset by low cloud, and perhaps it was this which accounted for the lack of enemy fighters. Or maybe they had struck lucky and caught the enemy on the hop. Either way it was beginning to look like a cake-walk. Charlie glanced down at the map and tried to estimate how long it would be before they were back on the ground at *Menidi*, he needed to pack for his leave. Then the sky exploded.

Flak guns opened up from below and sent an impressi display of fire into the air, black shell bursts appeared all around them. It was a mixture of light and medium flak and their tight formation, so perfect for dealing with fighters, now worked against them. They were an enormous target for the gunners and it was only a matter of time before they scored a hit.

'Hold on everyone.'

Peter's voice rattled in his headphones. Charlie steadied himself by gripping the chart table and gritted his teeth. The flak looked thick enough to get out and walk on, an overused phrase perhaps because it was so true, he mused. This was going to be an uncomfortable ride. The harbour was edging towards the bottom of the nose window, very nearly the bomb release point. He spoke into the intercom.

'Three minutes to target, stand-by.'

He glanced upwards at the aircraft in front again, just as a massive flak burst went off below its starboard wing. The aircraft seemed to jump in mid-flight, then the fuel in the wing tank exploded spectacularly. It sheared off the wing and sent the aircraft corkscrewing downwards with smoke and fire trailing from the stub of its ruined engine.

'Christ Almighty,' Charlie shouted. He was horrified at the sight of the flaming wreckage plummeting to earth, knowing that it contained three men fighting to survive. He forced himself back to the bombsight. Peter was speaking to Miller in his ears.

'See any chutes Miller?'

'No. Nobody got out.'

Over the wireless the C.O. ordered everyone to hold their course. And then the bombs of the lead aircraft could be seen falling. Charlie squinted down the sight at the harbour below. It was packed with shipping; it would be impossible to miss. He squeezed the bomb release button.

'Bombs gone, bombs gone.'

The formation wheeled south, turning away over the bay followed by the flak, which became less effective with every passing minute. Charlie stared down at the harbour. The 8,000 lbs of bombs dropped by the squadron was distributed unevenly across the target, but most of it found a home. There was a huge fire raging on the dockside and thick black smoke issued from the cargo vessel, as well as much debris in the water where lighters had been hit and sunk. He searched for the downed Blenheim and spotted what he thought was a patch of oil and wreckage offshore.

'I think it was Wardle's crew who bought it,' he said into the intercom, 'no sign of 'chutes, nor anyone in the water.'

'Understood,' Peter replied. Charlie was shocked by the extraordinary image of the Blenheim spinning out of control towards the earth, which he struggled to clear from his mind. An image of Wardle, tall and handsome, laughing in the mess or joking with his crew appeared in his mind. He was one of the old boys and was firm friends with MacNeish. This was going to have an enormous impact on the squadron. He rested his head back against the fuselage for a moment, he felt desperate for a smoke.

A few minutes later, the C.O.'s voice echoed over the intercom as he passed command of the formation over to Venner. Charlie only noticed now that he had an engine out and was slipping back from them. Another voice on the wireless warned of a pair of bandits trailing them. Miller reported that they looked like *Freccias,* but after a close look at the Blenheims they stayed back out of reach, following from afar.

'Keep an eye out for the C.O.'s aircraft, Miller,' Charlie warned, 'Those two sharks will be delighted with an easy kill today.'

*

Menidi was just clouding over as they touched down. Peter had the impression that, if they had been any later, they would have been forced to divert. A pretty problem that would have been, with the lack of suitable landing grounds and darkness approaching. The fuel gauge read just above the reserve for the last few minutes of the flight. He squeezed the brakes lightly at the end of the landing roll and turned off the airstrip towards the southern dispersal, where the engineers waited. One aircraft was already parked up even before the squadron landed. He realised *Yorker* had arrived back from *Araxos* whilst they were away. It was some comfort to him then when he saw Mellish, Crawley, and the others waiting on the dispersal.

Peter shut off the engines. He sat quietly and gazed out of the canopy into the middle distance. Losing two of nine aircraft was a blow, but the loss of the C.O. was a disaster. He also kept seeing Wardle's burning aeroplane in his mind's eye, it was a tedious, troublesome image that spoke of a deeper fear that Peter could not address. He reached up and slid the canopy back, admitting a cool, fresh breeze into the cockpit.

Miller was already out of the aircraft by the time Peter and Charlie emerged into the afternoon's grey light. He looked frustrated and angry, Peter remembered he shared a tent with Wardle's air gunner, a quiet young lad from Lincolnshire. He corrected himself silently, Miller *had* shared a tent with Wardle's air gunner.

'I'll put her to bed,' Miller said, turning to walk away.

'Mellish and the others can handle it, Miller. We'll debrief.' Peter's voice was neutral, but the order was implicit. Miller shot him a dangerous look.

'Debrief like a crew, you mean?' Miller's omission of 'sir' was pointed. It was a discreet *fuck you*.

'Well, we're a team, aren't we?'

'Sure. In the air we are, yes. But after landing, I'm back to being a Non-Commissioned Officer again. You both head back to the Officers' Mess for a sherry and your highfalutin chat about politics and the Season. I go back to my pigsty on camp.'

Politics was strictly banned in the mess and he knew nothing of the Season, Peter wanted to say, but Charlie spoke first.

'Being on a crew doesn't mean that we're equals, Miller. It's not even a matter of rank. Just look at the three of us: Peter is the skipper, but he isn't the most senior officer on board. Every team must have a leader, and your rank today is no predictor of future success. The RAF is a broad church.'

Peter was convinced that Charlie had not meant to suggest that Miller was not mess material, but Miller's face betrayed he taken it that way.

'All this chat is fine and dandy, but nothing changes for me. Whatever happens, it's still wealthy public-school boys ordering everyone else around. Just like it was before the war.'

'Class is the foundation of our society. You can't mean to criticise the importance of status and position, it's always been this way in England,' Peter said impatiently.

'I'm not the only one who thinks it should change. A lot of the lads are fighting for something greater than Crown and Country. We want to know that England after the war is going to be fairer and more equal. Otherwise, we're just as dumb as the Germans.'

'I quite agree, Miller,' Charlie said, defusing the argument Peter was forming in his mind, 'war changes everything. We need to learn the lessons from it to build a better future.'

'Well, until then,' Peter snapped, 'you can get the kite filled up.'

He turned on his heel and walked away. Charlie caught up with him about 50 yards later, having jogged to make up the distance.

'Don't you think you were a little hard on Miller back there?'

'Quite the opposite actually, I think I went easy on him.'

'Oh you do, do you?'

'Yes. He picks and chooses his arguments to suit his fancy. He can be a trade unionist at times. We're all tired.'

'You can't know how wrong that description is, Peter. He was just expressing his opinion. Plenty of people believe our society needs reform - across a whole bunch of things: health, education, workers' rights-'

'Look, I know you're very clever when it comes to this sort of thing, Charlie. But I think this debate rather misses the point, doesn't it?'

'And what's that?'

'If we don't beat the Germans, there won't be a society left to reform.'

*

The Air Liaison Officer waited impatiently to run the debrief, but the crews were in no hurry. They hung around obstinately outside the dispersal tent smoking and drinking tea from a large canteen brought over from the cookhouse, along with the now obligatory egg sandwiches. The mood was sombre, a third of the squadron's strength had evaporated in a matter of weeks. At this rate they would reach 50 percent attrition before the spring. Without replacements this was unsustainable.

Regardless of the circumstances, the debriefing was professional, they owed the C.O. that much at least. The key points from the raid were discussed and recorded: likely serious damage to, if not complete loss of, enemy vessel estimated to be approximately 2, 000 Gross Register Tonnes; severe damage to port facilities; and associated damage to small craft within the harbour. The Air Liaison Officer also noted the details of the lost aircraft, so that he could pass this back to headquarters. He told them that their bombing raids were having a material effect on the war effort, with the Greeks pushing the Italians out of Greece towards *Tepelene*. But no-one felt much better for hearing it, least of all Peter who was still fuming from his exchange with Miller.

By the time the debrief concluded, the airfield was completely clouded over, making any further flying impossible despite an urgent request from Air Intelligence for a photographic sortie across the border in Albania.

'I won't ask the crews to fly in this pea soup. I wouldn't do it myself,' Peter overheard Venner tell Brian, with no small surprise.

Peter slipped out and made his way to the medical tent. He wanted to tell Eve about the exchange of words he'd had with Miller, and to hear that he was right to be angry about Miller's attitude.

The area seemed deserted and when he ducked under the flaps of the tent containing the rudimentary ward, he found all the beds neatly made and quite empty. Searching around, he discovered an orderly sitting in an adjacent office.

'Excuse me, there was a girl here yesterday, well a woman really. Do you know where she went?'

The orderly looked up from his book and pushed his thick spectacles back up his nose.

'I'm sorry sir, she left a few hours ago. A couple of men arrived in a car to collect her, a civilian and an army officer, if I remember rightly.'

'Did they say where she was going?'

'No sir, they spoke to the doctor and then the three of them left in the car.'

'I don't suppose she left a note or anything?'

'No, sir.'

'I see. Thank you for your time.'

Peter left feeling completely deflated. Though he barely knew her, he felt Eve was someone he could confide in. He badly needed to talk, nothing seemed right. The C.O. was gone, Peter was at loggerheads with his gunner, and now this. Eve had come into his life totally unexpectedly and had left just as quickly. She remained a complete mystery to him.

Chapter 13

Charlie stepped down from the Bristol Bombay's hold onto the hard-packed sand at Heliopolis and felt the warm, dry air caress his weary bones. He shared the flight over to Cairo with a dozen bags of mail, two reclining stretcher patients, and a young Captain from the Army Pay Corps who wept silently for almost the entire journey. Consequently, he was very relieved when they touched down at the RAF base. In the operations building, Charlie picked up the telephone handset and asked for the Cipher Section at Helwan. A deep male voice answered. Charlie pictured an ageing, overweight senior officer who did not normally answer the office telephone.

'Ciphers, Squadron Leader Bennett speaking.'

Charlie smiled to himself.

'Good afternoon, sir. Flying Officer Kendrick here, from XXI Squadron. May I speak to Section Officer Dacre please?'

'Eh, Dacre? She's not here. Don't you know it's Christmas? They're all off on leave - as I should be.'

'Oh, I don't suppose you know her leave address?'

'Well I might. Is it urgent?'

Charlie sensed that Bennett would not be too troubled if Margot Dacre was bothered by a work matter on her leave.

'Utmost importance, sir. I've flown in especially from Greece.'

'Oh, I see. One moment then.'

The address that Bennett gave him was a block of flats in the Giza district of the city. It was a residential neighbourhood on the Nile's west bank, where greenery intermingled with turn of the century buildings set out along wide boulevards. His excitement at seeing her after so long occupied him; he forgot to buy flowers, his uniform was crumpled. But none of this mattered to Charlie as he arrived at her building, checked the nameplate on the entrance door read 'Dacre' and then took the steps two at a time.

Gramophone music echoed down the stairwell to him as he climbed. It was a lively little tune and he tried to name it. He had not done so by the time he reached the second-floor landing and heard Margot's laughter. It lifted his heart and he paused at the door to whip off his service dress hat, run a hand over his dark hair, and straighten his tie. He knocked, once, twice, thrice.

After a short pause, the door opened and a young man in army uniform appeared in the doorway looking inquisitively at Charlie. He wore no tunic, his tie was off, and his shirt sleeves were rolled up to the elbow. He held a champagne glass in one hand.

'Can I help you?'

'I was hoping to call on Margot Dacre,' Charlie said glumly, his mind racing.

'This is her place, chum,' said the young man and then, over his shoulder, 'Margot, darling, you've got company.'

Margot appeared in the doorway, she was wearing a pretty cocktail gown and her hair was up. Like it had been the night Charlie sat with her at dinner, he realised with a pang. The moment she saw Charlie her eyes widened in shock, which she then tried to conceal.

'Tony, just excuse me for a moment please,' she said, before stepping out onto the landing and closing the door behind her.

'Oh, Charlie, you might have telephoned ahead.'

Margot shot a guilty look back at the closed door.

'I'm sorry, Margot. I didn't realise that you were having a drinks party, I got your address from the office.'

'You've got a nerve, Charlie. I hear nothing from you in months and you just turn up out of nowhere like this.'

Margot folded her arms across her body, her face appeared suddenly drawn. It looked to Charlie like a number of emotions were vying for supremacy on her beautiful face. He tried to shift his lingering suspicions and the sense of dread that descended upon him like a stage curtain.

'But I wrote. I wrote several letters. In fact, it was one of those letters that I meant to speak to you about.'

'You've come all the way from Greece to ask me about a letter?'

'Well, ah, not entirely that. But it was an important matter, do you remember we spoke about the possibility of a leak. Peter and I have a theory that it's someone on our squadron and-'

'Charlie, I've received not a single letter from you. In any event, the service police caught a double agent working in Cairo. So any leak has been stopped. I said as much in my last letter to you.'

'You've got to believe me; I've had nothing from you either. I can't fathom it at all.

Charlie wanted to tell her that he had not just written about matters of operational security. He had also scrawled expressions of joy at their meeting, and ridiculous sweet nothings. In one note he had even attempted poetry, he grimaced at the thought of it now, that one that was better left unfound. He swallowed hard and wondered whether she noticed his eyes filling. When Margot spoke at last, her voice softened.

'Won't you come in and have a drink, Charlie. I hate to think you've come all this way on a fool's errand,' Margot said, realising the implications she added, 'I mean, all this way for nothing.'

So that was it, he had been replaced. This was the let-down. He could hardly stand there in Margot's flat like a gooseberry, celebrating god knows what. No man could bear that insult. He felt suddenly and inexplicably homesick for Greece, for his squadron.

'No. Thank you. I still have things to attend to before I fly back on Monday,' he said, stiffly.

'Please don't be sore with me. Let's blame it on the war?'

Margot squeezed his hand. Charlie brought her hand up to his lips and kissed it gently.

'Take care of yourself, Margot. Goodbye.'

He turned and descended the steps as quickly as his feet would carry him. Before he reached the next landing, he heard the door above open and shut again, by the sound of the music that reached him as he fled. The tune sprang to mind, it was Al Bowlly. He smiled grimly to himself as he sang the words.

My dream of romance ended in a friendly chat,
But more than that,

I knew I never had a chance.

*

'Come in.'

Peter stood to attention, waiting for Venner to look up from whatever he was writing at his desk. His desk, not the C.O.'s, who was still officially missing and had been for the last three days. Venner was running the squadron now, albeit until headquarters could find a substantive Squadron Leader to appoint to command.

'Ah, Denhay. At ease, old chap,' he beamed at Peter in an odd way. At least, Peter did not recognise this new, benevolent Venner.

'You'll no doubt have noticed that we're short-handed with only seven crews. Well, six really, because I won't be flying missions now - with all my additional responsibilities,' Venner gestured at the stack of paperwork in front of him, 'Supply matters, discipline, engineering, the list goes on. I won't bore you with it. Oh, how rude of me, will you sit?'

'Thank you.'

'Now, the reason I wanted to speak with you is because, in the C.O.'s absence, there are some long-overdue changes to be made. You may be aware that we are moving to a new base nearer Albania in January?'

'I wasn't, no.'

'Really? I heard it from the lady who washes my uniform,' Venner laughed heartily at his own joke.

Peter smile politely but said nothing.

'Well,' Venner went on when he had stopped chuckling, 'You need to take more responsibility now. You're rapidly becoming one of the older hands, so I'll be giving you temporary command of 'C' Flight. It's only you and one of the new boys, Brewer, but an excellent opportunity for you to rehearse for when the time comes for real.'

This was news to Peter, but he swelled with pride at the thought of being a flight commander. Even though part of him felt that Venner was somehow attempting to beguile him, his ego won through.

'Thank you for the honour.'

'Not at all, not at all,' Venner spread his hands in a magnanimous gesture, 'I've had my eye on you for some time.'

Venner leaned forward, clasping his hands, and spoke in a conspiratorial tone.

'Now. There's this other thing I needed to broach with you too. It's a damned difficult question. You see, your navigator-'

'Charlie Kendrick?'

'Yes, that's right, Kendrick. Well, I've been digging around and I've turned up some very troubling things about him.'

Peter stared at Venner mutely, it dawned on him why he had been offered this apparently prestigious role. It was a gobstopper.

'For example, were you aware that he was removed from his last unit for fighting? In the Officers' Mess?'

'I'll admit Charlie has some unconventional aspects. But he's a very fine navigator with a great record on the squadron.'

'That's as maybe, but this is a pukka unit and he doesn't fit. He doesn't fit at all, Denhay.'

Venner sat back, looking at Peter with something of his usual expression of displeasure. He fiddled with a letter opener, then put it down before speaking again.

'I don't like to do this, but I'm going to offer him a way out. No, no - I've quite made my mind up on this one,' Venner said, waving away Peter's protestations, 'Transfer to headquarters in Cairo. He's got a doxie there, hasn't he? Well, I think it's for the best all round.'

Peter wondered how Venner knew about Charlie's nascent relationship with Margot but dismissed the thought to address the discussion at hand. He sensed there was no point arguing with Venner, the man would simply talk over him as he had done throughout this interview.

'Can I at least keep him until the end of January? I'll need his help with bringing along Brewer's crew.'

Venner looked at him thoughtfully for a moment or two.

'Ok, sure it can't hurt. But then he's gone.'

Peter stood up and as he did so Venner gave him an ingratiating smile.

'Stick with me, Denhay. You won't recognise this squadron in a couple of months.'

*

Charlie awoke on Monday morning with a monstrous hangover and mounting alarm that he had missed his return flight from Heliopolis. He had spent the two days of the weekend drinking heavily and had fallen in with some Australians. The rest was a blur. In panic he threw his kit together and flagged down a taxi. He was relieved to find his transport flight was delayed due to engineering problems, so he joined the rest of the passengers stood on the side of the apron. They were a mixed bunch, all army or RAF, mostly returning to Greece after Christmas leave. They waited patiently in the weak morning sunshine, enjoying the last of the mild weather before the call to board.

One of the passengers, a staff officer, was chatting loudly to his neighbour about a great offensive that the British had launched in the desert against the Italians. Charlie was not fond of earwigging, but he had heard nothing of operations in Egypt in the echo chamber that was Greece, and this news fascinated him. The officer explained that the offensive had been completely hush-hush, to keep the Italians in the dark. When it came in an armoured hook out of the desert, it sent the Italians reeling back beyond the border.

'38, 000 Wops in the bag,' the staff officer exclaimed, 'never have so many surrendered to so few!'

If that was true, it meant the Italian invasion of Egypt was finished. Maybe even the Italian army in North Africa. Charlie's mind filled with the possibilities of what this meant for Greece. Perhaps the Italians would throw in the towel there too. As he considered the implications, a staff car drew up. Margot got out of it. Of all the things he expected today, this was not one. He had not prepared himself for another meeting and his stomach turned a somersault at seeing her. She was in uniform and, though this was not an uncommon sight these days, Charlie was conscious that the attention of his fellow passengers was drawn to her. He placed himself between the crowd of passengers and Margot to hide their stares.

'Charlie, I felt terrible when you left. There's so much left unsaid. I called about for you but none of the regular places in town had you listed. This was my last hope,' she said.

'You shouldn't have come,' Charlie replied, casting a glance over his shoulder at the other passengers who were pretending not to listen, 'I think the position is quite clear.'

Margot looked down for a moment, but when her eyes rose back to meet Charlie's there was a look of fixed determination in them.

'I don't expect you to understand about Tony. And I'm not looking for forgiveness, it's not like I never waited for you-'

'A couple of bloody months?'

Charlie could hear the anger in his own voice, he stopped himself.

'I've got needs too, Charlie. For Christ's sake, you think one afternoon together means a lifetime's commitment? It doesn't, and I thought your mind worked differently.'

The passengers were boarding the Bombay now, on the opposite side of the aircraft the starboard engine coughed into life. The area immediately around the aircraft had been cleared of all freight and people, a solitary airman stood next to the open fuselage door, waiting to remove the passenger steps.

Charlie looked back to her. God, she looked beautiful, he thought. And, moreover, he knew deep down she was right - it was no different for women than it was for men. She thrust an envelope into Charlie's hand.

'This is for you. I think it will give you the answers you're looking for.'

He took it wordlessly and, nodding, climbed aboard the transport. From his seat he saw Margot return to her car. He caught a brief goodbye wave before the aircraft turned and taxied away. Soon, it lifted away from Egypt and climbed out over the Mediterranean. Charlie studied the envelope for a moment, then tucked it away in his tunic pocket. All he felt now was abject misery. No letter in the world could lessen the sadness that filled his heart.

Chapter 14

Paramythia was about as concealed as aerodromes got in Greece. Nestled inside a wide, circular valley not far from the Albanian border, it became home to XXI Squadron in January when Venner led the remaining six aircraft over the mountains from *Menidi*. The airfield was used by fighters of the Royal Hellenic Air Force, so there were local anti-aircraft defences and Greek troops to protect them. Nevertheless, RAF support staff from an Air Stores Park had been there since December, preparing the ammunition and petrol dumps, and building a tented camp.

Peter's crew flew over a dozen sorties together by the end of January and the date for Charlie's transfer approached. He had taken it well, Peter thought, since his return from Cairo. It seemed like he had settled into his groove, applying himself professionally to his duties. Charlie had not told him anything about his time in Egypt, just that their fears about Venner were unjustified. He had looked so grim and serious when he spoke, that Peter hadn't pressed him for more. He'd stopped talking about Margot in the wake of the trip too; Peter drew a conclusion from that. Privately, Peter was relieved to hear that Venner could be trusted. He knew his own star was rising in the squadron and to discover that Venner was working for the Italians would have been inconvenient, to say the least.

The thirteenth mission, he scoffed inwardly, unlucky for some. For his first job as flight commander for 'C' Flight, Venner had given him a milk run, a simple attack on a road junction in the Italian rear. It was important because reinforcements were passing through it, on the way to the front. The two crews grouped around an unrolled map in the dispersal tent. Peter looked from man to man, from Charlie and Miller on his left to Brewer's air gunner and observer, and finally Brewer himself. He wanted to commit this scene to memory. The three men of the new crew stood uneasily, this being their first mission they were unsure of what to expect. Peter cleared his throat.

'Our target is this road junction at *Berati*,' he pointed with a pencil at the red mark that indicated the target, 'the Italians have been trying to reinforce their forward positions, which are under severe pressure due to the Greek counter-offensive.'

A line had been marked running between *Himara* and *Pogradec*, indicating the rough position of the front line, now well inside Albania.

'Their troops and lorries have to come up through this pass here at *Berati* and cross over a single bridge. The bridge is narrow, which causes traffic to queue on either side. Air Intelligence wants us to bomb concentrations of motor vehicles around the bridge, but not the bridge itself.'

'Why don't we just hit the bridge and leave it at that?'

It was Brewer, a chubby young man with wavy brown hair and a prominent nose. Peter was not sure what to make of him.

'Two reasons: first, achieving a direct hit is near-impossible, even if our bombs could damage it; and second, the Greeks want the bridges intact to support their push northwards. They won't thank us for ruining their route of advance.'

Brewer nodded.

'The plan is to head up the valley from the south-east and drop on any vehicles to the north of the bridge at 4, 000 feet. The payload needs to go out in one pass. I have no intention to re-attack because it makes us vulnerable to flak. If the target is obscured by cloud, then we'll fly north to look for targets of opportunity elsewhere. Any questions?'

There were none, how could there be when Brewer's crew did not have a clue what they did not know at this stage. Peter thought back to the so-called 'briefing' Venner had delivered on their first mission as part of 'A' Flight.

'This part is very important,' he fixed Brewer with a sharp look, 'Sit on my wing as close as you can and drop your bombs when we do. If, for any reason, we get separated in cloud, do not attempt to fly below it. In these mountain passes it quite often goes all the way down to ground level. Instead, trust your instruments and climb up to a safe height then make your way south-west to the coast. The cloud normally dissipates over the sea and you can follow the reference marks back to the airfield.'

Brewer swallowed hard, looking scared for the first time.

'Finally, if we're bounced by fighters, don't try to make a break for it on your own. That's what they want you to do. Just stick close and we'll fight them off together.'

They emerged from the tent into a damp, grey drizzle. Thick fog blanketed the airfield, but it was reported to be clear at 1, 000 feet. Peter weighed up the options and decided to launch, knowing that *Paramythia* normally cleared by midday. He hated the thought of searching for the hidden valley in low cloud on their return trip, but not as much as he did the prospect of telling Venner that he'd scrubbed his first mission.

*

The two aircraft rose from the airstrip and were swallowed instantly by the murkiness. They burst out of the cloud at 920 feet exactly into a clear blue sky and the sight presented to Peter robbed him of speech. The peaks surrounding *Paramythia* appeared to float like islands on a still white ocean. In the bright sunshine the mountains were ill-defined dark shapes, except for the snow that capped their every summit.

Miller called over the intercom to confirm that their wingman was still in company and he swung them onto their course, north-east towards Albania. To shake-off the boredom, Charlie nattered away about Greece's many mountains. He told them about Olympus and Parnassus, the mountain of the house of the gods and mythical home to the muses. The further north they travelled the more the cloud thinned, and great gaps appeared permitting them to gaze down into sunlit valleys below. Peter wondered whether life continued on for the people who lived in those valleys, whether they too were looking up at the two aircraft overhead and wished death to the Italians. The Greeks were a proud people, he had learned that in the short time amongst them.

'You've a good grasp of the Greek, I didn't have you pegged as a scholar,' Peter said.

'Just schoolboy classics really,' Charlie replied, looking down through the canopy perspex, 'some of it stuck. Generally anything about babies being eaten, or monsters, or chaps carrying away with goddesses. The bits I really enjoyed though, was all the divine retribution. When the gods got involved to really sort out the mess that mere people had made of things.'

'Like Zeus? He was a god wasn't he? He could fart great bolts of lightning down on people!'

Miller's laughter echoed across the intercom.

'Sort of, yes. Zeus was the god of the air and of thunder. And he was king of all the other gods, when he wasn't carrying on with all and sundry,' Charlie looked down at his map for a moment.

'The goddess Nemesis once took the form of a goose to avoid him,' he went on, 'but he changed into a swan and had his way with her anyway.'

Miller cackled down the intercom.

'Nemesis?' Peter asked.

'Nemesis was a goddess,' Charlie explained, a faint note of exasperation creeping into his voice, 'and her job was to bring retribution to those guilty of hubris, an excessive pride or arrogance before the gods.'

'Like the Lone Ranger?' Miller asked, with tedious insistence.

'Sort of. But really she's a metaphor for universal balance in life. No major injustice goes unpunished in Greek mythology.'

Peter and Miller said nothing in response to this.

'One hour and 20 minutes to the turn.'

Italian traffic was visible on the road leading north of *Berati* for some distance. From 4,000 feet it looked like a mixture of lorries and other vehicles, some of which towed light mountain artillery pieces, but there were far more horse-drawn wagons down there and marching troops too. The Italian army in Albania was like most other armies of the time, in that it relied heavily upon animals to support it, particularly the mules that supplied forces operating in snow-locked passes and atop of steep ridges.

Although it possessed armoured and mechanised elements, the character of the Italian army was in fact no better represented than by the 6th Infantry Division *Cuneo,* that was at that moment on the march to the front through *Berati*. It would not have looked out of place in the last war. In common with all towns that lay across major communication routes, *Berati* was also choked with support troops, who ran field kitchens, laundries, bakeries, and supply dumps. If any of the troops in the town noticed the attacking aircraft, they failed to raise the alarm. The high peaks that surrounded the town deadened the noise of their approach until they were practically on top of them, just as they had planned.

Peter twisted around to look behind, unable to see Brewer.

'Skipper to Gunner. Can you see Brewer back there?'

'About 500 yards back and low,' Miller said after a short pause.

It was understandable that any junior pilot would allow a gap to appear in the formation. Close formation was hard and dangerous work, and at medium-level in the mountains there were few options to escape if it went wrong. It was understandable, but intolerable, and Peter spoke angrily into the radio.

'Hello Tinker 2, hello Tinker 2. Close up on me immediately, over.'

His voice, harsh and metallic over the wireless echoed in everyone's earphones, and Brewer closed the distance. At the end of the valley the river beneath them switched direction, making a hard 90 degree turn to the west. Here the valley widened dramatically into a broad plain. The town of *Berati* spread prominently along the northern side of the slow-moving water, all white houses with brown tiled roofs and a narrow bridge crossing the Osum River.

Traffic was just starting to move southwards across the narrow bridge. Italian soldiers, who had clambered out of their lorries during the lengthy halt, rested alongside the river. None looked skyward until the first shouts came from the head of their column, '*Bombardiere, bombardiere*!' Some had the good sense to run, realising that the crowded streets and alleyways of the town offered them reasonable protection against all but a direct hit from a falling bomb. Others froze, staring mutely as the two aircraft screamed towards them.

If Peter even thought about the non-combatants in the
it was only in passing. Of course, he knew that there ___
civilians down there. They intermingled with the troops and
vehicles and were, therefore, as much at risk from the attack as
the soldiers. He had long told himself this was a feature of
modern conflict and his duty was to place the bombs as
accurately as possible. He did not consider *himself*
dispassionate, such was the character of war the airman fought,
dislocated and impersonal.

The few anti-aircraft guns in the town were poorly sited and
their crews were not alert. It was too little, too late when they
eventually swung into action. The sound of the guns frightened
the draught horses and one broke free. The agonised creature
cantered into the bottleneck at the northern end of the bridge.
The flak exploded well above the bombers and Peter knew it
would not catch them now. Some brave soul trapped the loose
horse between a lorry and the bridge long enough for its driver
to get a rope around it, although in doing so a second lorry
attempted to move past the knot of animals and men, only to
become hopelessly jammed against the low wall on the other
side. Traffic control ceased; command broke down. And then
came the bombs.

The Standard Small Bomb Load was designed for targets like
this because it represented a varied dish. The two 250 lbs
General Purpose bombs were the meat and vegetables.
Although the bombs themselves weighed 250 lbs, their
explosive content was actually only 25 percent of that weight,
or about 60 lbs' worth of TNT. This quantity of explosive was
quite low, but it had a blast radius of something over 150 feet in
which it might obliterate, wound, or disorientate. The 20 lbs
bombs were the dessert, because these fragmentation devices
were designed to target people and other soft targets. Because
they were lighter and there were more of them, twelve in total
in this configuration, they would necessarily carpet a larger
area.

The first of Peter's bombs fell short. It landed squarely in the
river and exploded, sending a fountain of water up into the air
that rained down upon the vehicles on the river road. The second

impacted twenty feet further on, burying itself into the road before exploding. Its subsequent blast disintegrated two nearby lorries and sent a third sideways into the river. The scattering of smaller bombs rained down about the column. Some blew up to no effect, but several found the field kitchen in the town square and scoured it of sheltering bodies.

Brewer's bombs went long. One landed in a garden and failed to go off. The other dropped in the main street, where it destroyed several vehicles and horse-drawn carts in a brief but violent explosion. It was, in fact, Brewer's scattering of 20 lbs bombs that caused the most damage. Falling amongst the congested traffic struggling to make its way onto the bridge, the blasts were merciless and tore apart man, horse, and vehicle alike. Leaving the wounded and the dead cast aside in a gruesome tableau. Peter saw everything and nothing, as he roared overhead.

'Good effect on target,' Charlie said over the intercom, peering down as Peter rolled the aircraft to starboard following its bomb-run. He did not see the devastation wrought on the Italians, only that the bombs appeared to have fallen within or very close to the aiming ring marked on the northern end of the bridge on their charts. Peter said nothing, but glanced back at their wingman for a moment, before rolling level and setting up for the cruise home. Behind him Brewer was lagging, he'd spent his momentum before even thinking about the climb out.

'Tell Brewer to close up again,' Peter instructed Miller.

As expected, the cloud dissipated over the course of the afternoon to usher in one of those clear winter days that were more common in these latitudes. As they climbed to cruise altitude, Charlie shouted a warning.

'Lone aircraft approaching on a reciprocal course, but maybe 1,000 feet below. I don't think he's seen us.'

Peter rolled the aircraft over to get a better look. It was a large three-engine aircraft in the unmistakable Italian yellow and brown camouflage. It stood out clearly against the white of the mountains below. He looked about for some sign of a trap, perhaps a squadron of Italian fighters was lurking just out of sight waiting to pounce.

'No sign of company' Charlie said, reading his mind.

Peter weighed up the options in his mind. There was no doubt they should attack a lone enemy bomber that was clearly in Greek territory. It was an easy target, lumbering along on its own. His hand was on the throttle when it occurred to him that Brewer's crew needed this more than he. They were raw and inexperienced and his role as leader was to oversee the business, not to do it for them.

'Hello Tinker 2, bandit eleven o'clock low. Do you see him, over?'

There was a pause. Brewer's crew had obviously not seen the Italian, otherwise it would have been them calling and not the other way around. Peter shook his head silently.

'Hello leader, Tinker 2. Yes I see him now, over.'

'Engage target. Leader out.'

Peter snapped off the wireless and put the aircraft into a gentle turn overhead.

'Keep your eyes peeled for fighters,' he told Charlie and Miller.

Brewer turned and descended upon the enemy bomber. Though his aircraft recognition was rusty, Peter thought it looked like a Savoia Marchetti SM.81 *Pipistrello*. An outdated bomber with three engines and a fixed undercarriage.

'He's going to overshoot,' Charlie warned as Brewer dived down on the Italian. They saw him fire his wing-mounted .303 machine-gun at the bomber as he closed rapidly. At the last safe moment, he dove beneath the *Pipistrello's* port wing, but Brewer's air gunner raked the aircraft as they passed. Peter looked from the Blenheim, turning away to set up for another attack, back to the bomber now trailing a thin line of grey smoke from its port engine. This quickly grew into a thick plume of black smoke as the engine caught fire.

What's wrong with him? He's not even trying to evade, Peter thought. Sure enough, the bomber continued flying straight and level as if nothing had happened. He must expect the inevitable second attack. The Italian gunners did not return fire. Then he saw them, a pair of parachutes blossomed behind and below the bomber, followed by another. There was a short interval in which the bomber descended sharply. The engine fire erupted along the width of the wing and as far inboard as the wing root. Then a further two parachutes appeared, drifting down behind the burning aircraft towards the mountains below. Without warning, the wing folded up and then came away from the bomber. It entered a tight spin and corkscrewed downwards. Flames still showed bright from both wing and aircraft until it eventually slammed into the snow-covered ground with an almighty explosion that echoed across the valleys. The five parachutists plopped gently into the snow some way behind it.

*

Paramythia was clear of cloud by the time they returned and both aircraft touched down on the field within minutes of each other. After shutting down, Peter followed his crew back to the dispersal tent for the debriefing. Brewer caught up with Peter as he walked. He was red-faced, having run the last few yards.

'I say,' Brewer panted, trying to catch his breath, 'I say there, Denhay. Do you have a moment to chat?'

Peter stopped and gave him a quizzical look.

'Look, Denhay, I don't want to carp on, but you come across quite blunt. I'm sure you don't mean it that way. However, I *am* a Flying Officer and you're a- well, damn it, you're a Pilot Officer-' Brewer's words died away unsaid.

'And what's your point?'

Peter smiled. He knew full well what Brewer's point was.

'I'm sure you can see it's a sensitive matter, old chap. You ordering me about like that in the air. It looks bad in front of my crew.' Brewer leaned forward to whisper the last bit with a conspiratorial look.

Peter folded his arms and set his jaw. He was conscious of a certain formal tone creeping into his voice.

'Regardless of our ranks, I'm the flight commander. If I give you an order it's because my life is in danger, or because your life is in danger. Either way, I need you to respond to it quickly and balls to your sensitivities. I trust I make myself clear?'

Brewer physically cringed away from him as he said this, although Peter never raised his voice.

'There's no need to take that tone with me.'

'Since we're on the topic,' Peter said, warming up to the subject matter now, 'Your flying is all to cock. You're too light on the throttles when you need to be firm. And hanging back from the formation will get you snapped up by an enemy fighter. You can't afford to make mistakes like that around here, otherwise you'll end up sitting out the war as a Flying Officer in a Wop prisoner of war camp - if you're lucky.'

Brewer fell silent. He looked absolutely wretched. Seeing this, Peter softened his tone a little.

'Look, I didn't mean to speak harshly. What's your first name anyway?'

'It's Michael.'

'Can I call you Mike?'

'Sure, why not?'

'Mike then. We all have to start somewhere. It helps not to get hung up on rank though. We make an awful fuss about it on the ground, but it doesn't matter so much when we're in action. You've got to rely on your crew to work together to get things done. If you give yourself airs and graces, they might work for you, but they'll never respect you.'

'They didn't mention any of that at the Operational Conversion Unit.'

'They never do. This stuff you learn on the job,' Peter started walking again, but looked back over his shoulder as he did.

'Why don't we have a cup of tea and I'll explain what I mean about pushing the throttles?'

Charlie waited for him outside the tent, he was puffing on his pipe and he gave Peter a wry look as he approached.

'What?'

'Nothing,' Charlie smiled, 'it's just that you've come a long way, Peter.'

Peter went to reply, but found himself lost for words, he closed his mouth again. Charlie removed the pipe.

'What I saw today was impressive. You led the formation like a veteran flight commander, *and* you nursed an inexperienced crew through their first mission. I suppose Brewer just tried to give you a mouthful and, by the looks of it, you told him where to go.'

Charlie gripped Peter's arm.

'You're the real deal, Peter. I feel like I can leave the squadron knowing that I was at least part of that,' Charlie smiled.

'Charlie, I-'

'It's alright, there's nothing more to say. I never expected that it would end like this either.'

Chapter 15

Under Venner's command the squadron flew far more sorties as the weather improved and, at one point, had aircraft on operations for an uninterrupted 10-day period. On their way back from one of these missions the formation was ambushed by a full squadron of *Freccias* and fought a desperate battle back to friendly lines. There had been no fighter cover and the Italians exacted a heavy toll on the squadron in consequence. MacNeish force-landed with his gear up and one engine out, and Milne made it home with most of his tailplane shot away. Two other aircraft, flown by newly arrived crews, were listed as Failed To Return. It was later discovered that one had been shot down with the loss of all on board. The other was abandoned over the Aegean and the crew picked up by an Italian corvette to become prisoners of war.

Charlie left the squadron but did not go far. He was seconded to work for Wing Commander Cranmer, as the intelligence officer for the Western Wing. His job was to motorcycle between the aerodromes within the Western Wing's territory sharing intelligence reports. In February a German Heinkel He.111 bomber was sighted by a XXI Squadron crew flying north of *Paramythia* and Charlie led the crew's debriefing in a dreary tent by the side of the dispersal. Brewer sat with the Air Liaison Officer, who asked questions as Charlie filled out a report.

'A Heinkel?'

The Air Liaison Officer's tone of voice suggested that this was impossible.

'There aren't supposed to be any Heinkels around here. Are you sure it was a Heinkel?

'Sounds like it,' Charlie interrupted, 'Elliptical tail plane, glazed nose, twin engines. It's basically the aerial recognition picture of a Heinkel He.111.'

'Well, what do you think he was up to?'

Charlie mastered a strong desire to be facetious. He found the soldier's questions unhelpful. Brewer looked confused, he shrugged silently at the question. Charlie tried to help him along.

'He's airfield spotting. Brewer, you said he was up at something like 20 or 25, 000 feet, flying in straight lines? We do the same when we take photos for mosaics.'

'Yes, that sounds like the measure of it,' Brewer replied.

'I don't suppose he was lost then,' the Air Liaison Officer's voice betrayed a hint of disappointment.

The news confirmed what Charlie knew was being whispered about at the Hotel Grand Bretagne, the Germans were planning to enter the war in the Balkans. He had seen an intelligence minute on this, which gave an indicative German order of battle, an operation name, and an estimated date for the first week of April 1941. How the British had come by this information was baffling to him. He suspected that it might have been by listening on telegraph wires. He had a faint notion this had happened in the previous war.

*

Grey clouds hung over *Paramythia*. Great curtains of water poured down from the sky and it rained for 5 days without ceasing. It turned the airfield into a wet misery. Even though drainage ditches had been dug by local labourers, the camp flooded. Peter sat in the tent he shared with his new navigator and stared at the roof. He wondered if he was going slowly mad, either because of boredom or because Ralph Monroe's conversation was stultifying.

Other than losing Charlie, Monroe was one of the greatest disappointments of becoming a flight commander. He had no idea where Venner had found him, but he suspected that whatever unit he came from was delighted when they foisted him onto XXI Squadron. Dumpy, prematurely balding, and a hypochondriac, Monroe would have been better suited in the Local Defence Volunteers rather than the RAF, in Peter's opinion. He was also a Twitcher and moaned incessantly about how the rain ruined his opportunity to watch birds. All this could be forgiven if he was good at navigation, but alas he was not. On their first outing as a crew, he had become hopelessly lost and they had to circle over Corfu to find their way back to base. The mere thought of it made Peter burn with embarrassment.

The first anyone knew of a major operation in the offing was when the Gladiators of 112 Squadron arrived at *Paramythia* after the rains. The Greek counter-offensive had ground to a halt in Albania during the height of the winter. They were desperate to bring the campaign against the Italians to a conclusion, because of strong indications of German movements in neighbouring Bulgaria. There was a need for a 'stonk', an operation to prise the Italians from their positions in the northern mountains between *Kelcyre* and the coast. This would restore movement to the battle, permit the Greeks to drive on *Valona*, and deny the Italians the ability to resupply their troops. It was agreed that the RAF's bombers would switch from interdiction to attacking the Italian's air power wherever it could be found.

'The idea is to fly a mixed formation of bombers and fighters to target their airfields,' Venner said, 'That way the fighters can protect the bombers and any Eyeties that get up will be knocked out of the sky. This will keep the Italian air force guessing and prevent them from playing a role in supporting their ground troops.'

The packed briefing included all the fighter pilots and three crews from 30 Squadron, lent to XXI for the purposes of this operation. A quick glance around the room revealed to Peter that no two men were dressed alike. The standards of 1940, never rigidly enforced in Greece, were completely thrown out of the window at *Paramythia*. Peter wore service trousers, suede chukka boots, and a scandalous brown woolly pullover. He also sported a blue silk polka dot scarf, to ease the discomfort of sweeping the horizon from the cockpit.

The entire formation took ages to pull together, even taking off in flights of three aircraft as they did. The bombers launched first and then flew circuits of the airfield as the little fighters, with their shorter range, climbed up above them. They broke out over the gap in the ridgeline north of *Paramythia* and turned towards the coast, a crucial part of the deception they had to maintain. Soon they were heading for *Valona*, the nine Blenheims in their box formation at 6, 500 feet and the half dozen fighters of the escort, stacked up even higher at 10, 000 feet. In this manner, the trap was set.

The target was the aerodrome at *Valona*, now home to increasing numbers of Italian fighters. A sense of retribution pervaded throughout the squadron. They would attack from the sea to avoid the heavy concentration of anti-aircraft guns around the port, carpet the airfield and buildings with 250 lbs bombs, and then turn southwards to escape.

Venner had laughed, 'With any luck there'll be a couple of fighters up for the escort to play with.' It was easy for Venner to joke about it, Peter thought to himself, Venner wasn't flying again. But there were more than a few fighters up, as it transpired. As the formation made its final turn over the great headland that shielded *Valona* from the sea, they spotted the Italians off to the east. It was a clear day and Peter knew they were positioned in expectation of an enemy attack over the mountains, not the coast. Seeing the bombers, they took the bait and turned to intercept them somewhere on the other side of the target. They too did not fancy the idea of being shot down by the flak.

'Good Lord. There must be three squadrons of Dagos over there,' Monroe said over the intercom, a tone of wonder in his voice. Peter craned his head to look through the starboard cockpit window and tried to count them. He stopped after a dozen, deciding that it was a pointless endeavour. Their part in the plan, he told himself, was not to worry about the enemy fighters, it was to deny them a home to return to. Their own fighters, the pitiful few of them, would sort out the Italians.

The formation released their bombs in unison, when the leader was overhead the runway. 9, 000 lbs of bombs delivered in a tight formation, was certain to make a dent in all but the hardest of targets. The effect was, however, not immediately evident to Peter because the Italian fighters swept in to attack.

The Italians, Peter thought not for the first time, lacked neither skill nor courage as he watched the leading *Falco* launch his attack on the formation. The air gunners fired back at him and the amount of defensive fire seemed overwhelming. He attacked high and from starboard, screaming down from above with his guns blazing at the Blenheim directly in front of Peter. Bullets struck the bomber and pieces of panel broke off and disappeared in the slipstream. Then the fighter roared between them, disappearing in a flash. The bomber flew on, untroubled by whatever damage it had sustained.

He had been so close that Peter could make out the oil stains on the fuselage around the aircraft's exhaust pipe, and the individual aircraft serial number on the tail before it dropped out of sight. Other fighters followed, some choosing to press their attacks right home and others preferring to pepper their targets from a distance. It hardly mattered because in no time their own fighter escort pounced.

The air was suddenly black with aircraft diving, turning, climbing and rolling. A *Falco* streamed beneath the formation with a Gladiator in pursuit. Another Italian fell away in a graceful arc, leaving a trail of black smoke behind him. To Peter's amazement a *Falco* picked this time to make an attack on *Yorker*.

'Bandits three o'clock,' Miller shouted. The noise of his machine-guns firing rattled back down the fuselage to the cockpit. A tick, tick, tick echoed on board and the Italian buzzed close overhead, chased by defensive fire from their formation. Peter glanced at Monroe who was curled up in a ball in the nose, he'd said nothing for some time. *Jesus, he's going wobbly on me*, thought Peter as he shook his head in disbelief.

'How does it look Miller?'

'Nothing serious. Although the engineers won't be pleased with the new air holes drilled in the aircraft,' he replied.

The dogfight slowly fell behind the formation as the Italians became more preoccupied with the fighter escort. A few parachutes could be seen in the air and Peter looked back at the damage they had done to *Valona's* aerodrome. There were craters in the runway and smoke was rising from a wrecked hangar that had received several direct hits.

'Pity anyone who has to land on that mess,' he said into the intercom.

'I suspect there won't be many of those. I counted at least seven aircraft going down to our Gladiators. They won't forget that in a hurry,' Miller replied.

'Did they get any of ours?'

There was a pause, then Miller replied.

'No. I can see all the bombers, not sure about the fighters though. This fighter escort thing really works!'

The escort re-joined them about 20 minutes later, all six fighters in a single formation stacked one below the other like steps. The leader waggled his wings and they made a long slow turn southwards. Their greater speed meant that they could get home faster and the job they had done on the *Falcos* meant that a fighter interception was unlikely in the short-term.

In any event the Blenheims were not long behind them and in no time were turning over the southern tip of Corfu, their reference point for the start of the route that led to the gap into the Valley of *Paramythia*. They shook out of their formation at this point and went into line-astern. Each aircraft followed another, and all followed MacNeish as he entered the circuit and descended gently onto the grass strip.

Peter was surprised at how quickly the ground had dried after the rains and had expected a much longer landing roll. Instead he had to open the throttle and taxi away quickly to the dispersal to create room for the aircraft following him to land. After shutting down, Peter waited until he heard Miller's hatch swing open behind him, and he could be confident that he was alone with Monroe. He turned to him as he was packing up his kit.

'What were you playing at back there?'

Monroe looked shame-faced and held his hands up, before he could speak Peter snapped at him again.

'Don't try to pretend you don't know what I'm talking about. You looked like you were going to disappear under the chart table when we got bounced by those fighters.'

'It's my medicine, given to me by the medical officer,' Monroe blurted out.

'Your what?'

'I suffer from air sickness, so the doctor prescribed some pills for me.'

'Air sickness?'

Peter put his face in his hands momentarily. *As if this couldn't get any worse*, he thought to himself. He looked at Monroe, whose fat jowls had flushed an unhealthy purple colour, for any sign he was pulling Peter's leg. Worryingly, he saw none.

'Yes, because of all the staring at maps when we're flying. It throws my balance out and makes me dizzy. So, I've got a set of pills to deal with that, but they leave me drowsy, so the doctor also prescribed another set of pills.'

Monroe dug around in his jacket and produced a battered carboard packet marked 'Benzedrine Sulfate'. He showed it to Peter, who took it and turned it over to read the reverse of the packet. It claimed to 'relieve psychogenic tiredness and restore optimism'.

'This looks like strong stuff,' Peter whistled, returning the pack.

'I dare say it is, but I don't like taking it. It throws out my sleep pattern and leaves me hungry. That's why I avoid it if I can.'

'You were *sleeping* in the nose today, not hiding?' Peter said incredulously; he could not work out which was worse.

'Yes, I'm afraid I had a short nap. Just after the fighters appeared.'

Peter shook his head and sighed, 'Ralph, if the doctor prescribed both pills, you need to take both. I can't have you sleeping on the job. Your eyes could be the difference between evading a fighter or not. Do you understand me?'

'Of course. I'm sorry, it won't happen again.'

Peter gave him a doubtful look. Even as a flight commander he still had a soft heart and he could not bring himself to chew Monroe out for this oversight, as serious as it was. Without another word, he pulled back the canopy hatch and climbed out to find Mellish waiting for him on the wing. Mellish's normally smiling face now wore a look of displeasure, presumably at seeing the state of *Yorker*. He stood with his hands on his hips looking up at Peter as he stepped out of the cockpit. Crawley was on the other side of the fuselage looking at their damage, he was complaining to himself loudly, 'And the stringer's split here, that will need riveting back. Two bleeding hours in this weather. They don't care about these 'ere fucking kites.'

Peter opened his mouth to speak but Mellish beat him to it.

'Don't you be listening to old Tom Crawley there, sir. He's only bellyaching. We're just glad to see you back safe.'

'Will it be a difficult fix?'

'We're used to these old Blenheims, Sir. They're built by craftsmen an' they needs a craftsman's hands.'

'Old, Sergeant Mellish? You could hardly call them old.'

'Well, that's as may be, sir. But they laid the design down in 1935. The Mark IV's got beefier engines and better guns, but the aircraft ain't changed much. Six years is an awful long time in aircraft production, you know.'

Mellish smiled at last but then his face changed as he looked up at the sound of a strange aircraft overhead. It was the whining of an engine in a fast dive towards the airfield. Following Mellish's look, Peter saw a sleek, low-wing monoplane was about to buzz the field at extreme low-level. It had a large engine cowling, retractable undercarriage, and was painted in the dappled yellow and brown camouflage of the Italians. It dawned on him they had been tracked to their base.

The fighter roared along the airstrip, narrowly avoiding the final Blenheim that was taxiing in, and pulled up sharply at the end of the airfield boundary. He kept climbing over in a half loop until he was fully inverted, and then he rolled the aircraft level at just over 500 feet above the aerodrome. It was a display of aerobatic flying known as an Immelmann, and it was worthy of any good RAF pilot in Peter's opinion. He expected the Italian to run away to report the location of the secret airfield to his superiors, the sensible thing under the circumstances. But instead he lined up to make a gun run along the dispersal where the Gladiators were parked amongst sandbagged pens.

The fighter dived down on them with both machine-guns blazing, a twin line of bullets impacting the earth and plinking the occasional aircraft, but thankfully no people. He whizzed by again and pulled into a tight left-hand turn, circling to come back for a third pass at the airfield. Peter watched transfixed as the Italian proceeded to beat up the airfield, something they were all familiar with from pre-war flying displays. It was at this point that the Italian's luck gave out.

As he crossed the airfield boundary a canny Greek gunner, crouched in a machine-gun pit, sent a burst of fire into the fighter's engine. The rounds stitched along the aircraft and hit the cowling, spraying oil up onto the canopy. The engine burst into flames, the propeller seized and there was a sudden silence above the field. In an impressive display of handling, the Italian flopped the fighter onto the grass with the gear up. He skidded along for about 200 yards, narrowly avoiding a parked aircraft, before disappearing into the thick bushes at the edge of the airfield.

Peter joined the press of people running to get hold of the Italian airman. Greeks with rifles keen to claim their prize and RAF aircrew and engineers, who wanted to ensure he was not burned to a crisp. When they reached the stricken aircraft, they found that the pilot had climbed out of the cockpit, and was sitting on the wing awaiting his captors, wistfully smoking a cigarette. Confronted by the fulsome welcoming committee, the poor startled fellow threw up his hands in alarm and shouted, '*Scusa, mi dispiace tanto.*'

Chapter 16

Paramythia improved noticeably in April's kinder weather. The rains fell less frequently, and the sun shone in cloudless blue skies, bathing the hills in its warmth. In the valleys the spring flowers grew and the colour of the grass and even the trees thereabouts seemed more vibrant too. It was easy to forget there was a war on, at times, or so Charlie thought. But with April also came the Germans.

Charlie had only visited *Paramythia* that day because Sinclair and Brewer were out on a photo recce sortie and he wanted to collect the film himself. He drove up early and ate lunch in the mess with Peter. He met Monroe returning from a morning spent birdwatching, who greeted him in his shirtsleeves with a pair of binoculars around his podgy neck. Charlie caught Peter's look and smiled.

He was smoking in the afternoon sunshine when the noise of a Blenheim racing into the circuit met his ears. The engine tone sounded urgent and, Charlie guessed, from the quick turning descent the pilot conducted, the pilot was in some hurry. He almost landed with his gear up, seemingly only remembering to lower the wheels as he crossed the airfield boundary. Though he cut the engines, it was not a delicate landing and the aircraft touched down on its main wheels first, bounced, touched again and ran along the strip for a time before the tail dropped. Charlie heard Peter click his tongue and he looked sideways at his friend, who he knew had done a few of those landings himself.

The aircraft headed towards them at a fast taxi and they saw it was seriously damage. The canopy glass was shot out in the nose, there were large holes in the fuselage and the turret was shattered. Charlie took off towards it at a sprint. The pilot didn't even shut down before he was standing out of the cockpit waving. It was Brewer shouting, 'I need a medic, my gunner's hit! Oh god, I think he's dead.' He disappeared back into the fuselage.

Others arrived now, opening the lower escape hatch and helping Brewer's navigator from the cockpit, a shocked and bloodied young sergeant. A utility truck raced towards them from the main camp area. They lowered the injured man from the aircraft. Charlie caught a brief glimpse of a pale white face, where it was not covered in blood; he was unconscious. Brewer shut down and staggered out onto the wing. Here he collapsed and slid down to the waiting arms of the crowd who had responded to his cry for help.

MacNeish helped him down to the ground where he stood unsteadily, gazing wildly about. Brewer's hair was damp with sweat and he ran a hand over his glistening face. Someone asked about Sinclair; Brewer shook his head. Charlie lit a cigarette for him, and it was accepted by a shaking hand. He took a drag and tried to explain in halting words what had happened. They had been flying near *Berati*, when they were ambushed.

'They were all over us in an instant,' Brewer said, 'There must have been half a dozen of them. I tried to turn to get away, but they anticipated every move I made. Sinclair didn't stand a chance - they got him even before we knew they were there.'

A silence fell over the group at this revelation. Sinclair was one of the most experienced pilots on the squadron and one of the few remaining old hands. Charlie recovered his wits first and asked, 'Did you see any parachutes, did anyone get out?'

'Not likely,' Brewer replied, 'they just piled in. I lost sight of them when I tried to break away. They must have bought it.'

'Come on,' MacNeish said, putting a brotherly arm around Brewer, 'Let's get you a cuppa. We can talk about this later.'

Charlie took the hint. He let the group head off towards the mess. Turning back to the aircraft he found Peter measuring the holes in the fuselage with his hand.

'These are cannon holes,' Peter said pointing to the damage, 'they were lucky not to get torn in half.'

'So what?'

'So there aren't any Italian fighters that carry cannons. All the fighters we've come up against are under-gunned, so what's this?' Peter folded his arms.

'German fighters have cannons. Both 109s and 110s carry them. God, I didn't even ask Brewer whether he could make out their markings,' Charlie said, frustrated with himself.

'It's bad news,' Charlie said finally, 'It's really bad news.'

*

'Intelligence believes the strength of the German air force allocated to the invasion of Greece to be between 600-800 aircraft of all types,' the A.O.C. told the packed room. He stood in the large marquee tent at *Paramythia* in front of an audience that included crews from 84 and 112 Squadrons, as well as XXI Squadron.

Peter's attention was grabbed by the numbers. He quickly worked out the appalling worst-case odds against them, 10:1. Looking about at his fellow crews, he wondered how many of them would survive when they were so badly outnumbered. Not many, he thought glumly.

The purpose of the A.O.C.'s visit to *Paramythia* was to offer some encouragement to the crews before kick-off, Peter decided. It was a pep talk. That's why Venner was here when he would normally be mooching in his tent or away in *Athens* for meetings at headquarters. Peter could see him now, sitting in the front row right in the A.O.C.'s eyeline, *the crawly bastard*.

'You in the Western Wing will continue to fly operations against the Italians in Albania, whereas the Eastern Wing will face the Germans,' the A.O.C. went on. Peter rolled his eyes, that was an unlucky break for those poor sods. He suddenly realised what it actually meant, the Germans would destroy the Eastern Wing first, then the Western. Any lucky break for them would last a matter of weeks, at best.

An unknown Flight Lieutenant said, 'Sir, what about the ground forces - what's their plan?'

The A.O.C.'s gaze shifted to the young man near the front.

'They're digging in along a feature known as the Metaxas Line. Our aim is to prevent the Germans from making any headway into Greece from Bulgaria. That's why we must intensify our operations against the Italians, so that we can ensure the Greeks can transfer forces from the Albanian front. We have to defend the Klisura Pass, that's your new objective.'

Venner held his hand up, 'Sir, what plans are being made for a withdrawal of our troops?'

The question generated some conversation amongst the audience, which ended abruptly as others hushed them to hear the reply. The A.O.C. appeared to straighten up so he physically stood taller. He fixed Venner with a serious look.

'There are no plans for withdrawal, indeed I see no reason why we should even think about it at this time when we are still on the offensive.'

In the silence that followed this, Peter heard Milne in front of him whisper to his neighbour, 'That's shut *his* trap then.'

After the briefing, Venner sought out Peter and MacNeish, his surviving flight commanders. He looked anxious, the first time that Peter had recognised that in him.

'I'm going to base myself here permanently from now on. With Sinclair gone I suspect that you'll need a hand. Brian has things under control at *Menidi* and we're expecting replacements any day now.'

MacNeish looked unimpressed, he replied in a tone that betrayed his frustration.

'We're down to 5 crews, and Brewer is pretty shaken with his gunner dying on him. The supply situation is critical and, even if I can scratch a crew together for you, six aircraft can't make much of a difference on this front. It's bloody hopeless.'

'Well, the A.O.C. has ordered us, and therefore that's what we shall do,' Venner replied stiffly.

So, the A.O.C. had rebuked Venner for dithering about and now he'd come up to take charge, Peter concluded. MacNeish clearly shared this opinion; he shook his head in silent rage before walking off. Venner turned to Peter, 'The A.O.C. also asked me to host some Americans. They've come up from *Athens* to see how we do business. You can take one of them up on a sortie over the front line. I'm sure they'd love to see how the RAF does Close Air Support.'

*

r had already flown one sortie on Easter Sunday when the American arrived. They were refuelling and rearming when Venner appeared with their passenger. Major Dan Schilling was a broad-shouldered giant of a man with jet-back hair, green eyes, and a firm jaw. He wore the uniform of the United States Army Air Corps, to which he belonged. Schilling studied his new crew a look of mild disappointment.

In his scruffy jumper, Peter looked like he had just spent the day mending a dingy. Monroe at least wore his RAF uniform, although his choice of plimsolls as a substitute for flying boots was somewhat incongruous. Only Miller in his Sidcot Suit would have looked *pukka*, as far as Major Schilling was concerned, but he was asleep inside the fuselage.

'Major Schilling, I'd like to introduce you to Denhay and Monroe. They'll take you up and give you a *shufti* over the lines,' Venner said. Schilling looked confused by the word 'shufti' and chewed his wad of tobacco thoughtfully for a moment until Peter reached out to shake his hand.

'Delighted to meet you, I'm Peter. This is Ralph.'

'Hullo there,' Monroe smiled, offering a damp hand.

Monroe looked strangely animated to Peter, who wondered if it was down to the Benzedrine he was taking. Monroe beamed at Schilling, 'Shall I give you the thruppenny tour of our aircraft?'

As they strolled off, Venner hissed at Peter, 'For god's sake don't take any chances; bring him back safe. We need all the allies we can get if we're not to fight this war alone.'

When Monroe returned from the walkround of the aircraft, Peter showed Schilling around *Yorker's cockpit*, paying careful attention to the aspects he thought would be of most interest. He pointed out the emergency escape hatch in the nose beneath the observer's position, the location of the life raft and flare pistol, and the folding seat that he would perch on next to Peter.

'You want me to sit on *that*?' Schilling exclaimed, spitting a great gob of tobacco juice expertly over the fuselage to land on the ground beyond the aircraft.

'Where do I put the other half of my ass, buddy?'

When Peter looked around at him, however, he saw that Schilling was grinning.

'Let's get you a parachute,' Peter replied.

The Air Liaison Officer marked the target for them on their charts. It was a battery of Italian field guns in a village near *Tepelene*. The battery was firing on Greek positions on the Trebeshine Massive, a geographical feature and bastion of the Greek frontline. They climbed steadily into a clear blue sky and soon the mountains and hills of Albania passed below them. There was very little to differentiate between Greece and Albania at this point, Peter reflected. The location they were heading for sat on the top of a plateau that was divided from the Greek position on the opposing ridge by a wide valley. Here was the defensive line, here was the enemy.

They circled at 6, 000 feet trying to identify the target, but Monroe couldn't pinpoint the village marked on the map. Peter searched the sky for enemy fighters that he knew to be prowling over Italian lines. He felt on edge, as if at any moment a German formation might materialise above them. Schilling was judging him too, he decided. Although he'd said nothing, Peter knew.

'We planning to be here all day, boys?' Schilling asked drily.

'Guns firing, bearing one o'clock low. Back slope of long ridge,' Monroe said over the intercom. Rolling gently to get a better view, Peter identified the Italian guns in an orchard, outside a village composed of about a dozen white-walled dwellings. The trees offered excellent natural camouflage. Had it not been for the full battery of four guns going off all at once, he suspected Monroe would not have seen them at all. The smoke of the discharge cleared, but the orchard stood out to one side of the village and was distinct from the small arable fields that surrounded it. It was marked.

'Tally ho,' Peter yelled over the intercom. At the same time, he rolled the aircraft over until the ground was visible through the upper canopy windows and, pulling the column hard back, entered a sharp dive towards the earth.

'Jesus Chr...,' Schilling uttered quietly. Peter saw out of the corner of his eye that he had blacked out. The sensation of speed when flying at low-level was exhilarating to Peter and as the ground rushed up to meet them, he felt the thrill of pure ecstasy. The force of the manoeuvre pressed his guts down into his loins and as he pulled out of the dive he almost whooped with joy. By the time Schilling came round again, the Blenheim was thundering along towards the ridgeline they had circled above just minutes before. Schilling reached down to grip the metal support running below his seat. As they passed the summit Peter glanced between the fuselage and the port engine and glimpsed figures on the mountainside looking back up at them. They were Greek soldiers, some of whom waved at the friendly aircraft as it flew over. Then the ground fell away again some 3, 000-odd feet to the valley floor and there in front, on the slightly lower plateau, was the little white village and the orchard, and the guns.

Peter pushed the stick forward to sink into the valley and then levelled off again. Looking ahead, he confirmed the orchard was lined up perfectly on the nose. Monroe said, 'Hold it there, its dead-on. Standby.' Another salvo rocked the trees, indicating the guns in the orchard had fired again, belching smoke and fire into the sky. Schilling's voice sounded over the intercom.

'Aw, I just swallowed my wad,' he said, and then after a pause, 'Why the hell don't those gunners run, they're still firing the crazy-.'

'Bombs gone, bombs gone,' Monroe shouted. Peter pushed the throttles fully forward, selected boost, and pulled the aircraft into a sharp climbing turn. The engines roared at full power. Ground fire zipped past the aircraft, clearly someone had noticed the bomber's approach. The gravitational force thrust Peter back into his seat. Schilling was straining to look through the canopy behind Peter's head at the orchard far below where their bombs had landed. He heard the explosion as they climbed away, much louder than a stick of four bombs normally warranted. That meant secondary explosions.

'Dang, boys,' Schilling whistled to himself, 'You pasted them - I swear I saw one of those guys running after us.' Schilling shook his head, as if in disbelief.

Peter said nothing until they climbed back up to 6, 000 feet again and levelled out. With the aircraft in the cruise he had time to chat and turned to Schilling.

'We should be home in about 20 minutes, Major. What did you make of our bombing display?'

'I think it was just swell. I used to consider myself a heavy bomber man. But you've opened my eyes to the advantages of flying in support of troops on the ground,' Schilling replied, 'I've seen plenty here to take back to Washington.'

'Do you think America will enter the war then?'

'I think you Limeys haven't got a chance in hell of that,' he replied. But when Peter looked at Schilling, he saw that he was laughing.

Schilling was less ashen faced when he stepped out of the aircraft at *Paramythia* than he had been over Mount Trebeshine. He thanked Peter for the opportunity to fly along and wished him the very best for the future. As he shook his hand he said, 'You never know when our paths might cross again. I'll be seeing you boys.'

Schilling strode off. Miller gave Peter a wry smile from the fuselage hatch before he ducked inside again. Peter shouted to Monroe in the nose, 'I think he was pleased, Ralph. Good thing you spotted those guns, otherwise we'd have looked a right bunch of clowns.' Peter chuckled to himself, there was no answer from Monroe. Probably asleep again, he thought, he'd have to have a word about it. This was completely unacceptable. Peter climbed back up to the cockpit and stooped forward to the nose section, where he could see Monroe slumped over the chart table. He shook him and Monroe rolled backwards off his seat, exposing a face frozen in the unmistakable mask of death. A horrific bullet wound in the top of his head had cruelly disfigured the young man's features. Peter recoiled in shock and shouted to Miller, who came crawling down the fuselage with an anxious look. When he saw Monroe's body he just sat and stared.

Peter spotted it a short while later. A tiny hole no bigger than a penny in the floor of the nose; the bullet's entry point. It had struck Monroe under the chin and exited through the top of his head, presumably shortly after he released the bombs.

'Gawd. You think he felt much? I didn't hear him cry out over the intercom,' Miller said.

'I don't think so, it looks like death was pretty much instantaneous,' Peter replied. It was just dawning on him that he had never really given Monroe the time of day. For all his complaints, his wretched navigation, and his bird watching, he was likeable enough. And yet he could never have matched up to Charlie Kendrick, either as a navigator or a friend. Peter leaned forwards to where Monroe's unseeing eyes looked skywards one last time as if in tribute to the one passion Peter knew he possessed. Peter gently closed them and said a silent prayer for the fallen airman.

'Blue skies and tailwinds.'

*

Charlie was lounging in the dispersal tent when the call came through on the field telephone from *Athens*. The Air Liaison Officer answered it and what he heard seemed to be of such import that the soldier sounded increasingly glum. He scribbled notes onto a scrap of paper with a stub of a pencil he produced from his pocket. Charlie stood up and tried to get a glimpse of what he had written. He could see some timings and a place name, *Monastir*. The rest was indecipherable. The Air Liaison Officer put down the phone and turned to Charlie.

'We're done for,' he said, before dashing out of the tent. He returned a short time later with Venner, who looked like he had just woken up. Venner gave Charlie a filthy look but said nothing as the situation was outlined to him. The Air Liaison Officer explained that the Germans had launched an offensive into Greece through Yugoslavia. Charlie knew that meant there were now two German axis of attack, one out of Bulgaria directed at *Salonika* and this new one.

'They're going to turn the flank on the Metaxas Line,' Venner exclaimed, after scrutinising the map laid out for him by the Air Liaison Officer. Charlie realised it must mean a withdrawal. There weren't enough troops to hold the Germans at bay.

'Headquarters has asked for a raid to slow them down. This road junction here at Monastir,' the Air Liaison Officer pointed to where he had marked the map, 'They want a full squadron effort.'

'But we've only got five crews,' Venner said.

'You've got six. If you include yourself,' Charlie interrupted. Venner swivelled to face Charlie with a look of pure hatred in his eyes.

'Five or six, it hardly makes a difference. Don't you have somewhere else to be?' Venner snapped.

'I think I'm in just about the right place now, actually. Want me to call your crews in for a briefing?'

Charlie thought Venner looked conflicted, as if he was considering alternate options. He wondered if Venner would try to squirm out of this one. If he did, he would have to explain to the A.O.C. why they had not put their entire strength into the air for this raid. There were no other options open to Venner; his duty was clear.

'Fine. Call them in,' Venner replied.

'All aircrew, all aircrew. Report to squadron operations, mission briefing in ten minutes.'

The shout echoed across the dismal collection of tents belonging to the squadron. They arrived well before they were requested, curious to know what was going on. Charlie spotted MacNeish, Milne, Brewer and their crews. Sandford, a new boy, and his crew looked lost and bewildered. Miller wandered in alone, followed shortly by Peter who looked pale and withdrawn. Charlie knew as well as they did that almost every one of them had flown at least twice a day, every day, since they moved to *Paramythia*.

'We've been given an urgent mission by the A.O.C.,' Venner said, indicating to the chart, 'Jerry is moving in force into Greece from *Monastir*, here, through this gap in the mountains towards *Vevi*. If they manage to get as far south as *Kozani,* they will be well on their way to encircling our troops, who are holding a blocking position around Mount Olympus. We cannot allow that to happen.'

Venner's face was a picture, the strain of command was obvious. Up until this point Venner had done a reasonably good job of running the squadron. At least, that was what they said about him in *Athens*. Charlie heard what the crews said behind his back, however, and he knew they felt he didn't fly enough and concentrated on matters of administration. Important enough on its own, but trivial when conducted at the expense of leading crews on operations. He had also heard that Venner was a drinker and had run up some pretty spectacular debts in *Athens*. Perhaps that was where his Rolex had disappeared to, he mused as he glimpsed the white band of flesh around Venner's wrist.

'We're to put in a six aircraft sortie against *Monastir*, with the objective of stopping traffic and disrupting the offensive. I want a tight formation at medium level. We'll target the centre of the town with a view to wrecking roads and halting movement.'

'Do we have fighter escort?' A voice from the back.

'No.'

'You must be joking,' MacNeish interrupted him, 'attacking like that in daylight makes us sitting ducks for Jerry. It'll be a massacre.'

'We could always go in a low-level,' Peter suggested, 'In pairs? That way the Krauts will find it harder to see us; we might slip in unnoticed.'

There was a hubbub in the room, but it appeared that there was broad support for the low-level option. Venner rubbed his face in frustration before slamming his fist down onto the table.

'Enough! Shut your traps,' he shouted furiously. The room quietened.

'I'm in charge and my orders are that we attack in tight formation at medium level,' he repeated, 'Our air gunners can reinforce each other and therefore we have strength in numbers. It's a tried and tested procedure.'

The crews grumbled. They had flown regularly, and they knew that whatever tactics had been effective against the Italians would not necessarily work against the Germans. Charlie had read numerous confidential reports about German fighter performance. They were not under-gunned as the

166

Italians were, and large formations of light bombers were easy prey for them. He tried to tell Venner this but was hushed by his next statement.

'Anyone who wants to sit this one out can hand in their brevet at the door,' he spat.

The effect of this was instantaneous, no-one was prepared to be named a coward in order to win an argument, not even if it meant avoiding what was likely to be a one-way trip. Charlie heard Miller speak behind him.

'Well, that's that then.'

Venner gave everyone a dirty look.

'Take off in 15 minutes,' he said and stormed out of the tent.

Charlie found Peter outside. He stood looking into the early afternoon sunshine with his hands thrust into the pockets of his flying jacket.

'Alright, Peter. Why so glum?'

'Monroe bought it. They're just scraping his brains off the canopy windows.'

Charlie hadn't expected this, he felt like an idiot for not reading the obvious signs.

'Oh, Peter. I'm sorry. You must feel dreadful?'

'I honestly don't know what I feel right now. Especially with this *Monastir* job. What are the odds of making it back untouched?'

Charlie sucked his teeth, 'I won't lie to you. Not good. The Krauts have a lot of fighters, and they're all superior to our Blenheims. You've got one thing going for you though.'

'What's that?'

'The best navigator on the squadron is going to be flying this one with you,' Charlie winked.

Peter stared at him silently for a moment, then his face split in a wide grin.

'Venner won't like it.'

'Balls to Venner. What do you say?'

'Reunited for one final job? You're on.' Peter offered him his hand.

'I'll just nip back to my tent to get my flying gear and then I'm your man.'

Charlie sprinted to the mouldy tent on the airfield boundary he had been moved to when he was exiled from the squadron. As he ran, he wondered to himself whether he should tell Cranmer about his decision to join the operation. He dismissed the idea. Cranmer was always away doing things without telling Charlie; it worked both ways. Ducking under the tent flaps, he found his leather flying jacket, boots, and helmet all stuffed into his trunk. He pulled his boots on quickly, but did not take time to tighten the straps, then he grabbed his pistol and ran out of the tent.

Within minutes he was back on the dispersal, where their aircraft were starting up. The engineers had performed another minor miracle in readying the six aircraft for an operation in such a short time. Venner taxied past him on the way out to the airstrip, Charlie looked up at his imperious face in the cockpit, but he did not look back. *Yorker* was turning over, both engines spinning at idle and Peter waved out of the cockpit hatch. Suddenly he was seized with the feeling that he had forgotten something. He patted himself down trying to think of what it was, but his mind drew a blank until he touched the tunic pocket in which he had placed Margot's letter. He had completely forgotten its existence until now.

He pondered whether it was an attempt by some part of his subconscious to limit the harm it would cause should he read it. There was nothing to lose now, since he faced the real prospect of imminent death. Peter beckoned him from the aeroplane again, Charlie waved back, but he slipped his thumb under the sealed flap of the envelope and tore open the gummed flap.

The letter was short, only a single page in length. As he read, his eyes widened. He couldn't believe it; he read it over again. This confirmed his first impression and he felt a sinking feeling in the pit of his stomach as he stood rooted to the spot. He crumpled the letter up and stuffed it into his pocket. The roar of a Blenheim taking off down the strip yanked him back to reality and he resumed his walk to the aircraft. As he did so, he shook his head.

'How could you have been so bloody stupid, Kendrick?'

Greece, April 1941 (Easter Sunday)

Chapter 17

Charlie beat furiously at the fire with his flying boot. There were sparks in the cockpit and then it was extinguished. Peter coughed, trying to clear his lungs of smoke.

'The Very pistol was hit,' Charlie shouted into the intercom, as the flare died out, 'It's made a right mess of the fuselage.'

Peter glanced at the seized starboard engine, where flames licked back from the cowling towards the wing. There was no way to stop that if it got out of control, and when it reached the fuel tank, it would blow them apart. He shut off the fuel feed to the engine as a precaution. The port engine was coughing too, god knows what was up with that he thought. The aircraft felt unresponsive and groaned with every movement of the controls. It was dying even as it flew on.

'I wouldn't worry about the fuselage now Charlie, I think this kite's finished.'

Charlie pulled on his singed boot and nodded to the flaming engine.

'You can set her down somewhere,' Charlie said, 'we've got enough time.'

Peter glanced at the altimeter, 1, 500 feet and descending. No chance, he thought, not with that Jerry still snooping about. If they were going to get out at all, it had to be here and now.

'Bail out, Charlie,' he said firmly.

Charlie shook his head despairingly but seeing Peter's pig-headed indifference to his opinion he pulled the intercom lead out. Peter could tell that he was swearing but heard nothing through his headset.

'Skipper to crew, bail out, bail out.'

He glanced back to see Miller kick open the lower hatch and clip on his parachute harness. Looking forward, he saw Charlie do the same and unlatch the emergency escape hatch below the nose. It fell momentarily, before being whipped away behind

169

the aircraft and out of sight. He watched Miller lower his legs through the hatch, looking strangely squat and lumpen in his baggy flying suit. Miller shuffled his backside off the edge so he was dangling in space, his legs buffeted by 180 mph winds, and then let go. He dropped out of sight. Charlie leaned over to speak to Peter, who pried the ear cup of his helmet away from his head to hear better.

'Miller's gone. I'm jumping now. Don't try to be a hero, Peter,' Charlie yelled over the noise of their remaining engine. Peter gave him a thumbs-up.

'Go on, I'm right behind you.'

Charlie gave him one last look. It was hard for Peter to tell what his look conveyed, sadness maybe or regret. He didn't make up his mind before Charlie dropped through the hatch.

The aircraft coasted along on its remaining engine, the wind gushing in through the holes in the fuselage and open hatches. Peter tried to set the aircraft up to fly straight and level but found that any reduction in pressure on the pedals or controls threatened to send it into a tight roll. Even gliding with the throttle back required command input; he knew that in the time it took him to loosen his straps, climb out of the seat, and dive through the escape hatch, the aircraft would be in a spin. He loosened his straps anyway, but a check of the starboard engine revealed that the fire had diminished slightly.

An Me109 thundered overhead, turning sharply to port in a flick roll as he passed the stricken bomber. He did not fire, he could see there was no need. The Blenheim was finished and now he was just watching for the inevitable. It occurred to Peter that this action was something like the single aircraft combat of the Great War recorded in books he had read by Captain W. E. Johns. He half expected the German to wave a salute before heading for home.

The altimeter revealed he was well below 700 feet, approaching the lowest altitude from which he would be comfortable making a parachute descent. No, he thought, it wouldn't do at all. It had to be a forced landing or nothing. Scanning the terrain about him, he tried to identify a suitable field on which to land.

The valley was not well endowed with landing sites, but he could see some flat ground on the fringe of a large lake beneath him. It looked like he might just be able to make the edge of that if he husbanded his height and committed to this course of action now. He made his mind up and eased the aircraft onto its new course over the water.

He ran through the normal landing procedure but decided not to drop the gear, he was worried that the resultant drag would reduce his airspeed and therefore his glide range. He kept the flaps up for the same reason. It suddenly occurred to Peter what an odd day it had been. He resigned himself to the thought this was it: he was damned to die unloved and unknown in an empty valley, miles away from home. So much for ambition.

'What a daft way to go,' he said shaking his head.

Drawing the port engine's throttle back slightly, he let the airspeed roll back to 85 mph. The ground came up quickly and he noticed for a fraction of a second how beautiful and calm the lake was off to his left. His eyes snapped back to the flat ground he had selected as the landing field. It was about a mile long and at least half as wide but broken at regular intervals by very low stone boundary walls. It was too late to do anything about that now. Aside from a dirt road that ran along one side with some trees and scrub in the distance, there were no other signs of life.

The altimeter dropped steadily, 200, 150, 100 feet, he counted. He lowered the flaps, flattened out and, at about 20 feet above the ground, chopped the throttle. Then, with pang of surprise, he realised his straps were still loose.

The tail struck first with a great thump before the belly slapped down, knocking the wind out of him as he was thrown forward into the instrument panel. The starboard engine disintegrated, sending chunks of metal flying and both propellers bent backwards in contact with the ground. His head struck the panel and he felt intense pain. A bright white light exploded behind his eyes, which was replaced instantly with blackness. A deep, warm blackness into which he slipped quite comfortably.

*

wanted to sleep. He dreamt about the empty desert in nd about Venner, and about Ralph Monroe's dead eyes staring up at him from the cockpit. But these dreams were all peripheral to the one he had about the girl in the hospital. He could not remember her name, so many other thoughts clouded his mind and clamoured for his attention. But he could see her face clearly and she called to him.

'Wake up. Wake up, Peter. You're in terrible danger,' she told him.

'But I'm comfortable here,' he said, 'it's warm and quiet, and I'm so tired.'

'Wake up. You have to go,' she replied, her voice louder now and more manly.

Peter was disturbed, he had no idea why she should be shouting in a man's voice. There was a sound much like the steady crackle of a fire and then the foul smell of gasoline and hot metal. His senses returned. A smashing sound above his head brought him round and he saw hands reaching down to undo his straps. Someone pulled him bodily from the cockpit and down the port side wing to the ground, which was higher than normal.

'Miller,' he cried, 'you saved my bacon.'

'Come on, sir. We'd better run or we'll both be grilled,' Miller replied.

They sprinted away from the wrecked aircraft, Peter looking over his shoulder at *Yorker* as he ran. She was a miserable sight, on her belly in a field with her canopy blasted out and pock-marked with bullet holes. Flame engulfed the starboard wing and spread to the dry scrub grass in the field too. He wondered for a moment whether *Yorker* had held on just long enough to see him return safely to earth. Then the starboard wing exploded in an enormous ball of flame that consumed the aircraft.

They dived to the ground as pieces of aircraft landed about them, mostly small chunks of panelling, but a flaming patch of tyre rubber narrowly missed Miller where he lay in the dirt. They waited there for a moment in case of any more explosions. What remained of the fuselage was still burning, but the starboard wing had gone and the fire had reached back as far as the turret. The ammunition began to cook off, bullets cracked and zipped into the sky.

'We should keep moving, sir. No sense surviving that crash only to get shot by our own guns. Are you fit to walk?'

Peter put a hand to his head,

'My head aches like the devil and I think my nose is broken. How do I look?'

'You look like shit,' Miller paused, and then added, 'sir.'

They both laughed, Peter felt like it was the first time in months. There was a short silence, which Peter broke.

'Thank you for pulling me out of that wreck, Miller. It took some guts to get in with the thing on fire. Especially when it might have gone up at any moment.'

'Don't mention it. We're a crew after all,' Miller winked.

Peter recognised his own words, and the associated implication, and felt like a fool. He knew he'd given Miller a hard time before, but the man was a rock.

'I was an ass to you a few weeks back. I got focused on my own self-importance; I get we don't have to agree on everything, so long as we have the same goal.'

'I can't fault you there, sir,' Miller smiled, 'so what's our goal now?'

'We should try to head south, find our way back to friendly lines,' Peter replied, feeling around for the chart he had stuffed in the straps of his parachute harness. Finding it was not there, he looked back at the remains of the aircraft and the blackened and smoking cockpit, where it had almost certainly fallen when Miller dragged him free.

'Charlie might have a map. In any case, we should try to link up with him. He can't have gone far. Did you see him when you came down?'

Miller shrugged. He reached into the pocket of his flying suit and pulled out a small tobacco tin. When he levered off the top, it revealed a small fire-lighting kit and a button compass. Taking the compass out Peter held it up and let the needle settle.

'We should pick up the road,' he indicated the dirt track running around the edge of the plateau, 'if we follow it in that direction it will take us towards *Kozani*.'

'Aren't the Krauts in *Kozani*?'

'I think the Krauts are everywhere now, sir.'

'Well, what are you waiting for? Come on.'

He set off towards the road, with Miller trailing behind. As he walked, he released his parachute harness, he had no need of it now. The loss of the thick harness exposed him to the fresh breeze and, shivering with the onset of mild shock, he took stock of his own escaping equipment. Other than his suede boots and sheepskin flying jacket he had nothing. Not even a hat, which was still back at *Paramythia* with all his other belongings. Stylish but hopeless, was his judgement on their current situation. But he felt more positive by the time they were on the dirt road, after climbing an earthen bank and stone wall to reach it. He waited for Miller to join him, who was slower because his baggy flying suit was built for comfort, not speed.

Peter turned back to the road as Miller mounted the bank, and what he saw there made his heart freeze. A grey open top truck was approaching from the north at speed with three helmeted figures on board. It threw dust up behind it as it accelerated towards them. It was about 500 yards away when he saw it and Peter knew that to run would be useless. Besides some bushes next to the road, steep hills on one side and open fields to the other rendered any escape impossible.

The truck pulled up and the driver and passenger leapt out, both wore the field grey of the Germans. Camouflage cloth covered their distinctive coal scuttle helmets, something Peter had not seen before. The driver carried a rifle, the passenger a machine pistol. He shouted at them.

'Halt, halt! Oder ich schieße.'

Though neither spoke German the tone was unmistakable; they raised their hands in response to his challenge. The soldier with the machine pistol nodded at the driver, who slung his rifle and searched them roughly. The third man remained in the truck and Peter noticed he had removed his helmet and pulled on a pair of earphones. A wireless operator then.

'These men are SS,' Miller whispered.

For the first time, Peter recognised the collar flashes on the man searching him. At his neck was the double lightning strike of the *Schutzstaffel* or SS, the Nazi paramilitary organisation. Their cuff titles denoted them as members of the *Leibstandarte SS Adolf Hitler* Brigade. Peter knew little of the SS, other than it had a reputation for brutality and was recruited from the most fanatical Nazis.

Peter's searcher found nothing on him except his watch, an Omega with a thick bezel and black leather strap he had been issued for flying training. The German signalled to him to remove it and, with little choice, Peter handed it over. The soldier slipped it into his jacket pocket and, pushing his foot roughly into the back of Peter's knee, forced him into a kneeling position, before turning to Miller. The sharp pain caused Peter to yell out.

The man with the machine-pistol spoke to the radio operator in German. Occasionally he gestured with his supporting hand towards them, but he never removed his other hand from the pistol grip. There was some debate going on. The man with the machine-pistol was a non-commissioned officer, Peter believed. He was giving the orders and he glanced back at the two airmen with an evil look in his eyes. In such small numbers the group could only have been some sort of reconnaissance force, perhaps they were looking for a way around the British flank.

The searcher discovered Miller's escape tin and, after checking inside it, flung it away into the bushes by the roadside. He found Miller's wallet and packet of Players. He pocketed the wallet and took a cigarette from the pack, which he offered to the man with the machine-pistol.

'You saucy bugger,' Miller shouted at being flagrantly robbed and he received a rifle butt to his stomach in return, which forced him to double over in agony and drop to the ground on his side. The German raised the rifle to strike again, but he was stopped by his machine-pistol wielding superior, who removed the lit cigarette from his mouth, shook his head and said with a wave of his hand, 'Nein, Hermann, nein.'

He rapped off a series of instructions in German that Peter could not decipher and then took a few paces back. Hermann cocked his rifle.

'Jesus, are they going to shoot us? We're in bloody RAF uniform,' Miller said.

'Be brave, Miller. Don't let yourself down in front of these creatures.'

'Bollocks to brave, I won't give them the satisfaction of thinking I give a damn.'

Nevertheless, Peter closed his eyes and tried to settle his heart, which threatened to beat out of his chest. The thought of dying in an aeroplane crash was nothing compared to this brutal, ugly and very personal execution.

And then the first shot rang out.

Chapter 18

Charlie found the sensation of falling from an aeroplane an unenjoyable one. The initial drop from the aircraft forced his guts up into his chest cavity and gave him the disagreeable feeling that they might evacuate in mid-air. With the aircraft disappearing above him, he grappled to find the ripcord. Locating it, he yanked it forcefully to deploy the parachute.

The parachute unfolded from its pack and the canopy filled, but the cords twisted above his head into a tight knot. It pulled him up with a strong jerk that removed the looser of his flying boots, which fell to earth. The twisted cords jammed his head forward under the risers, so that he descended to earth with his chin pressed painfully to his chest until they untwisted. In doing so, Charlie was pirouetted about the axis of the canopy several times in a way that would have been comic, had anyone been able to see it.

He braced for a parachute roll upon landing, as he had been taught, but this proved unnecessary as the canopy snagged on a large tree and he came to a rest about 12 feet above the ground at the edge of a small wood. Hanging there in his straps he was just beginning to feel relieved at his escape from death when he heard the unmistakable sound of a branch snapping and was dropped unceremoniously the full 12 feet to land on his arse beneath the tree.

Charlie swore, and then swore again. He climbed to his feet and rubbed his backside where he had fallen. His lower back felt sore and he wondered if he had done himself some harm. But then the Blenheim whistled low overhead with one engine coughing and flames emanating from the busted starboard motor. It left a thin smoke trail in the air behind it.

'Silly bastard,' he muttered to himself and, freeing himself of his harness, took off in the aircraft's direction of travel. He had some difficulty because his back and legs hurt from the fall and he only had one boot. His bootless foot was immersed in mud, and the wetness of the ground soaked his sock. It was with an odd, limping gait that Charlie made his way towards the likely landing site. He muttered to himself as he jogged along about the likelihood of blisters, and how inconsiderate it was of Peter not to have jumped like everyone else. The light was fading as the sun dipped towards the horizon. He performed the old trick of measuring the distance between the sun and the mountains with an outstretched hand, counting the minutes remaining until sunset by measuring how many digits fitted into the intervening space.

'One, two, three,' he counted out loud, '45 minutes. Probably closer to the hour if you account for the terrain.'

Pausing to gather breath, he found he was wet beneath his bulky sheepskin flying jacket, which he unzipped, wiping his face with his scarf. A loud explosion ahead startled him and, though he could not see it, it echoed through the forest. Now he ran, with no thought for his bare foot or the pain in his back. He ran as fast as his legs could carry him, dashing between the trees and leaping the occasional low stone wall that he came across. He did not know how long he had been moving but he had left the wood behind and was jogging through tall scrubland when he heard the running of a car engine and German voices close in front.

He skidded to halt and dropped to one knee behind some bushes at the roadside. His heart beat furiously and he took deep breaths to try to regain his composure. There was a truck in the road, a couple of Germans and, *blast it all*, Peter and Miller were kneeling on the ground before them.

Charlie reached down to the pistol holster at his side and withdrew the revolver slowly. He took great care to crack the barrel open quietly and peered into the chambers. The brass bottoms of six .38 cases met his eyes. There would be no opportunity to reload so they would have to count. He snapped the barrel closed, pulled back the hammer, and stood up. He suddenly realised the war that he had fought so far with great detachment was about to become an intensely personal affair. He steeled himself to do what needed to be done.

He stepped quietly towards the Germans, holding the pistol up with one hand. His gun hand shook with nerves and so he gripped his wrist with the spare hand to support it. The German cocked his rifle and pointed it at Miller's head, just as Charlie emerged from the scrub by the roadside. They were about 15 yards distant, and the Kraut had his back to him. Peter looked calm with his eyes closed, but Miller stared at the German with a look of pure hatred.

Charlie squeezed the trigger.

The round took the German just below the right shoulder and spun him around, Miller was on his feet in a flash and threw himself at another German with a machine-pistol. Charlie fired again at the rifleman and the second round caught him squarely in the throat. He dropped to the ground with a look of obscene surprise on his face, blood showing bright red around his mouth and the bullet hole in his neck.

The first burst of the machine-pistol was diverted by the force of Miller hitting the SS man with a flying tackle. It sprayed up the side of the truck and tore into the wireless operator, who jerked repeatedly as bullets tore into his stomach and chest, and then slumped sideways onto his smoking wireless set. The remaining SS man was on his feet quicker than Miller, however, and he scrabbled for the dropped machine-pistol. Charlie aimed for him but could not be certain to miss Miller as the two men grappled. The German reached the machine-pistol a fraction before Miller, he fired a second burst into him as he pounced. Miller crumpled to the floor at his feet.

The SS man turned back towards Peter, but only got so far before a rifle cracked and he slumped to the ground, dead before he hit the floor. Peter lowered a smoking rifle. Three dead Germans and Miller laid outstretched on the floor. He dropped the weapon and rushed to Miller. Charlie joined him, kicking the Germans' weapons away from their bodies as a precaution.

'How is he?'

Peter rolled Miller over. There were three bullet holes in his flying suit and a rapidly spreading dark stain across his midriff. Miller stared up at them with a vacant look. There was blood on his lips and in his mouth. He tried to spit it out, leaving a bloody trail down his chin.

'Jesus, it hurts,' he wheezed.

'You daft sod, you saved us,' Peter said to him, and then turned to Charlie, 'is there anything in the truck that we can use to help him?'

Charlie saw the ominous stain spreading across Miller's flying suit. Anyone could tell there was very little in a first aid kit that could help Miller now. He wanted to tell Peter that what Miller needed most was either a surgeon or a padre. But instead, he climbed into the open back of the truck to search for a medical kit. Opening the opposite door, he shoved the dead wireless operator so he flopped over out of the opening, to enable him to search the interior. The contents of the truck included several boxes of ammunition, and gasoline in the metal containers that the British referred to as 'Jerrycans'. There were some wooden ration boxes and, finally, a small wooden case with a red cross painted on it.

Miller was barely lucid when Charlie returned, his face was very pale and Peter cradled his head in his lap and talked to him in a low voice. Charlie knelt and upended the box, sorting through the field dressings, cellulose cotton, packs of gauze, and adhesive tape.

'Can't you hurry up?' Peter snapped. Miller gripped Peter's hand and closed his eyes.

'Come on, Miller, hold on. We've got something in the medical trunk that will sort you out, you'll see.'

Charlie shook his head. There was only a tube of tablets marked 'Pervitin' and a small bottle of Ether. Miller coughed again, obviously in great pain, and he spoke in a haltering voice.

'You were always a good skipper, Mr Denhay. I knew you'd bring us through in the end.'

Miller's eyes glazed over and he fell still.

Charlie was unsure of how much time passed before he managed to get Peter to let Miller go, so he could cover him with a tarpaulin. Peter looked in complete shock, he could hardly blame him either. He had turned out a bottle of Schnapps in his examination of the truck and now he removed the top and they took turns swigging from it, until something like colour returned to Peter's cheeks.

*

They buried Miller in a shallow grave in the scrubland to the side of the road, using the shovel strapped to the bonnet of the truck, which closer examination revealed was a Horch. Peter removed one of Miller's identification tags and put it in his pocket, then they covered him over with dirt. Although they knew they were running out of time to make their escape, he insisted they stood over the grave for a moment out of respect. Peter turned to Charlie in the half light and whispered, 'Should we say a few words?'

Charlie shrugged and said, 'Also I heard the voice of the Lord saying "Whom shall I send and who shall go for us?" Then I said, "Here am I; send me".'

'Isaiah?'

Charlie nodded.

'It seemed apt under the circumstances.'

They stood for a few minutes in silence. The wind whistled through the trees and Peter felt it caress his cheek, it was time to go. He turned back to the truck. They had dragged the bodies of the SS men into the undergrowth. Neither the shallow grave nor the Germans would be seen from the road. Peter hesitated for a moment before plundering the dead, eventually he decided it was morally acceptable because of their greater need. And also because they started it. His Omega was retrieved from inside the jacket where it was secreted, mercifully undamaged by fire. He handed Charlie a pair of jackboots, which he accepted with a grateful smile.

The Horch yielded other prizes and, by the light of an electric torch, they scrutinised the Germans' map. Charlie pointed out their current position to the east of Lake Prespa. Peter was surprised how far from the target they were, having dropped their bombs at *Monastir*, well to the north.

'We need to head south, sharpish, before their mates come looking for them,' Charlie nodded to the bushes.

'Fine, I'll drive.' Peter said.

'Not likely, you've done enough driving for one day.' Charlie grinned. He chucked the machine-pistol in the back of the truck and climbed into the driver's seat.

'Do you think anyone else made it out? I saw at least one of ours going down,' Peter said after Charlie had started the truck and they moved off down the track.

'I saw a couple. One got lit up right over the target, bloody enormous explosion. After that it was every man for himself.'

'Do you think they'll look it at like that on the squadron?'

'What squadron?'

Peter said nothing in reply. They rode in silence, the headlights of the truck picked out the rough vegetation at the side of the road. The light beams also caught the occasional fox staring back at them, before disappearing out of sight again. The sky had become fully dark in the short time since they left Lake Prespa and Peter looked up at the bright stars above them. He wondered where Eve was at this moment in time and whether she too was looking up at the stars and thinking of him. Probably not, he decided, she barely knew his name.

Charlie had been talking for some time, he suddenly realised, but Peter was not paying attention. He concentrated now, trying to make out the point of Charlie's chat and heard him say, 'Do you remember that fight that Miller got into in Cairo? He could be a real lout when he'd had a skinful,' he laughed.

'Lord, yes, he could really pack it away. I wonder if he had a girl at home?'

They both fell silent again.

'I haven't thanked you for what you did back there,' Peter said eventually.

'Don't talk rot, you would've done it for me. I just wish I popped both Krauts before Miller copped it.'

After a little while they reached a road junction where their dirt track joined a narrow, metalled road running down the centre of a long valley. A sign at the roadside pointed out the names of villages or towns in both directions.

'What does the sign say?'

Charlie squinted up at it.

'Can't tell, it's all Greek to me.'

They both laughed at this quip, which Peter thought was possibly the funniest thing that he had ever heard Charlie say.

'As long as we keep travelling south we're bound to avoid trouble,' Charlie said finally, wiping a tear from his eye. He turned right to take the road south. Not long after this Charlie slapped his forehead and turned to look at Peter.

'I had something I needed to say to you, but it slipped my mind in all the excitement-'

Peter looked down the road, anxious that Charlie was not doing that as he drove. He was first to see the roadblock formed of tree trunks bound together with rope and stretched across the highway.

'It'll have to wait, Charlie,' he said.

'Well, it's quite urgent-'

Charlie saw the roadblock and slammed the brakes on violently. Peter was thrown from his seat and the Horch skidded to a halt a matter of yards from the obstacle.

'That was close,' Charlie laughed.

Peter looked about for somewhere to turn. He felt uneasy, like they were being watched from the shadows. He turned to Charlie and said, 'I'll get out and watch you back, perhaps we can find another track that leads around this?'

'Wait, Peter, I need to tell you about Margot's letter,' Charlie replied.

Peter heard the click of a rifle bolt being made ready before he saw the figures loom out of the darkness towards them. They were hard, grizzled men with beards or moustaches who wore baggy trousers and military jackets. Some had forage hats or caps on their heads, others possessed long, dark hair that fell to their shoulders. They bore a surprising variety of weapons, and they were very curious about the inhabitants of the German truck. In a routine that he admitted was rapidly losing its novelty, Peter raised his hands.

Charlie hissed, 'Do you think they're Greek soldiers?'

Peter shook his head.

'No. I don't know what these chaps are.'

*

A white-painted room with one window and one door. A fusty and dirty white room, except for the stone floor on which they sat and the hearth over a small grate, blackened from the fire.

The grate was cold and empty now, much like their welcome, Charlie thought. The morning revealed these details to him because, though the window was shuttered, the rising sun filtered in around the edges of the rough wooden boards to lend a half-light to the interior.

They had arrived in darkness at the house after a forced march lasting, what he imagined, was a couple of hours across mountainous terrain. He only imagined it because the Greeks had robbed them blind. Peter's watch was taken again, along with their remaining cigarettes, Charlie's lighter and pipe, their weapons, and the little escape tin found in the bushes back at the lake. He'd heard Peter trying to explain that they were RAF and were fighting in defence of the Greek people. But the brigands showed no interest, it looked to him like they either could not understand or did not care.

Peter snored loudly, his head lolling back against the wall. Charlie had no idea how he was capable of sleep in conditions like this. His own sleep had been fitful and indifferent, but they'd both had a rough time the day before. He was just thinking about nudging Peter in the ribs, when a particularly loud snore brought him round, and he sat up in surprise.

'Morning,' Peter croaked, 'I suppose a cup of tea's out of the question?'

'Let me call down to reception. Would you like a paper too?'

Peter laughed weakly then said, 'What do you think they plan to do with us?'

Charlie considered the question for a moment. Much of the answer rested on the nature of the group who had seized them, he thought. If they were genuine criminals, then they might ransom them back to the British. Equally, they might sell them out to the Germans should they become occupiers. Another thought occurred to him, which sent a chill down his spine - if they were deserters, then there was no benefit in keeping the two RAF men alive at all.

'Difficult to say really,' Charlie said, patting his trousers for his pipe and remembering it had been taken, 'It looks quite dim, all things considered.'

'Don't say that, we'll come through. We always do.'

It was so typical of Peter to rely on sentimentality and avoid facing facts, Charlie thought.

'I admire your optimism.'

Charlie sighed. He shook his head and smiled wryly.

'You know, before the war we were so selfish. With our mouldy empire and our sense of superiority over everyone else, we were so wrapped up in our own narrow-minded affairs that we lost sight of what was really important.'

'What's that?'

'Democracy, Peter,' Charlie's voice was tinged with impatience, 'freedom. We led the world, and we squandered that power. Then the little unimportant men organised themselves in their beer cellars, with their vile politics and propaganda. And the dark forces grew and grew, feeding off the fears of a people who had only known poverty and conflict, and we ignored them until it was too late. What did our ignorance cost us: Czechoslovakia; Poland; Norway; Holland; Belgium; France; and now the Balkans.'

'Alright Charlie, this isn't Hyde Park,' Peter replied. Charlie realised that he risked sounding like a bore, Peter had lived through the same events as he had. It was not his intention to patronise.

He felt a slight twinge when he had talked about freedom. His own links with open socialists told him that the U.S.S.R. was not the model of freedom and equality he had imagined. Charlie wondered if now was a good time to tell Peter about his past. There was no need to keep secrets from Peter. Although he was not ashamed of his links with socialism in his youth, he knew that some would consider him something of a firebrand. There was a section of society that would deem him unsuitable for military service, which demanded loyalty, integrity, and subservience. He found it difficult to admit to himself that he was worried about being judged by his peers.

Then he remembered Margot's letter again. He opened his mouth to speak, when he heard the footsteps approaching beyond the door. There were Greek voices. An exchange of words, he thought, several voices speaking at once. Then finally, one single voice louder than all the others. Then a key rattled in the lock and the door opened inwards. A bearded Greek entered with a bunch of keys and a rifle slung over his shoulder. He looked momentarily abashed and then stared at the floor. More Greeks stood outside the room peering in, but it was the man who stood in the doorway that surprised them both the most.

'Good God,' Peter exclaimed, 'It's Jumbo Sutherland.'

Charlie thought he remembered the man's face from a dinner he'd attended in Egypt. He too wore the same costume as the Greeks, and he regarded his prisoners with a look of bemusement. Even more surprising for Charlie was the person who stepped through the door after Sutherland. It was the girl from the plane.

Chapter 19

'Peter! I can't believe it's you,' Eve cried, stepping forward past Sutherland. As Peter struggled to his feet, she grabbed his hands and gazed into his eyes. Charlie coughed discretely and Eve noticed him for the first time, dropping her hands to her sides self-consciously.

'You look dreadful, Peter. Where are your shoes?'

'It's a long story, I'm afraid,' Peter replied.

Jumbo Sutherland turned and spoke a few words to the Greeks, who busied themselves elsewhere. A German machine-pistol was slung over his shoulder and he wore a thin cotton scarf about his neck with an odd little grey fedora on his head. From a distance he looked indistinguishable from the others.

I think,' Sutherland said, turning back, 'we have enough time to hear it, if we may?'

'I'm Charlie Kendrick,' Charlie said, offering his hand to Eve and then Sutherland, 'I don't think we've been introduced.'

Peter told them about the raid on *Monastir* and how their formation had been bounced by German fighters on the way home. He described their desperate fight with the pair of Me109s and how it ended in a forced landing on the shores of Lake Prespa. But, above all, he focused on their capture by the Germans.

'You say they were SS?' Sutherland asked quietly.

'Yes. A recce patrol or something,' Peter replied.

'Then the position is much worse than we thought. It won't be long before the Germans can either link up with the Italians in Albania or encircle our troops around Mount Olympus,' Sutherland shook his head, 'They've made better progress than we estimated.'

Peter looked at Sutherland with surprise, 'You expected this to happen?'

Sutherland glanced at Eve, who folded her arms and said, 'We assessed that the Germans were going to intervene in Greece last year, we just didn't know exactly when or where. I obtained exact details of Operation MARITA, that's what the Germans call the invasion of Greece, from a contact in Bulgaria. But the Germans had me under surveillance, and they chased me to the point of extraction. That was when we met,' she smiled at Peter.

Sutherland continued, 'The Germans won't permit a British presence in Greece, because you can reach the Romanian oil fields by air from here.'

'But why is Romanian oil important to the Krauts?' Charlie said.

'We think of Germany as being an all-powerful nation that dominates Europe,' Eve explained, 'and, in a sense, it is. But Germany also relies heavily on other countries for their mineral resources, much of their foodstuff, and oil in particular. They need to safeguard their supplies, so that they can build up stocks for their strategic offensive.'

This was news to Peter, he could barely take it all in, he looked at Eve, 'What strategic offensive?'

Sutherland fixed them with a serious look, 'What I am about to tell you is so secret that very few people, even at the highest levels of the Government, are aware of it.'

Peter was suitably impressed with this statement and listened carefully.

'Come the summer, Germany will launch an all-out invasion of the Soviet Union. The aim will be to create a Greater German Reich running from the Atlantic to the Caucasus Mountains.'

'But the Russians signed a non-aggression pact with Germany, it was in the papers,' Charlie said.

'It just goes to show what a pack of rotters the Hun are,' Sutherland sniffed, 'Stalin's mob aren't much better frankly; they deserve one another.'

Peter was speechless. The implications of Germany going to war with the Soviets were huge, he realised. For one, it would take some of the pressure off the war in the Mediterranean if Germany's enormous war machine was focused on Russia.

'But if you knew this was going to happen, then why weren't we warned? We lost most of our mates yesterday.'

Eve opened her mouth to speak, but Sutherland interrupted her.

'The intelligence obtained through Eve's mission was sent through the appropriate channels. Our forces were warned, and that's why they've had time to organise a withdrawal. It is taking place as we speak. And not all of your fellow aircrew were killed yesterday either.'

Sutherland led them out of the dank little room and through the large house they had passed through in darkness the night before. Peter emerged onto a broad, shaded veranda that looked out onto a lush green valley. A handful of other white-washed buildings made up the small compound nestling in the fold of the surrounding hills, and Greeks were working in the simple gardens that sat between them. Olive trees ran up the lower slopes, placed in neat rows one after the other, it was an olive plantation he realised.

A table on the veranda was made up with a white tablecloth and five place settings. There were bottles of Retsina on the table, bowls of olives and unleavened bread. A man at the table was helping himself to the food and he looked up at their approach. Sutherland placed his machine-pistol down on the table and gestured to the other guest, saying, 'I think you both know Marcus Venner.'

*

Charlie stared disbelievingly, his mouth went dry and his heart pounded furiously.

'You utter bastard,' he snarled, lunging at Venner who leapt up, knocking over his chair and stepping back with a look of surprise. Charlie felt Peter's arm across his body, physically restraining him.

'Jesus, Charlie,' Peter said, 'what's got into you?'

Charlie took a good look at Venner, seeing for the first time that he had been encountered some misfortune himself. His uniform was blackened in places and his hair singed. Burns marked his face and, in place of the normal even tan the skin above his mouth and nose was a raw red colour. Someone had smeared a balm of some kind over it, so that it looked greasy in the morning light.

'Can't you keep him away from me,' Venner said to Sutherland, 'you can see I'm injured.'

189

'I'll tell you what you are, you're a damned Dago spy.'

Sutherland looked from Charlie to Venner with evident surprise.

'He's unhinged. Listen to him,' Venner said, inching away.

'Stand-still,' Sutherland snapped, before turning back to Charlie, 'What makes you say that?'

'We've had suspicions that a British officer was in league with the Italians because of some damned odd happenings in Egypt.'

Sutherland looked to Peter and asked, 'Is this true?'

Peter nodded wordlessly.

'I asked a woman, a friend of mine,' Charlie said, thinking sadly about Margot, 'At least, she used to be a friend of mine. I asked for her help. You see, she had contacts in counter-intelligence. But when I visited her in Cairo, she was with another man and I left none the wiser.'

'You can't trust a thing this man says,' Venner shouted, suddenly, 'He's a communist. I've done my homework about you Kendrick, oh yes I have.'

Peter frowned at Charlie, 'What's he saying, Charlie?'

Charlie shook his head and looked at Peter, whose face was clouded in confusion. He felt an idiot for not sharing this with him before now. Now he looked like he'd been keeping secrets too.

'He's right. I believed in communism before the war. I still do, to some extent. I only joined up because I had no other options and I could see the way things were going. But you must believe me, Peter, I would never sell out my country.'

'Sutherland, I warn you - this man is a threat to our security. I strenuously recommend that you restrain him,' Venner snarled. Charlie watched Sutherland's face as he turned from Venner to him. Sutherland looked doubtful. Out of the corner of his eye, Charlie saw Eve take a half step to his right. *They don't believe me.*

'Wait! I haven't finished. I can prove it,' Charlie said reaching inside his tunic.

'Easy now,' Sutherland said, his eyes flicked to the machine-pistol on the table.

Charlie held up one hand, 'When I left Cairo, Margot gave me this letter. She told me it would answer all the questions I had. But I assumed it was a farewell note, so I stuffed it in my pocket and forgot about it.'

'For god's sake get to the point,' Peter said.

'The British arrested an Italian spy. He was an Egyptian who worked in the mess attached to headquarters in Cairo, Ibrahim Bin-Farouk. Counter-intelligence assumed that was where he obtained his intelligence, but they missed part of the puzzle.'

Charlie withdrew the crumpled letter and handed it to Peter who unfolded it to read.

'Peter, there's a description in the letter of Ibrahim Bin-Farouk. Can you tell me if it fits your memory of the man you saw Venner meet with in the Khen-el-Khalil Bazaar?'

Charlie glanced at Venner, the mask was slipping. Peter scanned the note and when he came to the description read it out loud, 'Male. Aged 51. Medium height, medium build. Moustache. Blind in right eye. My god - that's him!'

Venner leapt for the machine-pistol on the table and grabbed it before Sutherland could react. He stepped back a couple of paces to where he could cover the entire group with a single burst.

'This madness ends here,' Venner said triumphantly.

'You can't get far,' Sutherland whispered, 'do you imagine the Greeks will let you just slip away after killing us. You don't have a chance; if you drop the weapon we can talk about your options.'

Venner looked panicked, he swung the weapon back and forth across the group as a warning.

'He's only half right,' Venner said, pointing the gun at Charlie who watched the barrel swing towards him again with unease, 'I gave the Italians a few grains of information. To start with, at least. They just wanted background details: numbers of troops, locations of bases. I needed the money, to fund my lifestyle in Cairo. So I obliged. I knew Farouk and he acted as an intermediary - there was no need to get my hands dirty.'

'It was more than a few low-level details you gave them though,' Charlie said through gritted teeth.

'I said *at first*,' Venner's tone was condescending, 'But you see, that's how they get you.

Breadcrumbs. Then they can wave your indiscretions at you whenever they want. They come asking for more information, times and location of fighter screens, priority targets, ciphers. And if you don't provide them-'

Venner drew his thumb across his neck, miming an execution, and went on, 'Moving to Greece was a gift horse for me. It meant I was out of contact with Farouk and everything was going to be fine, until I chanced on your letter Kendrick.'

Charlie closed his eyes in exasperation. So, Venner *had* seen his note to Margot.

'There was always something odd about the pair of you, I suspected it from the start. But he never writes to anyone,' Venner nodded to Peter, then turned back to face Charlie, 'And you're very chatty. Say all sorts in *your* letters. Not that Margot Dacre received any of them. I saw to that. And I made sure you didn't see hers either.'

Charlie filled with rage as a sly grin spread across Venner's face, he was shocked to hear that Margot had indeed written, as she had claimed. He told himself that Margot had never been sincere in her affection for him and now he regretted his angry words to her. He regretted everything.

'You destroyed her letters too?'

'All of them. Why, would you like to know what she wrote to you? All the private thoughts she scribbled down just for your eyes only, Kendrick,' Venner laughed.

'No. I'm just adding interfering with the King's mail to the list of charges to be heard at your court-martial,' Charlie quipped.

'Nice. But there won't be a court martial for me, Kendrick. Because none of you are going to be able to call for one. As soon as I've disposed of you lot, I'll head south and claim to be the sole survivor of the Easter Day raid - I'll be a thumping hero.'

Charlie caught a look from Peter, who said to Venner, 'You'll want this note back then, it pretty much incriminates you.'

'Hand it over,' Venner ordered, 'You could have been something special, Denhay. It's a shame it's got to come down to this.'

Peter put the note on the table and slid it over before standing back. Venner gave him a triumphal look, 'I'm not the only one either; there are others too.' Venner stepped forward to the table to take it. As he did so the barrel of the machine-pistol dropped towards the floor.

In a flash, Charlie snatched up a bottle of Retsina by the neck and swung it over in an arc to smash on Venner's head. Venner cried out and recoiled in agony, his hands reaching up to his wounded head and away from the machine-pistol. Peter went to grab for it, but five shots rang out in quick succession deafening him. Venner slid to the floor like a rag doll. He died in an instant. The first three shots were all within a hand's breadth of his heart and the final two in his forehead. In the silence that followed, Charlie saw that Eve had produced a small calibre handgun from her jacket. Smoke drifted lazily from its barrel, which remained pointed at Venner's body. Eve stood in the regulation position, firing hand up, body at a right angle to the target. She must have sensed the opportunity coming; Charlie realised she was a dangerous woman.

'I'm going to warm up the wireless,' she said firmly, 'the sooner we get them out of here the better, before any more of their 'friends' turn up.'

*

The Horch was hidden in a wooden barn a short walk from the main house and guarded by a loose picquet of Greeks. The barn smelt of cow dung and straw, dust motes floated in the beams of light that shone through holes in its roof. Eve told Peter the truck was important, because its battery was strong enough to power their radio. Peter noticed the wireless set installed in the German truck was holed in several places; it was useless.

'Who are your friends?' Peter gestured to their Greek guards.

'They're Andartes. Greek resistance fighters,' Eve smiled, 'They took to the hills when the Italians invaded last year and now they fight the Germans too.'

'They don't look much like resistance fighters.'

'Don't they? I suppose not but looks can be deceiving. They might be a little rough around the edges, but they're committed to their homeland and they're absolutely deadly.'

'I don't doubt it,' Peter said eyeing the wicked-looking knife that one bearded Andarte carried in a thick sash about his middle.

'How did you end up in this line of work? It's rather an unusual job. For a lady, I mean.'

Eve cocked her head to one side and looked at Peter, he had the impression that he'd said something stupid.

'I met Jumbo in Rome in 1936, where I was studying.'

'You're an artist?'

'I'm an archaeologist.'

'Forgive me, I don't see the connection.'

'Jumbo was heading to Jerusalem on business. I was looking to work with Petrie, but Jumbo took me under his wing. He gave me a job and I proved to be good at it. That's the funny thing about intelligence work, no-one ever expects a woman.'

'You're *working* for Jumbo?'

Peter tried to maintain a nonchalant tone of voice.

'Yes, Peter. Why, did you think I was sleeping with him?'

Peter blushed and Eve laughed heartily at his discomfort.

'He's a friend and a mentor to me. He taught me everything I know about tradecraft.'

'And you've been doing this since '36,' Peter asked, 'spying?'

'You can call it spying if you like. Our way of life relies on intelligence of all descriptions. We have eyes and ears everywhere, because that's how we protect ourselves. At the start of the war, we needed to know the relative strengths and intentions of both Germany and Italy. But spying was only part of what we did. Intelligence work is complex and dangerous. You have to lie and deceive, steal and-,' Eve looked directly into his eyes, 'occasionally, you have to kill.'

'So I see,' Peter replied, remembering way she'd dispatched Venner. She was stunning, he thought, and totally imperturbable.

Eve opened a wooden box on the bonnet of the truck to reveal a small wireless built into it. Under her instructions, the Andartes strung a length of wire from the barn to the roof of the big house. Eve attached the end of this to the terminal on the set and connected the truck's battery to the mains power socket. She removed a set of headphones and a Morse code keyer from a compartment and placed one ear cup of the headset against her head.

'Please look at that map and let me know whether there's anywhere suitable to land around here,' Eve said, handing him a chart.

As Eve tuned the set into the correct frequency, Peter studied the German map spread across the bonnet. The terrain in northern Greece was predominantly mountainous, where it was not a body of water. It was a nightmare for pilotage.

He considered their crash site near Lake Prespa, but dismissed it as too dangerous to return there, the place would likely be crawling with Nazis by now. There was an airfield at *Kozani*, although it was likely to be in German hands too. East of *Kastoria* there appeared to be ground suitable to land on, but without looking at it he could not be certain of that. He shrugged, it was as good as any option. He scribbled the coordinates down for Eve, who tapped out the message using the keyer. She was quick, well over the 20 words per minute considered acceptable for a good operator. Peter looked at her as she transmitted. If she was concentrating, it barely registered on her face. Aware of his gaze she smiled and looked up at him. His stomach turned a somersault.

'It's done,' she said, 'tomorrow at 1400 hours. Aren't you going to light me a cigarette, Peter?'

Removing the packet, he took a couple out. He realised with a pang they had come from Miller's flying suit. Placing both in his mouth, he lit them and handed one to Eve. Surreptitiously, he studied her as she smoked. It struck him that in so much of what she did she was like a man, her dress, her manner of smoking. Even the plain and direct manner of her conversation was so unlike the few girls Peter had known. He wondered idly if she preferred men at all. She looked at him as she smoked, and he felt like her eyes were burrowing into his very soul.

'You must be pleased to return to your squadron tomorrow,' she said after a time.

'I don't even know how many of the chaps made it back from the raid. There's barely any squadron to go back to,' Peter said sadly.

'The Andartes reported several crashed aircraft in the locality, but perhaps not all of them were RAF.'

'How many?'

'Four or five,' Eve said, looking closely at Peter.

'That many?' The knowledge stung him in a way he could never have predicted. Those men were all the friends he had in the world.

'They were your friends. It's fine to grieve for them; you have to let yourself grieve.' Eve seemed to read his mind.

'I just find it hard to know whether it's worth it. All this death, I mean.'

'Of course it's worth it, Peter. What's the alternative - stand by and do nothing? We don't have that option anymore.'

Peter stood silent. He knew she was right.

'Evil triumphs when good people hesitate. It doesn't matter if we lose a million people in the process, the cost of freedom is never too great.'

She paused and Peter sensed she was about to add something else. Eve looked at him, 'That's why Jumbo and I have to stay here. If we can keep resistance alive in Greece, the Germans will always be weak in the Balkans. They'll need to keep divisions of troops to garrison this place, troops that would otherwise be fighting the Russians.'

'So, you won't be coming with us tomorrow then?'

'No, Peter,' Eve said. She leaned over to touch his face and looked into his eyes.

'I'm going to stay here and raise hell.'

Chapter 20

The Horch rattled along the dirt track towards Kastoria with Sutherland at the wheel, throwing up a thick cloud of dust as it raced along. Eve sat in the passenger seat wearing a forage cap, a machine-pistol across her lap and the map on top of that. Peter was crammed in next to Charlie on the bench seat in the back, opposite an Andarte who had been introduced as 'George'. George gripped his ancient rifle and watched the country flick by on either side of the vehicle. It was a bright day, but Peter could see clouds forming in the mountains to the west of them, it would make any pick-up even more hazardous.

Occasionally he would meet George's gaze and the Greek would grin and make a punching gesture. Presumably, this was a demonstration of what he intended to do to the Germans. He seemed to know not a word of English, Peter not a word of Greek; it was a no-score draw. But he at least looked happy in his work.

Peter brooded. It seemed that fate was determined to separate him from Eve again. Whilst he barely knew her, he found himself repeatedly crossing paths with this woman and he felt sure she was attracted to him too. Looking up at the sky again, he wondered what kind of pilot would be crazy enough to even attempt to fly solo into what was, unquestionably, German airspace. Eve turned around in her seat, her face set in determination beneath the dark curls that spilled out beneath her hat.

'Once you've been collected we're on our way again,' she shouted over the noise of the truck's engine and the rush of wind, 'The Germans plan to push forward tomorrow to seize the airfield at *Larissa*, and that will extend their bomber range as far south as *Athens*.'

'What defence have you got against German aircraft?' Charlie looked puzzled.

'None. We're planning to disperse and head into the hills. We need to train and organise the resistance, then I expect we can keep the Bosche tied up with hit and run attacks for a good while,' Eve grinned.

Peter could not help but feel joy at the sight of that smile.

'About 10 miles to go, maybe 15 minutes or so,' Eve said to Sutherland then, looking up from her map as they cleared the edge of a small forest, she cocked the machine-pistol.

'German checkpoint ahead, slow down.'

The dirt track crossed the top of a ridge about a quarter of a mile ahead, where it met a metalled road. At this junction Peter saw a motorcycle and sidecar combination. A soldier sat in the sidecar armed with a machine-gun. Another German stood in the road waving them down. Sutherland glanced sideways at Eve as they approached the check point, he tapped her arm.

Wordlessly, Eve stood up from in her seat, braced one hand against the windshield and waved at the German. He hesitated out of surprise. Eve brought the machine-pistol up in a flash and fired a couple of tight bursts into him. As she opened up, Sutherland hit the accelerator pedal and the truck lurched forward over the German and past the motorcycle. The machine-gunner had no time to pull the trigger before Eve and George turned on him too. Peter saw his body jerk grotesquely as bullets tore into him, then he slumped back in the sidecar.

Sutherland hit the brakes and they skidded to a halt, unseating both Peter and Charlie in the process. He stepped out of the truck with George and they removed the machine-gun and ammunition from its mount, which George carried back to the truck. Sutherland dragged the dead German from the road over to the motorcycle and dumped him across the sidecar. Then he removed the petrol tank cap, took the Jerrycan off the back of the motorcycle and doused it liberally in gasoline. He lit a match and flicked it at the combination, which took light with an enormous roar. As they drove off the gas in the petrol tank ignited and there was an audible explosion.

'Did you mean for that to look like an accident?' Charlie yelled to Sutherland.

Sutherland shouted back over his shoulder.

'No. I meant for it to look like a warning.'

*

They reached the landing ground east of *Kastoria* with 15 minutes to spare before the agreed rendezvous time. Peter patted Sutherland on the shoulder and pointed out the long, flat grass field adjacent to the road that he'd identified from the map. It was in the centre of a verdant valley with tall Pines spreading up onto the low hills.

'That looks good enough to set down on, you can stop here,' Peter said.

Sutherland pulled over and turned to Peter, 'So, what happens now? Do you lay out some markers or something?'

'Not exactly. We could make a fire, that would give the pilot a reference and a wind indicator.'

'What are you waiting for - go to it,' Sutherland ordered.

Peter and Charlie ran about collecting wood. Soon they had a modest collection of branches and boughs stacked up like a campfire in the corner of the field. Eve lugged over the spare Jerrycan as Sutherland and George sat in the truck with the engine idling.

'I thought it might be easier with a little fuel.'

Peter smiled and returned to watching the skies, in the hope that the aircraft would soon appear.

'I've heard a watched pot never boils,' she said, studying Peter's face.

'We've barely had time to talk since we were thrown together again,' he said, finally.

'In my line of work you'll appreciate, Peter, it's wise to be circumspect over a great many things.'

'It must take a very heavy toll on you, to live in the shadows like this. Forever hunted, never knowing the comfort of home, or a lover's embrace?'

Peter glanced surreptitiously at her face in search of a response.

'It's all I know, Peter.'

'Well I think you're just about the most courageous person I've ever met.'

She smiled and said, 'Perhaps, we can arrange to meet someday. If we survive the war?'

'I'd like that. Just tell me the place.'

Eve looked thoughtful for a moment.

'Seven o'clock in the afternoon on the day after the war ends. The American Bar at the Savoy.'

'You're on-'

Peter was interrupted by the faint buzz of an aero engine. It was high above the clouds but unmistakable. The sound changed direction slowly and Peter guessed that the pilot was circling in search of a gap in the clouds. Eve removed the cap from the Jerrycan and sloshed gasoline onto the wood pile. The engine noise diminished. Peter started to think that the pilot had given up and was heading for home. But it suddenly grew much louder and then an aircraft popped out of the cloud base above them.

Peter lit a match and tossed it on the fire, which took instantly, sending a pillar of greasy grey smoke skyward. The pilot must have caught sight of this because, shortly after, the aircraft descended rapidly towards them. It was a twin-engine Percival, just like the one they had flown back from *Araxos* in.

The Percival passed overhead, performed a tight descending turn into wind and dropped nimbly onto the grass. The pilot taxied back to give himself a longer take-off run, then spun around and stopped with his engines idling. The propeller blast blew the grass behind the aircraft down in great swathes. Charlie ran out to open the door, he waved back to them and climbed aboard.

Peter turned to go, but Eve's hand on his arm stopped him.

'I wanted to say thank you again for rescuing me.'

'I think we're even now, aren't we?'

She leaned forward and kissed him forcefully on the lips. Surprised, he found himself kissing her back. He reached out for her and clasped her slender body to him.

'We are now,' she said, after what felt like only seconds, as she drew away.

Peter climbed aboard feeling thoroughly wretched, his head was spinning. He pulled the door shut and locked it, then groped his way forward to find a seat next to Charlie. Wing Commander Cranmer waved to him from the cockpit. When Peter looked out of the window to where the truck had been, it was disappearing along the track already lost in its own cloud of dust.

The aircraft was soon bouncing down the field before climbing steeply into the air. They ascended for less than a minute before entering the damp, grey embrace of the clouds. Peter hated flying in cloud because it was so easy to become disorientated or disbelieve your instruments. Cranmer, however, was a gifted pilot and they found the tops of the cloud at a little under 2, 000 feet. It seemed to brighten perceptibly, then melt away to reveal bright blue sky in every direction and the sun shone in through the fuselage windows. Charlie leaned over and said, 'I'm sorry I didn't tell you about my past. I was a fool. Can you forgive me?'

Peter looked at his navigator with curiosity, realising only now that he was his best friend.

'I wouldn't want to fly with anyone else,' he said, shaking Charlie's hand.

*

Brian Potterne stood in the operations caravan at *Menidi* and squinted at the signal form handed to him by a motorcycle despatch rider. A grim expression spread across his face. Normally signals were transmitted by wireless, but that was vulnerable to eavesdropping by German listening posts, whereas a hand-delivered message was not. The reason for this precaution became clear when he unfolded it from its buff envelope, marked 'SECRET'. It was addressed to the Officer Commanding, XXI Squadron, from Headquarters British Air Forces Greece and contained only four lines. These were:

EVACUATION OF RAF SQNS IN GREECE TO BEGIN WITH IMMEDIATE EFFECT. XXI SQN GROUND PARTY PROCEED KALAMATA BY M.T. BY P.M. 18TH INST/AIRCRAFT TO HERAKLION, SAME. ALL EQUIPMENT TO BE DESTROYED OR RENDERED INOP. DO NOT ACKNOWLEDGE, DESTROY AFTER READING.

'So the show's over then,' he mumbled to himself before dismissing the messenger. He was not surprised. Indeed, he had expected these orders and had already directed the squadron's ground party to return from *Paramythia*. They were due to arrive by road later that day. Venner had told him to hold onto all the replacement aircraft and crews that had arrived in the last few weeks. With accounting typical of the RAF, he now had three full crews and five Blenheims at *Menidi*, but insufficient engineers to service more than a couple of them at once.

Looking out across the field, he could see most of the aircraft parked in their earthen dispersal pens. One was in the hangar for maintenance and his crews were at the mess for the day. A pair of Hurricanes taxied by, just returned from a sortie by the look of it. Black marks on the leading edges of their wings showed they had fired their guns. Behind them came Cranmer's Percival. It was not an unusual sight *per se*, but he was certainly not expecting a visit today. He turned to Sergeant Tyrell, who waited patiently for instruction.

'Full squadron brief at 1900 hours this evening. And get hold of the Supply Officer, I need to speak with him urgently.'

He turned back to the Percival, spinning around on the apron as it turned to taxi back out again. The door opened and out stepped two dishevelled figures. As they drew closer, he recognised them, a realisation that drew a rare profanity from his lips. Peter Denhay was waving at him like an idiot and as he neared he shouted over the engine noise, 'Hullo Brian, pleased to see us?'

'Good lord, you look like you've seen a ghost,' Charlie said, and then in an aside to Peter, 'he's not pie-faced, is he?'

'I'm afraid I was rather lost for words for a moment. I didn't expect to see either of you again, that's all,' Brian said looking at them in disbelief. He yelled at the retreating Tyrell, 'Tyrell, bring some tea. Some tea Tyrell!'

'Did anyone else make it back?'

'I'm afraid that you two are the only survivors from the *Monastir* raid,' Brian said shaking his head. What the hell happened up there?'

Peter explained exactly what went on, the bad decision to fly in close formation, the ambush and everything that followed. Brian listened with mounting amazement at the story.

'Gosh. So Venner was a rat? I have to say I never warmed to the fellow. Didn't have him pegged as a traitor though,' Brian exclaimed. Now that he thought about it, Venner's nature had always been odd. He had just never really entertained the idea that an Englishman would sell out his country. Peter handed him Miller's identification tag, saying, 'Miller's buried near Lake Prespa, I'd like to write to his family when I get the chance.'

'There is one modicum of good news, however. The C.O. has turned up. He ditched near Corfu and got picked up by the Royal Navy. He was quite beaten about though and they've evacuated him to hospital in Egypt.'

'That's something I suppose,' Charlie said.

'Quite. It'll take more than a few Wops to kill Old Johnny Corbett - they can't touch him.'

Tyrell interrupted to say that he had put out the tea in the dispersal tent. Brian led them there and as they walked, told them of their new orders.

'We're being pulled out to Crete. I thought we were going to have to wreck the spare aircraft, but now you can fly one out for me.'

'When do we go?' Charlie's tone indicated that it could not be soon enough.

'Tomorrow. I'm just waiting for the ground party to come back from *Paramythia*,' Brian said, remembering the signal. The Supply Officer put his head through the tent door and Brian signalled him to wait outside for a moment.

'That's it? We just sneak off like we've been defeated?'

Peter looked angry and upset at this news. He had every right to be, Brian thought, after what he'd just come through.

'Peter, we *have* been defeated,' Brian said gently, 'I find accepting that fact makes it easier to move on. And I should know, I've seen a few of them. No, our orders now are to bring what's left of the unit safely back to Egypt so that we can build it up again. Just in case you were thinking of some alternative.'

*

Peter waited for Brian to leave the tent, then he turned excitedly to Charlie.

'You know, it would be such a shame not to fly one last sortie. A leaving gift, of sorts.'

'Like a Trojan Horse?'

'Exactly. Eve said the Germans would be at *Larissa* tomorrow. They won't be expecting an airfield attack on their first day as new tenants. It'll be like a game of Knock Down Ginger.'

'You heard what Brian said, we just need to make it back to Egypt alive.'

Peter could see the reluctance in his friend's eyes; Charlie looked away and sipped his tea.

'Come on Charlie, what happened to your passion?'

'The war happened! In the last three days we've been shot down, narrowly avoided being killed by Jerry, and held up by a renegade. Don't you think we've done enough?'

'I don't think you can ever do enough when it comes to duty,' Peter snapped, his frustration palpable. He wanted more than ever to bring Charlie into this argument.

'You told me yourself about Nemesis. The Greek God who punishes those guilty of hubris. She balances the books, doesn't she? Don't you think that the Germans have got something coming; they deserve a slap? If not for what they've done to Greece, then how about for what they've done to our squadron. To our friends.'

'You know, Peter, growing up I used to think that you were imbued with courage. Some had it, others did not. But in the last few months I've come to think differently. Now I believe that everyone starts with a cupful of courage, and over time the things you do set a drain upon it so eventually its contents are consumed.'

Charlie downed the last remaining dregs of his tea and placed the cup between them before saying, 'Some men have a larger cup than their fellows, and others die before their supply runs out. But a few have to live with the shame of knowing that their meagre supply is all they have to get them through their life. My cup is empty Peter, and I need a smoke.'

Peter followed him out into the weak afternoon sunshine, he watched Charlie fumble in his pocket for his pipe. Peter was about to embark on a monologue about the nature of courage, and how it was a decision and not an emotion. He knew it would blow Charlie's cup analogy out of the water and he opened his mouth to speak when a formation of aircraft appeared from behind the clouds above Mount Parnitha. A large formation of aircraft, he realised, perhaps two dozen or so. Not the kind of numbers the RAF could field in Greece any longer. His heart froze. Charlie saw it too and yelled at the top of his voice.

'It's the Bosche, Peter - run!'

A ringing bell alerted the fighter squadron and weary men sprinted to their waiting aircraft for what was the third or fourth time that day. To this cacophony was added the eerie warbling of the air raid alarm. Men were in motion everywhere. Peter ran too, but away from the aircraft and not towards like the fighter pilots must. Most headed towards the woods, where slit trenches had been dug for their protection. Looking over his shoulder, Peter saw a Hurricane lift into the air and climb steeply away from the field. Another followed it, but a third was less lucky. As it rolled down the airfield, the Germans struck.

The first wave of aircraft were Me110s, twin-engine heavy fighters. They caught the Hurricane on the strip and raked it with cannon fire. The little fighter bounced once, its wingtip dug in and it cartwheeled to explode in the middle of the airstrip. Peter gasped in shock, before he was pulled to the ground by Charlie. Behind them came Me109s, who buzzed the airfield at low-level, machine-gunning everything they saw.

Charlie crawled over to the lee of a sandbagged machine-gun emplacement. The crew of the machine-gun bravely sprayed away at any and all of the attacking Germans, but they were wildly outnumbered. Laying on his belly next to Charlie, Peter saw a couple of the engineers race out onto the field to check on the pilot of the crashed Hurricane. *Brave bloody fools.* They got no more than 100 yards before a German fighter picked them out and a trail of machine-gun bullets stitched into the ground all around them. The two men collapsed next to each other, unmoving. Fire raged in the hangar across the strip and smoke rose in a thick, oily column from one of the blast pens, blotting out the sun.

'You Nazi scum!' Charlie yelled skywards. At a leisurely pace, the Germans switched to the airfield buildings and shot up the wooden huts and the hospital. And then, just as soon as they had arrived, they were gone. Peter stood up and brushed down his uniform, taking in the results of the German raid.

An ancient fire engine plied its hose optimistically on the burning Blenheim in the hangar. People moved about the airfield to care for the wounded and collect the dead. A version of normality returned and one of the Hurricanes skipped back onto the aerodrome, deftly avoiding the burning remains in the middle of the strip.

Charlie stood too, a look of renewed determination on his face.

'When do we stick it to Jerry?'

Chapter 21

Brian only reluctantly considered the plan to attack *Larissa*, when Charlie outlined it to him. He gestured at the damage done to the airfield and the smashed aeroplanes and reminded them how difficult it was going to be to get everyone home alive, even without staging a suicide mission. Brian folded his arms with a disapproving look.

Peter argued that they must do it to avenge their fallen comrades. He seemed to be getting somewhere until he concluded with, '-and don't forget they destroyed the Squadron, Brian.'

Charlie thought it was a mistake to finish on this point. He was unsurprised when Brian turned angrily on Peter and replied, 'If you think the Germans have killed off the squadron, you're a fool. It takes more than the loss of a few crews to do that. A squadron is complex organism made up of hundreds of individuals working together for a common goal. All of us share the unique traditions and values of our squadron and we carry them wherever we go. So long as one single airman lives, a squadron can never die. Not even when its aircraft are scrapped, its standard laid up, and its people pensioned off.'

Peter fell silent, Brian stared angrily at him. Charlie attempted a new line of argument.

'Attacking *Larissa* will buy you time to conduct a withdrawal,' he said quietly, 'The Germans expect to move their bases forward so that they can attack ports and airfields around *Athens*. Their aim is to capture as many of us as possible.'

'You think a single aircraft attack will delay that?'

'It can't hurt. Perhaps it will give you a day, maybe two. But in that time how many thousands of troops can we evacuate - hundreds, thousands? It's got to make a difference.'

Brian studied Charlie thoughtfully, he looked like he was weighing it up.

'We've done it before, Brian. Peter and I pulled off another raid like this in Egypt with only a handful of aircraft.'

'Tell me your plan,' Brian replied.

In the dying light the airfield remained unusually busy with preparations for the squadron's departure in the morning. Engines ticked over outside as equipment was thrown pell-mell into their few lorries. Oil lamps shone inside the dispersal tent, illuminating the occupants by their strange yellowish glow and casting long shadows up the walls. The air stank of burning gasoline as the clerks destroyed sensitive documents, lest they fell into enemy hands. Charlie wondered if every retreat smelt like petrol and tasted like ash. God knows the British had seen enough of them in this war.

Brian called in Sergeant Mellish and the Air Liaison Officer, both recently returned from *Paramythia*, to hear the plan. The tired look on Mellish's face was replaced instantly by one of joy when he walked in. Charlie rolled out a map of the central portion of Greece, running from *Athens* as far up as the top of the *Larissa* Plain. He waited for quiet and then launched into his briefing.

'We received intelligence that the Luftwaffe intends to operate from *Larissa* Airfield tomorrow morning. This will put *Athens* in bomber range, and the Germans will be unable to resist the opportunity to launch an attack on the same day.'

'So what?' The Air Liaison Officer said, frowning.

'We anticipate that they will refuel and re-arm at *Larissa*. This takes time and makes them vulnerable to air attack. A single aircraft strike at low-level is liable to cause serious damage if they are caught on the ground.

The Air Liaison Officer laughed and shook his head, 'You'll need to time it to perfection, because if you don't they'll eat you for breakfast.'

'True,' Charlie shrugged, 'but we can limit the risk through logical deduction. For example, the Germans are predictable, and they don't like to fly at night. The best time of day to bomb is before the sun reaches its zenith, because the lack of shadows at midday makes it harder to identify targets. So, if they intend to strike *Athens* it will come at about 1000 hours. That gives a take-off time of approximately 0920 hours.'

'Don't forget sir, you need to allow time for refuelling,' Mellish said.

'Quite right, what would you plan on for refuelling time?'

'Oh, well there's a difference if they use fuel tankers or Jerrycans. But a couple of squadrons or more could take a couple of hours to park up and refuel.'

'Let's say 0700 hours for first landing at *Larissa* then. They could be airborne from their bases in Bulgaria and make that in daylight!'

'What if they leave guard fighters up to protect them?' Brian was tugging at his chin, he still looked undecided.

'We'll use their tactics against them,' Peter smiled mischievously, 'The sun will be up in the east; if we approach from the coast, they'll be blinded to our attack run until we're over the airfield.'

'You'll be chased, nonetheless. Any airborne fighters will see you make a run for it.'

'Yes, but they can't chase us far,' Charlie said, 'Me109s don't have the legs to get to *Athens* and they'll have been airborne for a couple of hours. If we maintain the element of surprise, we stand a decent chance of getting away.'

'What about your air gunner?' Brian's question was met with silence. Charlie had been considering this privately. He felt that it would be wrong to ask anyone else to fill Miller's shoes for this mission. In any event, plan hinged on the theoretical possibility they would not run into enemy fighters. If they had to fight it out, they were already dead.

'We don't want to break up another crew, and it seems wrong to expect someone else's gunner to fly this mission in Miller's place,' Peter said, as if reading Charlie's mind.

'I can handle the guns on the way back,' Charlie added, 'At least until we're over the sea.'

'I see you've thought this through, but it's a very risky plan,' Brian said eventually, 'Undoubtedly bold, but very risky indeed.'

Charlie knew this when he and Peter had planned it, of course. The odds for success were long, but if it failed the loss would be minimal. It was a hard thing to balance, nevertheless a single aircraft and crew was a drop in the ocean in the grim accountancy of total war. If it succeeded, it might mean whole army units would continue to fight on. And every solider counted in this campaign.

Finally, Brian gave Charlie a firm nod, 'Very well then. You two better get some rest. I've some things to attend to, but I'll leave written instructions for Sergeant Mellish to pass onto you in the morning.'

Brian stood and shook Charlie's hand, and then Peter's. There was a moment of silence as Mellish and the Air Liaison Officer disappeared out of the tent into the cool of the evening. Brian gazed at them with a certain sadness, he opened his mouth to say something and then shut it again. Finally, he said, 'I always had a good feeling about you two, you know.'

*

Peter sat bolt upright from a dream of being trapped in a burning aeroplane. Insistent knocking at the door startled him.

'Yes, yes. Fine. With you shortly,' He shouted groggily. He swung his legs off the bed and sat there blinking in the darkness. All sorts of worries crowded his mind, but he could not shake the nagging feeling that Eve was in trouble. Charlie groaned beneath his blanket

'What time is it?'

'0500 hours,' Peter said, pulling his sweater over his head.

'What odds do you give us today?'

'3-to-1,' Peter said robotically, surprised to find he didn't think better of their chances.

'That good?'

It was a brief, silent journey to the airfield by car. Even though the light had not yet begun to show, Peter could see a thin ground mist had formed overnight. At the aerodrome, the vague dark shapes of silent aircraft peered at them through the gloom. Each wreathed in its own private fog-bound study. One aircraft was dimly lit by a couple of safety lamps that the engineers lit during bombing-up. Mellish and his team had prepared everything for their departure. Their driver waited for a fraction longer than was necessary for them to climb out before driving off. He vanished from sight into the mist, leaving only the diminishing sound of his engine as a sign he was ever there.

'Mornin' sir,' Mellish smiled.

'Is it?'

Mellish handed Peter a sealed packet. He glanced at the writing on the front, which was addressed to 'Aircraft Captain'.

'Mr Potterne said I was to hand you that. He also wished you the best of luck and a happy return, sir.'

'Thank you Mellish,' Peter said with a smile as he tore open the envelope and pulled out the note. Standing closer to the lamps, Peter read the orders. As he did so, Charlie conducted the pre-flight inspection with Mellish and his words drifted back to Peter.

'It's dear old *Queenie*! Hello my friend.'

Charlie ducked under the fuselage where Mellish pulled back the bomb bay doors to expose their load of four 250 lbs bombs. All were neatly attached to their cradles with fuses screwed in. Some wag had scribbled on the bombs in chalk, the one closest read 'Berlin Express'. Returning to Peter near the wingtip, Charlie pushed his Service Dress hat back on his head.

'Special instructions?'

'It's mostly reserve radio frequencies and procedures to follow in case we have to abandon the aircraft. But there are coordinates for an emergency landing ground near *Kalamata* too.'

Charlie scribbled the frequencies and coordinates down in the corner of the chart he had marked up with their route details the previous day.

'Destination?'

'*Heraklion*, Crete, is the primary. Our diversion is *Argos*. We're not to return here under any circumstances. Think we can get airborne in 20 minutes?'

Charlie glanced up at the cloud and shrugged.

'I guess it tops out at maybe a couple of hundred feet. I can just about make out a clearing in the east. Yes, I think it's possible if we shake a leg.'

Peter nodded and tore their orders in two. He handed them to Mellish with instructions to burn them.

'I love this time of day,' Peter sighed, 'just before the sun rises. It's so still and peaceful, and the day holds nothing but promise.'

Charlie smiled back, 'Today's promise is to stick our foot up Hitler's arse.'

Mellish shook his head, as if questioning how anyone could joke on a day like today.

'But I'll miss this, when it's all over,' Charlie added, without looking at Peter. He picked up his gear and clambered up onto the wing. Peter asked Mellish if he would guide them through the fog to the aerodrome boundary and appoint someone to check the airfield was clear. Mellish nodded in acquiescence but remained standing there with an unhappy look on his broad face.

'The lads and me, sir, we put some provisions aboard for you. Jus' in case-,' Mellish said, seemingly at a loss for the correct phrase, 'you're waylaid, sir. It's just a flask of tea and sandwiches, that's all. But my old girl never lets me out the house without a full belly; we felt you and Mr Kendrick ought to have the same courtesy, sir. As regards eating.'

Peter was touched by this small but significant gesture. These men had doubtless been up all night preparing the aeroplane for its mission, still their thoughts were not for themselves, but for their crew. Peter was reminded, not for the first time, that it was because of men like Mellish and Crawley that Britons will never be slaves. He had to clear his throat before he replied.

'That's awful kind in you. But you needn't have gone to the trouble, you know. We'll all be having lunch on Crete later today.'

'Course you're right, sir. Well, I suppose we ought to be starting if you're to make your appointment with Jerry. This is goodbye for now.'

'Thank you, Sergeant Mellish,' Peter shook his hand, 'Thank you for everything.'

They taxied through the fog behind Mellish, who carried a safety lamp to guide their way. Peter tried to shake the image in his mind of a hearse drawn through the streets behind an undertaker. In spite of the circumstances, it felt good to be back at *Queenie's* controls.

At the airfield boundary, Mellish waved the lamp above his head to show they were at the beginning of the airstrip. Peter braked the starboard wheel and spun the aircraft until the compass pointed to their take-off heading of north-east.

He looked across at Charlie, who had the map laid out across his knees and a look of steely determination in his eyes. Charlie nodded, and Peter advanced the throttles. With a terrific roar, the Blenheim disappeared into the morning fog. It motored along to begin with becoming faster and faster, until the tail lifted and eventually she left the ground altogether. In its wake came silence, restored to its rightful place once more. The clouds swallowed them up and *Menidi* fell away to await the uncertain light of a new day.

*

Charlie looked up from his map at the Greek coastline rising steadily above the dark blue sea as they raced towards it. The mountains beyond *Larissa* had been visible since they made their final turn back towards the land, none more so than Mount Olympus far off to the north. The sun was just beginning to inch above the water behind them, it bathed the land ahead in an orange glow that made Charlie think of the saying, *red sky in the morning; sailor's warning*. The light played on the water's surface, picking out individual waves as they rolled and collided with one another, and he suddenly realised how low down they were, even by Peter's standards. He coughed and said into the intercom, 'Would you describe this as "below tree-top height", Peter?'

Peter looked like he was concentrating and replied without taking his eyes off the horizon.

'Oh, I don't know, I suppose so. What do you think?'

'It looks like "below wave-top height" from where I'm sitting,' Charlie replied with a wince. He glanced back at his map, studying the large plain on which *Larissa* sat. It was bordered by mountains in all directions, except in the east where it met the sea. Their route took them over the airfield at *Larissa* before making a sharp turn southwards to get into the passes near Mount Othrys. If they got that far, they had a reasonable chance of staying out of sight of the Germans and, passing over *Athens*, make good their escape. The blue of the water flashed white briefly and then they were over land again.

Charlie let his straps off and moved forward to the nose. Crouched here over the bombsight he felt the ground racing past at over 200 mph. Hues of brown, green, and yellow blurred beneath the nose and in the periphery of his vision. He was oblivious to the anything but the target, which he expected to appear in a very short time.

'I don't see any fighters up,' Peter's voice rattled in his ears. Charlie felt the impulse to look skyward, but fought it. Nothing mattered now other than an accurate pattern. He entered their height and speed into the sight, but the truth was they were so low that they could not fail to hit something. The airfield loomed in view, a flat expanse of ground ahead, distinct from the patchwork of fields that surrounded it. Then he saw the hangars, and the Germans.

They had been correct in their assumption that the Germans would mount their attack from *Larissa*. There must have been upwards of a hundred aircraft on the ground, and he recognised both bombers and fighters. Dispersal must have been a challenge for them because the wrecks of several abandoned Greek and RAF aircraft still littered the field, this forced them to bunch up. A large concentration of bombers, Heinkels by the look of it, were parked along the northern edge of the field. His intuition told him the crews would be busy overseeing the bombing-up of their aircraft. In amongst those aeroplanes would be bomb trolleys and stacks of petrol cans, and men working feverishly to put the whole damned lot in the air. This was it. This was their most vulnerable point. He passed instructions to Peter, 'Right a bit, Skipper.'

The aspect shifted a little, but the aircraft did not point directly at the centre of mass, a large group of Heinkels on the northern side of the strip. They sped towards the release point, almost too quick to be sure of an accurate drop.

'Come on, Peter. A little more right rudder.' The bombers slipped into the gap just above the sighting notch.

'We've got company,' Peter warned over the intercom, 'Two bandits high up at eleven o'clock.'

Charlie didn't reply, he squinted down the sight and waited for the right moment to push the bomb release. As he did so, he reflected on what a rum war it was to be bombed mercilessly by the Germans one day, and return the favour the next. He knew he didn't hate the Germans; he didn't know them. But he harboured a strong desire to harm them anyway. He wanted to right the wrong done to Miller, MacNeish, Sinclair, Wardle, and all the others. At their memory, he became conscious of something building deep within him. An unquenchable thirst for revenge. His mouth ran dry and his temples pounded with the blood coursing through his body. The German bombers filled his sight. Charlie hit the bomb release button.

'Bombs gone, bombs gone,' he yelled.

The aircraft lurched violently over to the left in a tight roll, throwing Charlie across the chart table. Alarmingly, through the nose canopy glass he saw the port wing pointing directly at the ground. There was a sharp *pop, pop, pop* from somewhere, but no hits. The ground fire whistled away harmlessly into the empty blue sky. They rolled level and crossed the main runway on their new course. He looked down upon black-suited German mechanics refuelling a *Stuka* who gazed back up at him open mouthed. They were so low he could see the pilot in the cockpit wore a yellow scarf and a look of utter amazement as they roared overhead.

Just behind them the four bombs exploded in quick succession. They were followed by other explosions, sharp cracks that caused Charlie to crane his head around to look back at the Heinkels. He could not see a great deal, there appeared to be one huge conflagration where the bombers had been parked and he could just make out smaller explosions before Peter's cry called him back to his senses.

'I could do with a hand here. These Krauts are on our tail.'

*

Peter had long held the view that there were really two types of people in life. One type was the artists, they were ruled by their instincts and were naturally creative. He thought Charlie belonged to this group. The other, to which he previously felt he belonged, was the scientists. This group based their actions on what they knew or could prove. They were logical, methodical, and in his view they were fair.

He reflected on this now because, whilst it was a matter of physics that in a headlong chase of a Blenheim by a Me109 the fighter would win, it did not necessarily mean the chase would end in a kill. This remained true even if the fighter had not begun the chase with 10, 000 feet of altitude to play with. A scientist would believe it statistically probably that the larger, slower bomber would be defeated, but an artist might pause to consider the other variables. For example, the closing speed of the chase aircraft would be something approaching 150 mph and the pilot of the Blenheim could increase that approach speed by careful manipulation of his own airspeed. An artist might reflect, as Peter did now, that *there's many a slip 'twixt the cup and the lip.*

Peter drew back the throttles and held the nose up to bleed off the airspeed. He practically sensed the on-rushing fighters and saw their fire pass by him, several hundred yards in front, before the two aircraft broke overhead and turned away in a sharp turn to chase the Blenheim's tail. That was close, he thought as he wiped sweat off his brow, they won't fall for that twice.

Charlie squeezed past Peter in the cockpit, fell flat on his face, and hauled himself back up again. Yelling, 'Selector!'

Peter, leaned forward and switched hydraulic power to the turret. He heard Charlie's voice back on the intercom as he reached the turret.

'Miller must have been gifted to hit anything with these peashooters.'

'Do try, won't you?' Peter said coolly.

Peter tore his eyes away from the retreating fighters to the ridge line that lay ahead. It was crowned by Mount Othrys, standing proud of the surrounding hills. To the west, a broad v-shaped valley snaked away, offering one potential avenue of escape. The only other option was to go over the top of the ridge. Peter dismissed this. To scale the ridge would sacrifice crucial airspeed; the valley must do. He yawed towards it, hoping to enter before the fighters caught up with them. Canon fire from behind told him it would be a close-run thing. He gripped the control yoke tightly. The valley loomed up ahead, its narrowness was safety; it was freedom.

The Blenheim was giving its all, *Queenie* strained to make it. And then they were through the gap. The hillsides rose up on either side, channelling the Germans into single file, the three aircraft zipped along below the hilltops. Their defensive machine-guns leapt into action, Peter could hear their dull metallic thumping through his helmet.

'We need to throw these krauts off, they won't miss a second time,' Charlie warned.

Peter pulled every trick he knew to shake off the fighters. He rolled, jinked and even tried to Yo-Yo, but the lack of manoeuvring space told against him. It was all to no avail as the fighters sat on his tail, determined to wait him out. When he reached the valley's end, he realised, it would be all over. The hillsides flashed by on either side of the cockpit, so close it seemed he could almost reach out and touch the earth. The further they travelled the smaller the gap became until the valley narrowed into a U-shape. Here the hills dropped almost vertically down to the green floor below and rock faces protruded on either side. Ahead he sensed, rather than saw, a fork in their path as a large hill sat squarely in their path. He had no idea which way to go. At this stage it hardly mattered.

He pointed the bomber as if intending to take the left-hand branch, feinting to lure the fighters into following him. At the very last moment he pulled the aircraft into a tight roll to the right with full rudder and emergency boost. *Queenie* answered with a shudder, turning onto its new course with only tens of feet to spare from colliding with the hillside. There was a pause broken by a dull explosion well behind them.

'Christ. One of the Jerries just piled in,' Charlie shouted, 'his wingman's still with us though.'

Peter was overwhelmed by a sinking feeling as he gazed down the valley he selected. It ran for a few miles before ending in a trough. This would force them to climb up and out, and in doing so they would be a sitting duck. It was literally a dead end.

'Guns are jammed,' Charlie yelled.

So this is how it ends, he sighed to himself, shot whilst attempting to escape. The moment they began their climb the airspeed would drop away. The fighter would advance from below and, pulling up beneath them, would drill them with canon and machine-gun and they would cease to exist. He saw it clearly in his mind's eye. He could not conceive of a way out.

'Here he comes. Look out,' Charlie said.

Peter pushed the throttles forward to the stops, raised the nose so it pointed over the top of the ridge, and waited for the inevitable.

Machine-gun fire sounded close by, several short bursts, and then an explosion. But it was not the Blenheim, Peter realised; it was the German. He blew apart in a great orange ball of fire as its fuel tanks detonated and a Hurricane swooped over them, waggling its wings as it climbed back up to its formation several thousand feet above.

Charlie whooped down the intercom, 'It's one of ours, you beauty. Right in the nick of time.'

Peter watched him go, realising as they crested the ridge that they were free. They'd made it. Charlie returned to his seat next to Peter, thumped him on the back in congratulation, and strapped in. They sat in silence as they flew south, both men lost in their thoughts. Charlie was first to speak.

'I've been thinking about what Venner said at the Olive Plantation.'

'What was that, I barely recall anything he said,' Peter replied.

'He said "there are others", like he knew the identities of other agents.'

'He'd say anything to get himself out of a fix. The bloke was a pathological liar.'

Charlie considered this point, 'But he said that when he was holding the gun. He didn't volunteer it to save his skin, he was gloating.'

'Look, Charlie, I can well believe that there are other people out there prepared to sell out their country for a few bob, but I really can't see how it's going to affect us from now on. Now, what's our new course?'

Charlie gave it to him and stretched his legs out in the cockpit, silence prevailed again. Peter tried to dismiss the troubling thoughts that now entered his mind following Charlie's question.

'Crete, then Egypt. Then a decent spell of rest for us,' Peter said into the intercom, more to reassure himself than anything else.

Behind them, the mountains and valleys of Greece slowly disappeared below the horizon until nothing remained except salt water and blue sky.

Author's Note

To write historical fiction is to walk a thin line between fact and storytelling. But writing *Out of the Desert* was made a lot easier precisely because the facts make such a great story. I hope that it stands as a tribute to the brave men and women of Great Britain and the Commonwealth who stood firm in the face of evil in those early years of the Second World War, which is what I intend it to be.

I relied heavily on the history of 211 Squadron RAF, on which XXI Squadron is loosely based. Their operational record is followed faithfully, albeit with some abridgement. It was learning of their near-destruction at the hands of the Luftwaffe in Greece on Easter Day in 1941, that inspired me to write in the first place.

I must admit some artistic licence in changing the aircraft type from the Blenheim I to the IV, with which 211 Squadron did not re-equip until later in 1941. My reasons for doing so were both technical and nostalgic. First, its performance was more appropriate to the type of action in which I placed it in Greece. Second, the long-nosed Blenheim IV was one of the first model kits I made as a child; I still think of it today as a better looking and more interesting aeroplane.

Readers who wish to know more about what it was like to fly the Blenheim IV should look no further than the excellent *Six Weeks of Blenheim Summer by Alastair Panton*. He was undoubtedly a very brave man and typical of the hardy soul you had to be to fly light bombers in 1940-41. The Air Ministry's *Pilot's Notes for the Bristol Blenheim* was also an invaluable guide in visualising the cramped and oddly designed cockpit.

It is difficult to avoid developing a soft spot for the Bristol Blenheim. It was so clearly a product of the eclectic British aviation industry in the 1930s, with its civil aircraft origins and light payload. I have the utmost sympathy for any pilot that accidentally shut off the fuel feed for the engines, when all they meant to do was change the propeller pitch! Our popular focus on the RAF's early fighters (Supermarine Spitfire and Hawker Hurricane), and later bombers (Avro Lancaster) is probably responsible for the venerable Blenheim's relegation to airshow curio. But I flatter myself to think that a little has been done here to redress the balance.

Air operations in the Mediterranean between 1940-41 were not the immediate priority of the Imperial General Staff, or the RAF for that matter. So, the air force in the Middle East tended, at least initially, to have the older and less technologically advanced aircraft. It is impressive to reflect on what they achieved despite this, particularly when the Italians were rolled out of Egypt and as far back as *El Agheila* during Operation COMPASS.

I take the view that the air campaign in Greece was really a forlorn hope for the RAF, even though the Air Officer Commanding (Air Vice-Marshal J H D'Albiac) put a brave face on it in his dispatch in the London Gazette (dated 9 January 1947). There are plenty of good books that describe the campaign in greater detail, such as *Wings Over Olympus* by T H Wisdom, but my personal favourite remains Roald Dahl's *Going Solo*, in which he describes his experience of flying as a fighter pilot with 80 Squadron in Greece.

As an aside, there really was a visit to 211 Squadron by American officers. Alas, history does not record whether they were taken up over the lines by the RAF and treated to a 'show'.

Having been more than decimated in April 1941, 211 Squadron was eventually pulled back to Egypt, before being sent to the Sudan for a long-overdue rest. It had been in continuous action for over 10 months. The next stop for Peter and Charlie, however, is Crete - and one can only guess at what adventures await them there. It is my sincere hope that I will be able to tell that story too, before long.

If you enjoyed this story, why not share your thoughts and comments. Check out my Twitter page @Tom_Walker_RAF or email me at tomwalker188d@outlook.com.

Acknowledgements

Like running a squadron or a wing, writing a book is a team effort, and I am really fortunate to have the best team behind me. First, I wish to thank everyone who helped beta read the early drafts of *Out of the Desert*. Matt and Louise Symons gave their time and support freely as ever (sorry it's not going to be called Zombie Squadron), as did Mark (Aaron) and Vicki Fulton. I was also aided by a real-life pilot and navigator, Sam Fletcher and Rob McCartney, both gentlemen aviators and stars of their own tales of adventure. Your help, advice and company propelled me along my way.

I owe a debt of gratitude to my development editor, Mike Jones, for helping me find my voice and to Alexandra Balsom for putting up with months of copy editing and listening to me read back out-of-context prose. I realise what a nightmare this must have been for a professional journalist.

It would be remiss of me not to mention Richard Foreman for his invaluable guidance, and the team at Sharpe Books, without whom the novel would never have seen the light of day. It goes without saying that any mistakes are entirely mine.

Printed in Great Britain
by Amazon